Born in Scotland in 1910, Jane Duncan spent her childhood in Glasgow, going for holidays to the Black Isle of Inverness. After taking her degree at Glasgow University she moved to England in 1931, and when war broke out she was commissioned in the WAAF and worked in Photographic Intelligence.

After the war she moved to the West Indies with her husband, who appears as 'Twice' Alexander in her novels. Shortly after her husband's death, she returned to Jemimaville near Cromarty, not far from her grandparents' croft which inspired the beloved 'Reachfar'. Jane Duncan died in 1976.

Also by Jane Duncan

MY FRIENDS THE MISS BOYDS
MY FRIEND MURIEL
MY FRIEND MONICA
MY FRIEND ANNIE

and published by Corgi Books

MY FRIEND ROSE

Jane Duncan

CORGI BOOKS

MY FRIEND ROSE

A CORGI BOOK 0 552 12878 3

Originally published in Great Britain by
Macmillan London Limited

PRINTING HISTORY
Macmillan London edition published 1964
Macmillan London edition reprinted 1974, 1979, 1983
Corgi edition published 1987

This book is set in 10/11pt Plantin

Corgi Books are published by Transworld Publishers Ltd., 61-63 Uxbridge Road, Ealing, London W5 5SA, in Australia by Transworld Publishers (Australia) Pty. Ltd., 15-23 Helles Avenue, Moorebank, NSW 2170, and in New Zealand by Transworld Publishers (N.Z.) Ltd., Cnr. Moselle and Waipareira Avenues, Henderson, Auckland.

Printed and bound in Great Britain by
Cox & Wyman Ltd, Reading

This book is dedicated with my affection to
MR AND MRS ADAM EDDIE

CHAPTER ONE

In 1935, when I first met Rose, I was twenty-five years old and I was quite certain that I knew right from wrong, but I do not blame myself entirely for this youthful conceit. I think that part of the blame must be laid upon my upbringing by certain grown-up members of my Highland family who, although no longer youthful, still harboured the aberration that led them to draw a rigid line across the fabric of life and place on one side of it actions which, by their canons of judgment, were indubitably right and on the other side of it actions which, by the same canons, were indubitably wrong. It was a rigid code that took no account of how, where, when or why the actions were performed; circumstances did not enter into the matter; this was right and that was wrong and there the matter ended. It was a simple code; it precluded the problematic, thus leaving the mind free to concentrate on the urgent daily business of earning a living.

The most voluble giver of judgments and placer of actions on the right or the wrong side of the line in accordance with the code at my home, which was a small farm called Reachfar that stood on top of a hill in Ross-shire, was my grandmother, a woman of such considerable personal force that even now, when my childhood is well over forty years away, my pen without my volition still tends to write '*MY GRANDMOTHER*' in the panoply of capital letters. I suppose that if my grandmother had been asked to formulate the moral code according to Reachfar, she would have admitted that its foundation was embedded in the Ten Commandments, but she would probably have added a rider to the effect that the sins decreed against therein were of such mortal degree as to be what she would call 'outlandish'. No Sandisons of Reachfar needed to be commanded 'Thou shalt not steal', for they would never dream of doing such a thing: no Sandison of Reachfar would dare not to honour his or her father, mother and, particularly, grandmother or grandfather as long as my grandmother was about; and as for coveting one's neighbour's ox or ass — although cattle and horses were more common with us — no Sandison would dream of that either, mainly out of conviction that the Reachfar cattle and horses were better bred than those of our neighbours anyhow. The part of this commandment that referred to coveting your neighbour's wife my grandmother would have ignored entirely, and I am quite sure that if one had pressed the matter she would have said: 'That bittie has been in it since the days of Moses when people were very, very ignorant and sinful and foreign besides.'

But, on the deep foundation of the Ten Commandments, the Reachfar code rose spreading and majestic as a tall, strong tree of such vigour and luxuriance that it was possible to climb the main trunk of 'what a Sandison would do' on to the branch of a major virtue named 'work' and along that to a lesser branch labelled, say, 'Housework' and go on up and out on lesser and lesser branches until you came to a small twig which told you which was the 'right' and which the 'wrong' way to iron the folds in a pocket handkerchief. In every department of life, in physical activity as well as in mental attitude, the code held good all through my childhood and adolescence; the tree stood firm with never a wind strong enough to shake its smallest twig. By that code I made my judgments and, having made them, went on my way without further question. I judged; I gave merit or I condemned, and when I condemned I felt certain that hell-fire awaited the sinner who had transgressed.

At the age of twenty-one I left Reachfar and burst upon the

south of England as one of the workers of the world, and in the course of my first few jobs was, I think, too carefree and full of the wonders of this new world I was discovering to give any thought to the code of my upbringing at all, although, of course, I continued instinctively to behave according to its rules, so deeply were they dyed into the very fabric of my being. I was slow of development out of childhood into young womanhood and I have always been a slow-witted creature. It was not, therefore, until I was about twenty-five that I began to discover that there were situations in life for which there were no guiding branches in the tree of the code; that hell-fire had not my grandmother's accuracy of discrimination as to whom to consume and — this was the important thing — that for all my grandmother's ignoring of the coveting of neighbour's wives and such things, such things did indubitably happen.

In the sixties of the twentieth century it seems almost impossible to believe that in the tens and twenties of the same century people could live in a district where human behaviour was very much like human behaviour anywhere else — if not even slightly more red in tooth and claw than in many places — and that my grandmother and many more people could maintain this attitude of the blind eye to the neighbour's wife part of the commandment. But it was not impossible, because it was done. And even more extraordinary than the passive attitude of the blind eyes was the fact that, without ever a direct word being spoken, it was instilled into every young woman that the sooner she got herself a husband and a home of her own the better. No guidance was given as to how to achieve this end, except for the passive precept that one must not behave in a way that would 'cheapen' one in men's eyes. Indeed, in my own case, I was in one sense guided away from this matrimonial end that was held to be so desirable by being educated to provide for myself so that I had no need to find some man who would 'look after' me, as the euphemistic phrase went. And so it was all very puzzling.

However, when you are in the early twenties of life, in process of discovering a whole new world, it is easy to push puzzling things into the background and go on from day to day, taking what comes, especially when, as in my case, most things that came were pleasing and interesting.

In 1935 I was working in Kent as secretary to an old gentleman called Mr. Carter, a post I had obtained through the good offices of his daughter-in-law, Angela, who was an acquaintance of mine. Angela, who was only a little older than myself, had a nursery with three children in it and a husband who went up to the family shipping business in the city of London every day, and I spent my days with old Mr. Carter, who was beguiling the tedium of his retirement from shipping by writing a book about shipping. He had a weak heart, was crippled with arthritis and lived mostly in a wheel-chair. He was extremely bad-tempered and had sacked a line of secretaries as long as the line of Bourbon kings. He never addressed me as anything but 'Here, girl' or 'Dammit, girl', but we were friends for the whole happy time that I knew him, and then he died leaving, in the drawer of his desk, an envelope addressed to his son. It contained a dated, witnessed codicil to his will which would have been a very orderly document had it not referred to his lawyer as 'that old mumbling woman, Sibley' and it directed beyond legal argument that I was to have five hundred pounds from his estate.

Those few lines there, where I have told of Mr. Carter's death, are very cold and stark, but that is how death seems to me to be, at the moment when it happens. It also strikes me, though, that one of the happiest conditions of our human experience is that the impact of death should be dulled by space and time. Life is governed by space and time; life is lived within these dimensions but it is not annulled by them as is death. Life uses these dimensions but death is at their mercy. Over the years, a memory of happiness remains unaffected by space or time — indeed happiness remembered is often greater than it was at the moment it was experienced — but sorrow, subjected to space and time, can be eroded away.

My mother died when I was ten years old, but by the time I was twenty-five the sorrow of that death had gone and I remembered only the happiness of the years when I had known her. My grandparents died when I was twenty-four, a year before the death of Mr. Carter, but at the time of their death I was in Kent, five hundred miles away from Reachfar, and even then, at the moment when I opened my father's telegram, the impact was softened for me, because that five hundred miles of space intervened. When Mr. Carter died, there was for me a moment of full impact, when neither time nor space operated, when the dimensions of life were annulled, when I stood in a timeless void beside his bed until the beating of my own heart told me that, in time, this was an early morning in July of 1935, that the place was Mr. Carter's bedroom and that I, Janet Sandison, had just come in with his tea tray and letters as I had done every morning for nearly three years, but that, this morning, Mr. Carter was dead.

Mr. Carter lived, as I have said, with his son, daughter-in-law and their children, but inside the house, in a very short time, he and I had made a world of our own which consisted of the library, his bedroom, which was a converted room opening off the library, and a terrace that ran along outside the french windows. Within this area, he and I lived in a comfortable, slovenly jumble of books, papers, tea trays, half-eaten biscuits and uninhibited thought and speech. It was a very lively world. Mr. Carter had the weakness of many clever men in that he could not spell. I have the gift of many fools, a photographic memory, so that I spell from a picture of a word that is written in block capitals in black, on a white card which slides as required into a frame I have for the purpose inside my skull on the inner side of my forehead. Mr. Carter also had a strong sense of the fitness of things, coupled with a well-defined faculty for looking facts in the face. He therefore felt, logically enough, that, being an old, clever man in relation to his 'girl', it was not reasonable that I could spell and he could not, so we would get into arguments which invariably came to a crisis of: 'Hand me the dictionary, girl!' I would hand him the dictionary and try to remove any breakable object that was within reach, such as an ink-bottle or tea-cup, whereupon he would say 'Sit down, dammit, and don't fidget!' I would sit down, there would be a sulphurous silence until: 'EI it says! Damned rubbish!' and the dictionary would go flying across the room. He would then spend half an hour accusing me of being born out of unholy wedlock between Mr. Webster and Miss Oxford-Concise; of having looked up the word beforehand because by the devilish second sight that my Highland birth had given me, I knew in advance that he was going to question it; of having no more brains than a ticker-tape machine; of being not worth a penny of what he was paying me; and of not knowing the difference between a stun'sail and a hole in the wall, by which time he would be breathless and I would say: 'What exactly is a stun'sail, Mr. Carter?'

'Stun's'l, girl! Good God, no sailor would say stun-*sail* like that! And you don't know what a stun's'l is? Well, now, just hand me that book third from the left over there — not that one, you idiot! The *lower* shelf!' and we would spend a little time on sailing ships and then: 'What am I paying you for? To educate you? Come, come now, where were we when you started arguing and asking questions?'

'We were checking page 82, Mr. Carter, at the paragraph that begins: "To obtain a mental picture of Venice at this time, you must conceive —"'

'Yes, yes. All right, girl. You really must *not* waste my time. My time is limited. All right, read on —'

That limit to his time had been reached, as I have said, between my saying goodnight to him and my getting up in the morning. In those days five hundred pounds was a fortune to me, but it was on that morning that I discovered that five hundred pounds — or five million, for that matter — did not compensate for the fact that all that irascible, lovable, unpredictable liveliness was dead and that never again would I jump out of the spell of concentration at the angry shout of: 'Here, girl, dammit!'

Angela and all his family were more than kind to me and I had a curious feeling that I must not cry for Mr. Carter more than his own people did, for that seemed presumptuous, but during the time I had been with him I had seen a great deal of him and they had seen comparatively less. In a way, he was nearer to me than to them in that period at the end of his days, for, although they had known him for a long time, I felt that I was the last friend he had made, that I was the last person who had learned to love and respect him.

As a ten-year-old child, at the time my mother died, my mind became anaesthetised for a few months so that I cannot remember much of the period between March, when she died, and July of that year 1920, although my memories of earlier periods are very clear. In a similar way, I do not remember much of the few days after Mr. Carter's death. I went up to my home in Ross-shire for a short holiday but I do not remember the train journey nor my arrival there, but memory takes up again with the end of the meal on my first evening at home when my father said what a pity it was that my job had come to an end when I had been so happy and well-paid in it and followed this remark by asking if I had any plans. I remember feeling a strange isolation, of looking round the table at my father, my uncle, my aunt and Tom — these four people who all loved me, who had made endless sacrifices for me, who wished the very best for me — as I realised that all that the death of Mr. Carter meant to them, who had never known him, was that I was out of a job. They did not — they could not — share my sense of loss. What had been between Mr. Carter and me had been a private happiness of our own; and now that he was dead, that death was a sadness of my own that no-one could share. But we all have a defensive armour, and this armour covered the sense of isolation in sorrow.

'I am going back south almost at once,' I told them all. 'I've got a new job as private secretary to Mr. Andrews, my friend Angela's brother.'

'Oh? At the same place? In Kent?'

'No. It's in London, in the City. He is in shipping too, like the Carters, but another firm. It's called Andrews, Dufroy & Andrews.'

I saw a look of relief and pleasure settle over the faces of my family. They had not forgotten my emergence from my university in 1930, fully trained, into a world in the grip of the Great Depression which had no jobs to offer. They had never ceased to wonder at the luck that had carried me from one post to another from then until now, and they told each other several times, with solemn gratitude, that it seemed to be an incontrovertible fact that the world felt it owed it to me, Janet Sandison, a living, no matter how many cleverer, better qualified, less flighty people went jobless and doleful. This was not, I think, so much a criticism of me and my abilities as a manifestation of the race-consciousness of the Scottish Highlander that starvation is always just around the corner; but, be that as it may, my family impressed on me, not for the first time, that I was a very lucky young woman indeed.

Many people, I know, would find my native Reachfar nothing more than a remote, barren hilltop, but it is a place that has always been able to do a great deal for me and, given my own way and uninfluenced by my family, I do not think that I would ever have left it; but having left it, I have always found that when things go wrong for me my instinct is to return to it, and its healing power has never failed. Nor did it fail to heal the hurt of Mr. Carter's death. I would always remember him with love, I felt, and I still do, but after about a week I left Reachfar again and travelled to London, to take up my new post with Mr. Andrews.

I had met Angela's two brothers for only a very short time on the day of Mr. Carter's funeral, and not until I reported at the office for my first day's work with their firm did I look at them properly or even differentiate them. Clive, the elder brother, I now saw, bore a strong resemblance to my friend Angela, but in Roy, who was about two years younger and 'my' Mr. Andrews from a secretarial point of view, the family resemblance was less marked and he had a distant, self-contained air so that when he said 'You have found a place to live, Miss Sandison?' I had a feeling that the kindly question was asked because it was the correct question — maybe Angela had indicated that he should ask it, I even thought — and not that he was interested in where I lived or, indeed, if I happened to die.

'Thank you, yes. I have taken, just on trial, a small flat in Chelsea,' I told him.

'Travel from Sloane Square?'

'Yes, Mr. Andrews.'

'The office calls me Roy — differentiation, you know.'

'Thank you, Mr. Roy.'

'You will find my work different from Mr. Carter's, but you apparently adapted yourself to *him* —'

'I was very happy with Mr. Carter.'

'I don't throw the furniture about,' he said disapprovingly, and then the mail for his attention was brought in and we got down to work.

I do not intend to write a treatise on shipping lines and shipping brokerage, although, like most other things, the more you know of them the more interesting they become, so that by lunch-time on my first day I had decided that I was probably going to like my new job very much. At about noon Mr. Roy finished a long letter he had dictated about refrigerated cargo from New Zealand and said: 'Have you met Miss Slim yet?' When I said I had not, he rose and conducted me along the passage to a door similar to the door to his own office, except that this door carried the legend 'Mr. Clive Andrews' instead of 'Mr. Roy Andrews', and when he opened the door I walked into an office which might have been the one allotted to myself, except that, instead of being occupied by me, it was occupied by one of the largest, fattest women I have ever seen.

'Miss Slim,' said Mr. Roy, 'my new secretary, Miss Sandison.'

'How do, Miss Sandison?' Miss Slim said in a fatly wheezy voice. 'I came along at coffee time but Mr. Roy was dictating.'

'Sorry,' said Mr. Roy. 'Miss Sandison will have to remind me of your coffee vice . . . My brother in?'

'Yes, go in, Mr. Roy. Mr Stewart is with him.'

He turned to me, 'Miss Slim will look after you.'

'Thank you,' I said and he went through the communicating door into his brother's office.

'Sit down, dear,' Miss Slim wheezed, putting a large manila envelope into her typewriter. 'I want to mail this myself at lunch-time. Won't be a minute.' She rattled an address on to the envelope, took it out of the machine, put a sheaf of papers into it and said: 'Where are those perishin' matches?'

The matches were unearthed and she began to drop gobs of sealing-wax on the closed flap of the envelope. 'Scotch, aren't you?' she asked.

'Yes.'

'With old Mr. Carter, weren't you?'

'Yes.'

'You'll find this easy after that.'

'I liked being with Mr. Carter,' I said a little abruptly. He had been my friend and it seemed to me that these people in this office were critical of him.

'I liked him too — all bark and no bite.'

'You knew him, Miss Slim?'

'Twenty years ago when I first came here to work for old Mr. Andrews. Mr. Carter was a great friend of his. Great old boys, both of them.' She jerked her head at the inner office. 'Used to have rows in there that would make your hair curl and then go out and drink sherry till train time at night.'

'You have been here for twenty years, Miss Slim?'

'Twenty-three to be exact. Started outside there, licking stamps.' She nodded towards the general office which lay across the passage. 'My father was chief clerk in those days. Dead now, of course.'

'You must know this business backwards.'

She cocked her grizzled bobbed head at the three seals she had made and laid the envelope aside. 'I suppose I know quite a bit. Anyway, if you are stuck any time, come along and I'll do what I can. In the meantime, let's go and get a bite of lunch.'

The telephone on her desk rang. 'Oh, eff it!' she said and picked up the receiver. 'Slim here. Yes, Mrs. Roy. Yes, I'll tell him. Yes, I'm sure he will. Yes. Goodbye.' She leaned so much weight on the top of her desk that it creaked as she rose to her feet. 'Excuse me.' She waddled on short legs into the private office and came out again after a moment or two. She nodded at the telephone. 'Mrs. Roy,' she said. 'Met her?'

'No.'

'You wait. Most beautiful woman I've ever seen in m'life. And dress? M'dear, regardless!' She took a bulgy handbag from a drawer, stufffed a carbon-stained handkerchief, a packet of cigarettes and the matches into it and wheezed: 'Well, come on. Let's get our coats.'

Over our lunch of chops and vegetables and a glass of beer in a semi-basement restaurant underneath a busy City bar, Miss Slim reverted to the subject of Mrs. Roy Andrews. She described to me in a detail that was almost stitch by stitch the dress that Mrs. Roy had worn to the firm's last Christmas dinner, and in similar detail she described to me the last street outfit that she had seen Mrs. Roy wearing, down to the clasp on her handbag. I became more and more bored with Mrs. Roy, as her mink coat got tangled in the green peas I was eating and her perfume gave a cloying taste to my beer.

'Is Mr. Clive married too?' I asked.

'Oh, yes. Mrs. Clive's a dear and the boys are pets.'

'How many boys?'

'Three. Richard, Desmond and Roy. Richard and Desmond are at Harrow but Roy's just at prep. school — he's only nine.' She looked thoughful for a moment. 'Mrs. Roy — '

I broke in, looking as if I were concentrating on the boys. 'I like young boys. Do we see much of them?'

'Off and on in their holidays, but not much. Mrs. Clive likes the country. They spend most of their time at home — near Frinton, it is, in Essex.'

'Oh.'

'Mr. Clive only keeps a small service flat in town. But Mr. Roy has the house in Sloane Crescent — Mrs Roy is *smart*, you see. They have a house in Bucks, but they only go down at weekends. Great big place it is. Nice enough, I suppose, if you like the country, but I often wonder why Mr. Roy didn't sell it. It was left to him by his uncle. But then I don't care for the country myself . . . Have an ice, dear, do. I'm going to.' She did. She had two ices and two cups of very milky coffee and then wheezed contentedly and accepted a cigarette.

I am not at all one of these hearty, hockey-playing women, but this was the first morning in all my life that I had ever spent in the gold-paved, gold-walled City of London and my country legs itched for movement while my country lungs bawled for air, but Miss Slim put her elbows on the table and began to tell me of the evening dress that Mrs. Roy had worn at the last dinner given by the Lord Mayor.

'And has Mrs. Roy any children?' I enquired, after we had dealt with the last accordion-pleated inset of ice-blue satin.

'Only the one little girl, Delia — Dee they call her. She's eight. I went to her last birthday party and Mrs. Roy was wearing the most gorgeous —'

At long last it was time to go back to the office, and as we went through the outer door into the big general room I was almost muttering aloud with exasperation at Miss Slim and, by transference, at the unknown Mrs. Roy.

CHAPTER TWO

My days resolved themselves into mornings of taking dictation from Mr. Roy, afternoons of translating the shorthand into type, and evenings spent in my small flat or at cinemas, concerts or theatres or walking about the fascinating streets of London, and at the end of three weeks I had acquired Mr. Stewart, the firm's accountant, as my admirer. I had achieved what, from the time I went to the university nine years before, had been my ideal. I had an interesting job that was well-paid, I had an admirer who had money in the bank and the light of matrimony in his eye, I had a small flat of my own in the metropolis of London, that sophisticated Mecca of ambitious young people of my countryside and period, and, having achieved all this, I was conscious of nothing but a vague, uneasy unhappiness which I could not define but which brought into my mind some words spoken to me once by my old friend Mr. Rollin: 'It is better to travel hopefully than to arrive.'

The true meaning of those words came home to me now for the first time, and a very sad meaning it was, that brought me my first taste of dust and ashes, but there also came to my mind words that I had often heard spoken in energetic tones by my grandmother: 'If things are not pleasing you, do something to improve them. Don't just sit there with a face as long as a fiddle!' This was good practical Reachfar advice; but with the contrariness that is a permanent feature of life, it was Reachfar and its people that prevented me from following it. If I left my good post with Andrews, Dufroy & Andrews at the end of the first month, my father, my uncle, my aunt and my friend Tom would consider that I was flying in the face of a very kindly providence, and in the evenings, when I thought about my dilemma, the tree of the Reachfar code would spread over my bed-sittingroom one of its biggest, strongest branches, the branch called 'Loyalty', and in a shadow of shame I would see how impossible it was to leave this post with my friend Angela's brother that my friend Angela had been kind enough to find for me. Frequently, it seems to me absurd to say that we live our lives — our lives are largely conditioned for us and directed by the people we know, the people whom we term loosely our 'friends'. At least, it is in this way that my life has been conditioned and directed and the few times I have taken a decision entirely to please myself it has always entailed rebellion against the influence of some relation or friend.

And so, uncertain and dissatisfied, but trying to forget the taste of dust and ashes and to prevent my face from looking as long as a fiddle, I muddled along from day to day, supported by some half-formed idea that I would continue with Andrews Dufroy & Andrews for six months or perhaps a year — what I termed a 'decent' period — in the Micawberish hope that something would turn up or that I would settle down, and beyond this six month or year period I did not think, for, at the age of twenty-five, it was not my way to think very far, very long or very deeply and it did not occur to me that to stay with Andrews, Dufroy & Andrews for six months was to involve myself more deeply in a new set of relationships.

It was in early September that this was brought home to me when, one lunch-time, Miss Slim said: 'Well, you'll see Mr. Roy's country place on Saturday when we all go down.'

'I don't think I'll go,' I told her. 'After all, I haven't been with the firm for very long.'

It was the custom for the younger, unmarried employees to make an excursion by bus each year for a day in the country, and of recent years their objective had been, by invitation, Mr. Roy's and Mr. Clive's country homes on alternate occasions.

'Oh, but you must! It's a really lovely place and you *like* the country.'

'Oh, well, I'll see.'

'Mr. Roy would be hurt if you didn't go.'

'Nonsense, Miss Slim!' I spoke sharply because I was so sure that what I said was so.

'Better call me Lily,' she said, sitting down at the lunch table and heaving her huge bust into a more comfortable position. 'I must say you are the best thing that has happened to me in years.'

'What do you mean?'

'You and Mr. Roy. The secretaries he has put through his hands you wouldn't believe. Complain? Hard to please? You've no idea. And fussy? Every little mistake picked up. I tell you it's been no joke. I thought of telling you that first day how tricky he was, but I missed you at coffee-time and by lunch-time he was so pleased with you seemingly that I didn't bother. And he *is* pleased, thank God. The way that man can complain and the things he can complain *about*! This one had ugly teeth and spat when she read dictation back. That one had dirty nails and her shoulder-straps were always showing. The next one seemed to think she was a chorus girl and that he was interested in nothing but her legs. The other one had sweaty hands and made the telephone sticky. I tell you, what I've gone through has been no joke. Of course, I suppose it's living with Mrs. Roy that does it — groomed to the last hair, you know. Always absolutely perfect. Last Christmas when she came down to the office she was wearing — '

For the remainder of the week the office was dominated by the 'outing', and but for the insistence of the older, more staid, married departmental managers no work would have been done at all. All the girls skimped their lunches and ran off to buy new hats or new stockings, and tennis rackets that had been brought to town to have a string repaired stood about the offices pending the moment when they could be rushed to a sports shop.

I was in a quandary about the outing. I did not want to go because I felt that it committed me still more to Andrews,

Dufroy & Andrews, but I was afraid of being stigmatised as a snob or worse if I did not. Quandaries are situations that have always made me cross. I visualised a quandary as a cross between a quarry and a penitentiary, a deep circular hole with steep, slippery sides of hard shiny stone, so that every time you try to climb out you get only a little way up before sliding back to the bottom, and the more often you try to come out the more polished and slippery do the walls get.

I do not honestly think I am a snob about outings. It is that I am quite incapable of enjoying myself as part of a mass, and I am not even capable of being merged into the mass sufficiently to be swept along and give even some semblance of enjoyment. I fended off any definite commitment about the outing all the week, but by Friday, under the coercion of Miss Slim, I fell back on what I can only call my last bastion. I invariably feel unbelievably sick in a motor coach. I can travel on a horse, behind a horse, in a train, in the front of a car, in a ship and in an aeroplane with comfort and enjoyment. I do not know how I shall feel in a rocket going to the moon, but it is comforting to know that I cannot feel worse than I do in a motor coach.

'Oh, you'll be all right, dear,' said Miss Slim. 'My cousin is just the same, but she takes a teaspoonful of milk of magnesia before she starts and she is all right. It never fails.'

If there is anything as bad as being sick in a motor coach, it is someone telling you of an infallible precaution against being sick in a motor coach. It is odd that people cannot understand that if one is determined to feel sick, one will feel sick. I became quite exasperated with Miss Slim for implying that my will was no stronger than a teaspoonful of milk of magnesia.

On the Saturday I went on the outing to Mr. Roy's home, but not in one of the coaches that carried the rest of the staff. I had not reckoned on the strength of Miss Slim's will nor had I reckoned on her organising ability until I found myself being told by Mr. Roy that, since being driven in a motor coach made me feel sick, I was to drive down with him and stay for the weekend, that we might spend Sunday working on a charter agreement. I felt utterly helpless and consequently very cross with Miss Slim, Mr. Roy, myself for being so weak and the world in general, but I could think of no way out and went home to my flat as instructed to pack a case for the weekend.

I am very subject to having feelings about things, but the exasperating thing about them is that they feel as if they should be helpful but they are not. I am often a little envious of Moses, as portrayed in an early film, whose feelings came whirling down from the heavens and engraved themselves clearly on tablets of stone so that all he had to do was read the instructions on the stones and carry them out. My feelings are not like that. One of the ways in which they manifest themselves is in slight itches at the small of my back and on top of my head so that, on this occasion, I stood in front of the clothes cupboard in my bed-sittingroom with my right hand scratching one place and my left hand the other and wondered what clothes to take for a weekend visit to Mr. Roy's home. In the end, I settled for the tweed suit that I felt most comfortable in, a plain black dinner dress with long sleeves and a short black dress with short sleeves and comforted myself that I was doing the world in general — little as it deserved it — a good turn, for Miss Slim, when she described what I was wearing when I met Mrs. Roy for the first time, would not be able to bore her listener for too long.

Mr. Roy and I reached Daneford Court well ahead of the motor-coach party, and when I first glimpsed the garden I was mean enough to wish that the rest of the people were not coming at all. It seemed to be such a long time since I had seen a patch of untrodden grass or a tree that did not have park chairs in its shade and I wanted to be able to look at them for a little as a landscape without figures, especially Miss Slim's figure.

The house was of no definite period or style but it had been there for long enough for its red bricks to have taken a weathered look and for its walls to have settled in and become a natural part of the landscape. We entered the grounds through gates with a lodge, obviously occupied by a gardener because of the rigid rows of choice sweet-peas that were impaled by professional raffia knots against a wire trellis. The long drive wound about between flat stretches of grass dotted with trees until it made a final turn that brought the house into sight, all the windows of its length seeming to smile in the sun.

'What a beautiful place!' I said.

'I am very fond of it,' said Mr. Roy and pulled up at the front door. 'The bags are in the back, Woolmer,' he told the manservant. 'Is Perky about?'

At that moment Perky herself appeared in the doorway. She was a tiny, thin creature, like a town sparrow, but with bright blue eyes instead of dark ones and an Edwardian knot of silver hair on the top of her head. Her skin was like pink and white wrinkled porcelain and she might have been the oft-described 'French Marquise' except that her hands were lumpy and stringy from years of hard work.

'This is Miss Sandison from the office, Perky, for the weekend. Have they got her room ready?' Mr. Roy turned to me. 'Miss Perkins, Miss Sandison.'

'How d'you do?' I said.

'Pleased to meet you, miss . . . You'd like to come up now?'

I had a feeling that Perky would like me to come up now, that to her it was infinitely desirable that I should come unprotesting into her charge, so 'Yes, please,' I said.

'Just come with me, miss.' She turned to the manservant. 'The green room,' she said.

I followed her across the wide hall from which archways led away to right and left, across an inner hall that went up through two floors of the house, up a wide staircase from which two passages turned away and along one of the passages to a door which she opened.

'I like this room,' she said. 'A proper young lady's room, it is.' She went to the casement window and opened it wide and, of course, I followed her. This window looked out to the opposite side of the house from the front door and was indeed a magic casement, for here the garden fell away steeply in a series of terraces, from a formal terrace garden just below the house through different levels, each level wilder and less gardened than the last, to the smooth water of the Thames which lay like a coiled silver ribbon at the bottom of the slope.

'What a lovely place! And that's the Thames, Miss Perkins?'

'So they tell me,' she said in doubting tones. She looked down at the river and at the rolling country beyond. 'I'm not much of a one for the country. I'm a Londoner but it's pretty in its way. You'd better call me Perky.'

'Thank you, Perky. My name is Janet.'

She looked up at me. 'You'll be comfortable in here, Miss Janet. Your bathroom is just there. I'll be in the hall when you come down. There's no 'urry.'

It was the first 'H' she had dropped and I felt it had significance. Perky did not want me to come downstairs. I sat down in a chair by the window. 'I can be happy here for a long long time,' I said.

'That's right. Make yourself at home.'

She went out, closing the door with a quiet click.

From the chair by the window I looked out over the fair, lush countryside. As I sat, the bulk of the house was behind me and the Thames valley in the green and gold of its early autumn beeches was before me. Behind me was the dark constraint in the house conveyed by Perky's manner and before me was all the brilliance of the sunlit distance. Mentally, I made my escape from that dark constraint out into the light and distance, and even as I made the escape I recognised that this was something that I had done frequently since I had been ten years old but I was now conscious for the first time of doing it. Mentally, as I sat at this window above the Thames, I ran away from this house, from its constraint, from Andrews, Dufroy & Andrews, from my London flat, from this 'outing', back to my home at Reachfar. I do not mean to convey that I was homesick or unhappy in any way, but, in a wavering, dim flicker at the back of my mind, I recognised on this forenoon that Reachfar was an insulation between me and unhappiness as I looked out over the beautiful river and said to myself 'So this is Buckinghamshire and the Thames' and discovered that my mind was seeing neither. While my eyes looked out on the pale sky, the autumn beeches and the silver ribbon of the river, the sight of my mind saw the Top Classroom at Achcraggan

School as it had been when I was a small child, when I first heard that there was a river called Thames.

I loved all my lessons at school and, in retrospect, I cannot but think that the teaching was of a very high standard in spite of the fact that all the lessons for some fifty children of all ages between five and fourteen were given by Mr. Stevenson, the Dominie, and Miss Inglis, the lady teacher. Mr. Stevenson took the geography lessons himself twice a week and Miss Inglis sent in from her room to the Top Classroom pupils, no matter how young, who she thought might absorb the lessons. I was one of the absorbing sort, for I learned at the age of six or so that the world was so big that its picture covered a whole wall of the Top Classroom, and yet Reachfar, my home, was such a small part of this world that you could not even see it on the picture. The other salient fact that I absorbed at this age was the political one that the red parts of the picture belonged to 'us' and that the rest belonged to the 'rest' who were a despicable lot, being mostly Germans. This was at the time of the twentieth century's first war and we used to bounce our balls in the school playground to a gay tune with the words:

'Down, down down went the *Lusitani-ah*,
The *Lusitani-ah*, the *Lusitani-ah*!
Down, down down went the *Lusitani-ah*,
And we will all remem-ber!'

On the final syllable of the verse, as well as on every '*-ah*' at the end of the ship's name, we jumped both legs over the bouncing ball and landed in time to bounce it down again and maintain the rhythm.

I had not sat for very long in the warm winter firelight of the Top Classroom before I learned that the nearest country to Scotland was England, but Mr. Stevenson was at pains to impress on us that, although near in distance, it was very, very different, and especially was it different from our own part of Scotland which was the Highlands. England, Mr. Stevenson told us, was a rich beautiful country, especially in the south and east, with grass greener than we had ever seen, deciduous trees of noble size in vast number, fine houses, some of which had been standing and lived in since the time of Queen Elizabeth and even earlier — 'You, Ian Sinclair, what was the date of the battle against the Spanish Armada?'

— and churches and cathedrals of a magnificence unrivalled anywhere in the world —

'Lizzie Bain, what was the tune we sang the second psalm to in church last Sunday?'

'The tune called York, sir.'

'That's right. Mary Macrae, what do you think that tune is called after?'

'The place in England called York, sir.'

'Well — Tom Smith, what is the most famous building in York?'

'The Minster, sir. It's a great big kirk.'

'Church, in English, Tom. We are speaking about England.'

'Yes, sir.'

'And the psalm tune is called after the Minster. A glorious edifice. Some day you will all go and see it for yourselves.'

In addition to all these glories, the Dominie told us, England had a river, a special river that was, like Scotland's own Clyde, known all over the world. It was a rich river, straddled near its estuary by London, the capital city, but it was rich in other things besides fame and money, for it was one of the most beautiful rivers in the world and had led a man, long ago, to speak what was one of the most musically beautiful sentences in the English language.

'Listen now,' he said and we all listened while the soft Highland voice said: 'Sweet Thames, run softly, till I end my song.'

And now, some twenty years later, as I looked from this green-curtained window, it was that voice, speaking those words, that I heard again. There was a far-reaching effect about the tuition of geography as given by Dominie Stevenson at Achcraggan School, something as far-reaching and as indelible from the mind as the moral code of Reachfar.

I was still by the window when Perky tapped and peered round the door.

'Oh, book-reading,' she said, looking at the volume on my lap. 'Miss Dee is just the same. Read books for hours, she will. Never was a one to settle to it myself . . . The buses will soon be in. Mr. Roy and Madam are in the drawing-room. I'll show you.' I put aside the book, took a last look at the Thames and followed her downstairs.

The large inner hall was now transformed into a dining-room, with tables laid to seat about forty people and two efficient-looking caterers' men were unpacking and polishing glasses from a hamper in a corner.

'This way,' said Perky and we went along the outer hall to a door at the far end.

'Come along, Miss Sandison,' Mr. Roy said when she opened this door.

At this time of which I am writing, it was the custom of what were called the 'society magazines' to publish full-page photographs of what were known as 'society ladies' taken against the background of their homes. Very often, the lady was posed by a fireplace, one forearm resting on the mantel, one foot, perhaps, poised on the kerb of the hearth. These photographs were almost invariably captioned: 'The Countess of So-and-so, chatelaine of Such-and-such Hall or Manor or Castle.' When Perky closed the door behind me, leaving me on the inside, I had a curious sensation that I was looking at one of these photographs, for the tall fair woman had the exact pose and the mantelshelf carried the exact period ornaments. Above the mantel, a huge mirror hung, reflecting the head and shoulders of the woman, the room and, beyond that, the steep terraces of the garden down to the shining river where a little tree-grown island lay sleeping in the sun. The effect was one of photo-montage and a little uncanny, as if the lovely golden head of the woman had been superimposed on the landscape of garden, river and island and belonged there yet did not belong, as figures sometimes are yet are not part of the landscapes of dreams.

'Come along,' Mr. Roy repeated, making me aware that I was indeed dreaming. 'Rose, Miss Sandison.'

She turned, smiled, held out her hand and the society magazine photograph dissolved.

'— And Miss Calvert and Miss Roland,' Mr. Roy continued.

I turned as he turned, towards a sofa at right angles to the fireplace and was, somehow, surprised to find that two women sat there. I had not seen them when I came into the room. One was fat, one was thinner, one a little older with thick-lensed glasses, one a little younger without glasses.

'How d'you do?' I said.

'And now for God's sake, Roy darling,' said the voice of my hostess, 'push the bell and let's have a little strengthener before the horde gets here.'

I had a quick consciousness of being one of the horde myself who had got here too early, but the older and fatter of the two women was patting the big sofa and saying: 'Sit down, Miss Sandison. This is your first firm's party, isn't it?'

'Yes,' I said.

'I think they are a splendid idea. I angle for an invitation every year. I do — '

'Lorna,' said Mrs. Roy, 'don't be so damnably enthusiastic. Sherry or martini?'

'Martini, Rose, thank you.'

'You are from Scotland, aren't you?' said the gentle voice of the younger thinner woman. 'What part?'

As we all raised our glasses, Mr. Roy said: 'Miss Sandison is from Ross-shire, Helen'; but before anyone could speak, Mrs. Roy screamed: 'Russia? I thought you said she was Scotch?' and then laughed with great enjoyment at her own wit, before going on: 'Talking of Russia, I heard a good story at the Masons' party last night, Lorna. It was the only thing about the party that *was* any good. There was this Russian woman called Olga and she was in Paris and she wanted to get a job in a brothel, so —'

When the story reached its dénouement, Mrs. Roy led us in a chorus of laughter, but I think the only one of us who was genuinely amused — with the exception of Mrs. Roy herself — was the fattish woman with the glasses called Lorna. Helen, the young fair woman, although she tried to laugh, was much more embarrassed than amused and I saw a faint flush suffuse her forehead, while hoping that a similiar flush was not suffusing my own.

'God, look at Helen blushing!' said Mrs. Roy. 'Roy, give me another cocktail and I'll tell a really funny one that I heard from Guy.'

'Rose has the most wonderful sense of humour,' Lorna Calvert told me while she raised her glasses and wiped tears of laughter from her eyes.

Mrs. Roy, now provided with the drink she had asked for was just beginning: 'There was this husband and wife and it was their wedding anniversary and —'

'There are the buses coming up the drive,' Helen said.

'Oh, damn!' said Mrs. Roy and tossed off her drink.

Lorna, Helen and I stood a little apart from and a little behind Mr. and Mrs Roy while they welcomed the staff one by one, and Miss Slim, as soon as she had been greeted, came over to join us. She was bulging cheerfully out of a printed silk dress, beaming with pleasure under her be-flowered, eye-veiled hat and carrying a large bag of American cloth from which the corner of a coloured bath-towel protruded. She already knew Lorna, who introduced Helen and then said: 'The room for the girls is the same one as usual, Miss Slim. Let's collect them and go up.'

We all went up to the bedroom and bathroom which had been allocated for the day to the female staff and we sat around while the girls washed, combed hair, powdered faces, exclaimed, giggled and enjoyed themselves. I found myself feeling more outside of them all than I had ever done.

'I *am* looking forward to the swimming-pool!' said Miss Slim, which made me understand the function of the protruding bath towel.

'You are fond of swimming?' the quiet-voiced Helen asked.

'Love it. I'm not mad about the sea, like Margate and that — too cold — but I've been going to the baths twice a week since I was a kid.'

'I didn't know there was a pool,' I said.

'Oh, we'll lend you something —' Lorna began.

'No, thank you,' I said. 'I don't swim, but I like to watch people do it.'

'The pool is new,' Lorna explained then. 'It was only put in last Spring. Dee is very fond of the water.'

Lunch was a very cheerful affair. My Mr. Stewart sat on one side of me and Helen Roland on the other, and Mr. Roy was at the head of our table. Mrs. Roy was at the head of another and Lorna's rich laugh came across to us from her place at the head of a third. When the meal was over, everybody disappeared as if by magic and I found myself on a seat in the terrace garden above the river with the quiet-voiced Helen.

'Do you smoke, Miss Roland?' I asked.

'Thank you.' She took a cigarette. 'This is your first visit to Daneford, Miss Sandison?'

'Yes. I have been with the firm for only about a month,' I told her. 'I think it is about one of the loveliest places I have ever seen, this.'

'It is beautiful, isn't it?'

There was a gentle, dreaming quality both in her face and in her voice as she looked down at the river. She had a strange, wistful charm, I thought.

'Maybe you find all this a little lush,' she said. 'I have a Scottish cousin who says it is cloying, but I love it. Of course, this is my home county.'

'That always has an effect. I have an affection for my own county, although a lot of it is as barren as the day before the Creation.'

'I have never been to the Highlands of Scotland. I have never been farther north than Edinburgh, but I love all of Scotland that I have seen.'

'You still live here, in Buckinghamshire?'

'Yes. I have a tiny cottage on the river — I work in Marybourne, you see. I have a little bookshop there and Miss Calvert, Lorna, has the antique shop next door. It was she who first brought me to Daneford — she and Mrs. Andrews were at school together.'

The terrace began to fill with people, some carrying tennis

rackets, some swim-suits and towels, while a group of some six of the younger staff were already running, laughing, down the winding paths of the terraces to the river. Mr. Roy, in immaculate white flannels, came over to us.

'And what about you two?' he asked.

'I think we are quite happy, Roy,' Helen told him.

'Not want a game?'

'Later, perhaps. Where's Lorna?'

'Gone to the pool with the swimming crowd.'

'Shall we go and look, Miss Sandison?' I rose from the seat. 'Go and have your tennis — we'll watch you later, if you make it interesting.'

'We'll do our best,' Mr. Roy said and went away with his tennis players.

I wondered in a passing aside where Mrs. Roy was as Helen and I walked round the house and down a back drive to the long low bungalow that housed the swimming-pool, but she soon passed from my mind. The staff was enjoying its collective self in what my friend Martha would call 'no ordinary way'. With the exception of Mr. Stewart, who was a Lowland Scot, and myself they were Londoners to the last, small bespectacled office boy, and one of the things that makes London such a lovable city to the stranger is the capacity of the Londoner for enjoyment. There is a deliberateness about the enjoyment of the Londoner, as if to enjoy himself were a duty that he owes to the fountain-head of life, and he goes about that duty wholeheartedly and enjoys himself right through to his very soul.

Miss Slim, with typical versatility, was the queen of the luxurious, blue-painted swimming-pool. Enormous in her tight black suit with the club badge on its ample breast, she was a shocking sight on the tiled floor at the bottom of the diving-board, but in the water she was as agile, graceful and lovable as the jovial porpoises who gambol round the ferry-boat that plies to and fro across my native firth. At one moment her broad laughing face under its tight cap would be grinning at us from the deep end and at the next her huge, shiny rump would be rising like Atlantis refloated from the water of the shallow end. The typists and despatch clerks, white and spindly, the girls a little shy in their red or yellow suits, the boys inclined to strut a little in their royal blue or black, were all glad to take lessons from her, some in the elementary strokes of swimming, some in their attempt to dive.

'I think Miss Slim is a most remarkable person,' I said to Helen Roland as we watched a dive that took her enormous bulk into the water as a bullet might go through a slab of cheese. 'There is a generosity about everything she thinks and does that I have seldom met before.'

But Helen did not seem to be listening. She made no comment. She was not interested in Miss Slim or, indeed, in anybody. I had the impression that she found me a bore, so I made no further attempt at conversation.

After a little, at her suggestion, we left the pool and walked back towards the house and then by a path between herbaceous borders to the tennis courts, one of which was hard and one grass.

'This is a wonderful place,' I said then. 'It has everything.'

'Everything,' Helen Roland agreed, and she looked away with obvious pleasure across the lawns to the trees of the park.

On the courts two sets were playing and Mr. Roy was sitting on a garden seat with a shy young typist who was pink with pride and enjoyment.

'And how is it going, Roy?' Helen asked.

'We two are walloping everybody,' he replied with an attempt at schoolboyish enthusiasm which sat oddly upon him. 'I picked Miss Mudie here for my partner because she is the youngest and I am the oldest, and it turns out that she was her school champion.'

'Oh, Mr. Roy!' Miss Mudie blushed.

'So we are very unpopular, but we are going to take on Stewart and Miss Glover next. You don't play, Miss Sandison?'

'I'd rather watch. I don't play well. I am the spectator-sports type.'

'No games at all, Miss Sandison?'

'No. I like to walk and dance. I like to ride too, in an untutored non-Hyde-Park sort of way.'

'I should have thought you would have been good at games,' he said in a regretful near-disapproving tone.

'I have never been sufficiently interested to try,' I said, simply to annoy him, for I could not see why my being employed as his secretary gave him any right of approval or disapproval of my chosen pastimes. In my mind, there are two sorts of people — those who like to chase balls and those who do not. I happen to belong to the latter group.

Helen Roland and I sat watching the tennis and Woolmer and Perky came out with jugs of lemonade and the afternoon wore on towards the fading light of evening. The tennis players, together with the river party which had now returned, decided to end their sporting day with a dip in the pool, so we all trooped back to the building which housed the shouting and the splashing. From the moment that Mr. Roy dived into the water and, rather like a sportive curate at a Girl Guides' summer camp, I thought, raced after Miss Slim and pulled her under by the ankles, joy became unconfined. Even the shy Miss Mudie and my reserved, dignified Mr. Stewart began to indulge in what can only be described as horse-play as the day worked up to its climax. Eventually, Miss Slim and Mr. Roy constituted themselves captains and began to pick sides for an all-in water polo match as a grand finale and everyone became comparatively quiet while the teams were chosen, some going to one side of the pool and some to the other when their names were called. Lorna Calvert and I were to act as joint referees.

The picking of the sides had just been completed when the door of the women's dressing-room opened and Mrs. Roy came through, a golden-haired, cream-coloured Juno in a tight, flame-coloured backless swim-suit of shining satin, a large yellow towel trailing from her left hand.

'Miss Slim,' she said into the silence, 'you do look coy with your two great big balls!'

There was an embarrassed titter and giggle from the young men and women and then Miss Slim looked down at the coloured beach balls, one of which she was holding under her arm while the other lay at her feet, and her muscles seemed to relax involuntarily, the held ball falling on to the one on the tiles and both rolling away into the water.

'We're going to play polo, Rose!' Mr. Roy shouted. 'Want to come in?'

'How appallingly hearty! No. I shall sit and have a cigarette.'

She sat down and arranged her beautiful legs gracefully on a long chair.

The game started, but the spirit had gone out of it. The timid young typists who, a minute before, had been screaming and giggling beyond themselves with gaiety and enjoyment, were conscious now of their shy white limbs, the wisps of hair escaping from under their caps, the shoulder strap that would not stay in place. The young men kept glancing at the long chair, missing the ball, then feeling foolish because they had missed it, so that all of them became steadily more nervous. It seemed to me that the long building was full of nothing but this lounging figure in its skin-tight flame satin and pair after pair of wide, searching eyes. It was not only brightness but a sort of innocence as well that had fallen from the air. I was glad when the game was over.

As soon as it was finished, our hostess went away back to the house, taking Mr. Roy with her, but Lorna Calvert and I sat on the diving-board and waited while Helen Roland and the girls dressed and then we all walked back to the house in a group. On the way, Miss Slim drew me to one side.

'Isn't Mrs. Roy just lovely? Have you ever seen anything like that figure of hers? And, m'dear, that *suit*!'

'She certainly has a beautiful figure,' I agreed.

Drinks were now served in the large drawing-room where our hostess, in semi-evening dress, was in position by the fireplace; a buffet supper was available in the dining-room and the tables had been cleared from the large inner hall so that the floor was open for dancing to a gramophone in one corner. For an hour or two, things went gaily enough, Mrs. Roy dancing with Mr. Roy, Mr. Stewart and one or two of the younger men who had obtained a little Dutch courage from the beer at the buffet, but then, as Miss Slim was changing the records at the gramophone, the high hall was filled with different music, a long run of notes from the grand piano which stood in a corner by the staircase.

'Oh,' Miss Slim whispered to me, 'Mrs. Roy is going to sing. She has a lovely voice — trained, y'know.'

We all turned our attention to the figure on the long bench and listened to a rendering of the ballad that opens with the words: 'I have so little to give, oh, my dear, won't you live for love alone – ' The voice was a mezzo-soprano and the song was rendered with a throbbing, eye-rolling melodrama that made me fix my eyes in embarrassment on a spot on the floor two yards in front of me. I do not think that I was the only member of the audience who felt like this, and, as Miss Slim went on applauding and requesting another song while the rest of us gave only the applause that politeness demanded, Mrs. Roy went on to render some five ballads in all, and all in the same manner, before Mr. Stewart, who was not over-sensitive, said to one of the young men of the Cargo Department of the firm: 'Well, Fullerton, what about a rendering of "Andrews, Dufroy & Andrews, the looniest mad-house in town" for a change?'

'Come on, Jimmy!' the others began to shout, largely out of relief, I think, at the chance to get away from the soulful ballads which were so out of character with the day.

'What's this?' Mr. Roy asked.

'Nothing, sir,' said Jimmy, kicking his feet about.

'Go on, Jimmy,' said one of his colleagues. 'That's a far better piano than the one in the Three Tuns.'

Mrs. Roy rose, Jimmy sat down at the piano, the Cargo staff gathered round it and, in contrast to the throb of the mezzo-soprano, we had a little staccato tune from the piano and an intimate, mischievous voice which yet sent its commentary on Andrews, Dufroy & Andrews and all its staff right home to every corner of the room. Jimmy, in a small way, was a real artist.

It was my Mr. Stewart who had been the instigator of Jimmy's song, and while verse followed verse, with everyone joining in the chorus, he stood nonchalantly in a corner while the other members of the staff fidgeted as Jimmy made his mischievous personal comments, with a smug look that said: 'Serve you right for giving him the chance to comment!' But suddenly, when everyone thought the last chorus had been sung, Jimmy went into one more verse.

'Mac Stewart looks after the money in the backroom labelled "Accounts".
His favourite words are "Ca' canny" while he dishes out minor amounts.
But since the advent of Miss Sanny, the guardian of Mr. Roy's door,
Old Mac is forgetting ca' canny and his ties are costing him more.'

'Oh, Andrews, Dufroy & Andrews –' the staff bellowed as never before. I did not know what my own face looked like, but I did not care, for the discomfiture of my rather smug Mr. Stewart gave me the greatest gratification.

I do not remember any details of the end of the party. I remember only the buses pulling away into the darkness and, shortly afterwards, Helen Roland and Lorna Calvert leaving in the latter's small car, but I remember being very clearly aware that Mrs. Roy was sulking.

CHAPTER THREE

The next morning I awoke with the light as I have done since my childhood, so I got up and dressed very quietly, went downstairs and let myself out of a french window from the drawing-room on to the terrace. I did not know in what part of the house Mr. and Mrs. Roy slept, but I made my way silently towards the yard between the kitchen and the garages from where, I had observed the day before, a path would take me by a roundabout route down to the river. I had just reached the place where this path joined the back drive when I heard Perky's voice calling to me from a pantry window.

'You are an early bird, Miss Janet! Come in the pantry here and get a nice cuppa before your walk.' She opened a door for me and I went into the pantry. 'I have your early tray all ready here, but I forgot to ask you last night when you would like to be called. I'm not forgetful as a rule, but it was a big day yesterday. Do you think they enjoyed themselves?'

I began to drink tea and eat thin bread and buter. 'We had a wonderful time, Perky. Especially Miss Slim — she spent the whole day in the swimming-pool.'

'She is a very nice lady, Miss Slim, and a great help to Mr. Clive. Been with the firm since she was a girl, she has.'

'Like you, Perky?'

She smiled. 'That's right. I started at twelve as nursery-maid to Mr. Clive — not this Mr. Clive, his uncle that's dead now.'

'When was that?' I am always inquisitive about people I like.

'Before your time, Miss Janet. 1881 it was.'

'And you have been here at Daneford all that time?'

'Oh, no. I'm not here, you know. My real place is the London house with Mr. Roy. He only sends me down here when something special's on to give a hand, like. Like yesterday.'

'Well, yesterday was a great success,' I told her. 'It must have taken a great deal of work to make it such a success.'

'Oh, not so bad with the caterers and everything. As long as it was all right — and no unpleasantness. That's the main thing.' She frowned momentarily and sighed, then she smiled. 'There now, you can go for your walk. It's not good to go walking in the morning on an empty.' Perky's habit of dropping out words that could be taken as said amused me. 'Mr. Roy has breakfast about nine on Sundays.'

'And Mrs. Andrews?' I asked.

'Madam always has breakfast upstairs.'

'I'll be back well before nine,' I promised her and went out into the sunshine.

As I followed the curving path between the trees down the slope to the river, I wished that Perky had never called me to the pantry, that she had not talked to me, for it seemed that, now, the brightness of the morning was tarnished. When I reached the tow-path and stood looking along the rippling, sparkling curve of the river at the little wooded island, I tried to hear in my mind the voice of Dominie Stevenson reading aloud to us 'The Lady of Shalott' at Friday afternoon poetry lesson, for here I was, standing on the very spot that might have been trodden by the burnished hooves of Sir Lancelot's war-horse, but I could not hear the words of the poem or the voice of the Dominie. All I could hear was the husky voice of Rose saying: 'There was this Russian woman called Olga –' Instead of dreaming romantic dreams by the morning-misted river as I wanted to do, the voice of Rose insisted that I must think of Rose, or Mr. Roy, and of reality, and, unhappily, I walked along the path, full of uncertainty, wondering what I was going to do.

I had never before met anyone like Rose, anyone who

behaved so badly according to the code by which I had been reared, with nobody to say her nay, with nobody seeming to notice, even, that her behaviour was bad. This was how it seemed to me at the time; it seemed to be a question merely of social behaviour. I thought that I did not like the thought of Rose, because by her remark to Miss Slim at the swimming pool she had 'spoiled things', because by sulking at the end of the party she had 'spoiled things'. It did not occur to me that Rose, in relation to myself, was something more fundamental than a woman who offended against the Reachfar code of social behaviour. I did not realise that she was the personification of reality breaking through my dreams; that her voice was a voice similiar in character to the uneasy whispers that came to me when I was alone in my bed-sittingroom, the whispers that I tried not to hear but which told me insistently that a well-paid job and a flat of my own in the Mecca that was London did not add up to happiness. In a similar way the voice of Rose telling of Olga and her job in a Parisian brothel was the voice of reality beside the lovely Thames, and because of it I could no longer hear the 'Tirra-lirra by the river' sung by Sir Lancelot.

But all this, that morning, I did not recognise. I walked along the tow-path wishing that I were anywhere but there, wishing that I need not go back to the house at all, wishing that I need never see Mr. Roy or Rose again, but when my watch told me that it was a quarter-to-nine I began to climb back up the steep path with a dreary sense of inevitability.

After what Perky had said, I was a little surprised to find Mrs. Roy formally dressed in the hall when I returned, but was relieved to find that I was not the only member of the household who was surprised when Mr. Roy, in riding clothes, came in and said: 'Good morning, Rose. What brings you down so early today?'

'I thought we should go to church,' she said.

'Church?' Mr. Roy look startled. 'Well, Miss Sandison and I were going to put in a little work — a job we should have done yesterday forenoon—'

'My dear Roy, you can't ask your secretary for the weekend

and then sweat her!' She looked at me and laughed.

'But I don't mind in the least—' I began.

'I'm sure you don't.' She turned back to her husband. If I were really truthful I would say that it was that she turned her back on *me*. 'I thought that having done the lady of the manor yesterday to the horde, I might as well make a do of it and take in the vicar as well. After all, Roy, you are always saying we ought to be around the place here a bit more.'

'Oh, all right, Rose. I'll change after breakfast. The work isn't all that urgent. Like to come to church, Miss Sandison? It's a nice old building and —'

'Roy, don't be silly! Miss Sandison is bound to be a John Knox or something,' said Mrs. Roy with a loud laugh.

'You are quite right,' I said. 'Besides, I would rather stay in the garden. I am appreciating my change from the pavements.'

We had a lavish breakfast, although Mrs. Roy, I noticed, ate very little, and when it was over I excused myself and went away into the garden.

The morning passed very quickly for me and I was watching the carp in a chain of small ponds in the sunken garden when I heard the car come back to the house; but when I went along the drive, two cars stood at the door, Mr. Roy's and Lorna Calvert's unassuming little saloon. When I went into the house there was a cheerful hail from Mrs. Roy in the drawing-room: 'Hi, Miss Sandison, come in. Had a nice morning?'

'Have a drink, Miss Sandison,' Mr. Roy said and handed me a glass of sherry.

'We saw Lorna and Helen at church,' said Mrs. Roy gaily, 'and I made them come back for lunch. Cheers, everybody!'

She was in a very gay mood and lunch went past very pleasantly, with Mr. Roy chatting amiably to Lorna Calvert on one side and Helen Roland on the other, while Mrs. Roy told me at great length what bores and how very unsmart her neighbours round Daneford were. When the meal was over, she said brightly: 'Helen, I suppose you want to go and see your darling horses? Roy has ideas of making Miss Sandison work, Lorna — did you ever hear of such a thing? I think you should take her for a drive instead — she doesn't know the Thames valley at all.'

I felt embarrassed to the degree where red spots danced before my eyes and began to make some sort of stuttering protest, but Lorna Calvert seemed to be genuinely pleased at being dragooned into entertaining a stranger in this way.

'That's a splendid idea, Rose. I'll be delighted. I want to run over to Maidenhead, anyway. Will you come, Miss Sandison?'

I accepted gratefully and got into her little car with her at once.

We spent a very pleasant afternoon. Lorna Calvert was an unhurried person who was interested in everything, and we stopped to examine some tall mulleins growing in a field and again at a little churchyard that she might show me a gravestone with an amusing epitaph, and so we came by devious routes to an old cottage near Maidenhead, where she gave some appreciated advice to a fashionable actor and his wife on how to destroy a worm that was making holes in the leg of an antique coffin stool. On the way back I said: 'I have fallen completely in love with the Thames valley, Miss Calvert.'

'Lorna will do nicely,' she said. 'I like the valley too. I was born in Putney, but my father and mother came from Marybourne and I came back here after they died.'

'I'm Janet,' I said.

'Janet,' she repeated. 'Nice and non-committal, the kind of name I like. I am always sorry for people with committal names. I have a friend called Honor. If I had a name like that it would get on my conscience — I would never be sure that I was living up to it.'

'Isn't it odd, how names get — well — coloured for one?' I offered hesitatingly.

'Just how do you mean?'

'I have a friend called Muriel. She is sort of messy and untidy and colourless and rather a bore; but even if a great actress or musician or someone were called Muriel, I would always envisage *my* Muriel first every time I heard the name.'

She gave her rich laugh. 'You are quite right. That does happen.'

'And the flower names can be awful,' I pursued. 'They so seldom fit. Miss Slim is Lily, you know.'

I suddenly realised with horror that Mrs. Roy, Lorna's friend of long standing, was named Rose and inwardly cursed my wandering tongue which always played me such tricks when I was at ease with someone, but Lorna was laughing heartily as she drove along. 'It is a shame, isn't it?' she said at last. 'But I don't suppose it worries her — nothing seems to worry Miss Slim much. Rose is very apt, though, for Rose Andrews, isn't it?'

'Yes,' I said thankfully. 'She is even a bit like a rose — one of those tawny-golden ones.'

'Yes, she is a lovely creature. Even at school she was lovely, and you know the awful pudding or skinny phases that girls go through. But not Rose — she was lovely at every age.'

'You have known her for a long time?'

'Since she was a child. We lived next door to one another in Putney and went to the same school. I am a good bit older than Rose, of course. I didn't see much of her for a time, but since she married Roy and has been coming down to Daneford I have found her again. Roy is a very agreeable sort of person, too.'

I agreed with her and went on to ask if she knew my friend Angela, his sister.

'No,' she said. 'You see, I meet only the people they know around here and they only come down at weekends. I think Roy would like to come down more often, but Rose is a town bird. You seem to be a perceptive sort of person, Janet. Do you like Helen Roland?'

I was startled. I felt that this was one of those questions that were socially unfair and it surprised me that a woman like Lorna Calvert should have asked it. I took a little time to reply, and before I had formed the words Lorna was continuing:

'I know it is a peculiar question, but I brought Helen to Daneford in the first place and I feel responsible.'

Responsible for what? I now thought that the question was merely silly, a sign of over-conscientiousness or some such thing on the part of Lorna. Helen Roland was obviously, I thought, what was called 'a perfect lady' — much more of what was meant by that term than Rose herself was — and fit to be introduced anywhere.

'I think Miss Roland is charming,' I said, 'but I shouldn't think she would be easy to know intimately.'

'That is rather the point,' Lorna said in a puzzling way. 'She is actually a sort of local tragedy. She was the only child of the Rolands of Ockleigh Manor, a big old place on the other side of the county. Her mother died when she was a child and her father seemed to lose his mind or something. Anyway, he died a couple of years ago. The place had to be sold, and when the taxes and debts were paid Helen was left with her two horses, a few hundred pounds and nothing else. She has been very courageous. She started a little bookshop and stationery business in Marybourne, the county rallied round and she is making a living. I feel very sorry for her, but one can't do much. As you said, she is not easy to know. Roy and Rose have been very kind to her.'

'She told me that her horses are at Daneford.'

'Yes. Rose is unusual in some ways. Most very attractive women don't, as a rule, care for other women, but Rose likes to have women around her, even if they have interests quite different from her own, like Helen and her horses.'

This was precisely true, I thought, more true than Lorna quite appreciated. Rose literally liked to have 'other women around her' as long as they were not of a type to compete with her in any way.

'She likes to have Helen about,' Lorna went on. 'That's why I bring her with me when I come up. You enjoy working for Roy?'

'Very much,' I lied or half-truthed politely. The work was interesting enough. 'He has such a rigid routine that it makes the work very easy. My last employer was old Mr. Carter, you know — Mr. Roy's sister's father-in-law, if that isn't too complicated a description — and with him there was no routine at all. My job with Mr. Roy is child's play.'

I went on to tell her a little more of Mr. Carter and Angela, and in no time at all, it seemed, we were back at Daneford and my country weekend was nearly over.

Lorna and Helen Roland went away shortly after tea, and the rest of us decided to go early to bed anent an early start for Mr. Roy and myself in the morning.

'I hope you don't find it dull of us, Rose,' he said to his wife. 'After all, you had your rest in the afternoon and might like to do something this evening?'

So that is where she goes in the afternoons, guests or no guests, I thought.

'No, thank you,' she said in a bored voice. 'I'll come up to Town with you in the morning.'

'But, Rose! We'll be leaving at seven!'

'I know — the crack of dawn — but I have a lot to do tomorrow. I have a fitting in the morning and my hair's a mess, and there's the Ormerod's cocktail squash in the evening.'

Very shortly after that we all went to bed, and in the morning we drove back to London in the sulky silence emanating from a too early risen Rose.

CHAPTER FOUR

The routine of the office took over, blunting the sensations of the weekend, although each day, for several days, Miss Slim at lunchtime turned over aloud her treasured meditations on Rose's swim-suit and the cocktail dress she had worn on the Saturday evening, and I did my best to do justice, by description, to the clothes that had been worn on the Sunday. Mr. Roy dictated to me his idea of a charter agreement with some machinery concern, while Mr. Clive dictated to Miss Slim his idea of the same agreement, and then the brothers got together with their legal adviser to beat out between them the final form of the contract, which fell to my lot for typewriting.

'A perfect job if you can manage it, dearie,' said Miss Slim, 'and I'll take care of the interruptions. Just close your door and I'll tell Nellie to put Mr. Roy's calls in to me. How long do you think it will take you?'

'The whole day at least,' I said, rolling the first sheets of crackling paper and carbon into my machine. 'I'm not very fast.'

'Just take your time and don't rush things.'

She shut the door and went away. Mr. Roy was out at a meeting, and by lunchtime I had the first six sheets — more than half of the job, I estimated — completed and all word perfect as far as I could see, so that I came back after a quick lunch feeling more confident than I had in the morning and had rattled my way three-quarters through the ninth page when I became aware of a small girl standing at the side of my desk. I stopped typewriting.

'Who are *you*?' she asked with a self-possessed stare.

'Janet Sandison. Who are *you*?'

'Dee Andrews.'

'And did your father bring you here?'

'No. I came.'

'Oh. How?'

'In a taxi.'

'Alone?'

'Yes.'

'Why?'

With precise little fingers she raised the lid of the inkwell and let it click back into place again.

'Because I wanted to. I don't like London.'

'But *this* is London,' I said.

'You are silly,' she told me. 'This is the City. I like the City. I don't like *London*.'

'Oh.'

'I want to type,' she said and reached at the keys of my machine.

I caught the little wrist quickly. 'No. Not now, Dee,' I said. She made a struggling lunge at the keyboard and yelled: 'I *want* to! I *want* to!'

By the Reachfar code children did not behave like this, not as brought up by my family, at Achcraggan School or anywhere that I had known as a child, so I administered a good sharp slap on Dee's held hand and said: 'Behave yourself, you little brat!'

She backed away from me into the middle of the floor, her round eyes staring, her mouth a round 'O' and her two mousy little pigtails sticking straight out like spikes from the sides of her head. Golly, I thought, I might have got away with her mother not liking me, but this has really torn it. She drew a deep breath.

'And don't start to bellow!' I said, throwing care to the winds, for I have always been the in-for-a-penny-in-for-a-pound sort. 'Just behave yourself till I finish this page, that's all.' I turned to my machine.

'Please,' she said in a quiet little voice, 'could I come near and watch you work it?'

'Yes, if you don't touch anything.'

'I won't,' she said and came to stand at the end of the desk again.

I was just taking the completed page from the typewriter when Miss Slim came bounding into the office, talking before the door was open.

'Janet, the kid — she's got away — she's lost —' She saw Dee.

'Gawd Almighty! How did you get *here*?'

'I came,' said Dee and turned to me. 'Now, can I get to type?'

'You come with me, Dee. I'll let you type. Miss Sandison's busy.'

'I want to stay here,' said Dee and began to click the lid of the inkwell.

'Oh Gawd!' said Miss Slim. 'Obstinate as a mule, she is. Oh heavens, I must go and phone them at the house.'

'You go, Lily,' I said, turning the next sheet of paper into my machine. 'Come back for her after you've telephoned.'

'I won't go,' said Dee.

'You'll do what you're told,' I said to her and went on with my work.

She stood there, a silent presence, watching my fingers on the keys. I felt nervous. If I make a mess of this page, I thought, so help me, I'll pick up this machine and brain her; but the page became completed, and when I turned over to the next sheet of script to be copied I suddenly found that a large section of it had been deleted and that the whole job was much nearer to completion than I had thought.

'Well,' I said to the child, 'want to have a go now?'

'No,' she said, and added, 'no thank you.'

Sulky little beast, I thought. 'Why not?' I asked.

She stared hard at me. 'I like you,' she said suddenly and disarmingly. 'You are ugly and cussed.'

'Really?' I asked because I could think of nothing else to say.

'Yes. That's the kind of people I like.'

'Oh.'

'Well, I suppose I had better go home now.'

'How will you go?'

'In a taxi, like I came.'

'But didn't you come to see your father?'

'Yes, but he's not here. I've been in.' She nodded at the inner office.

'That is not true. You haven't been in.'

'All right then, but I *looked* in through the scratchy hole in the passage window.'

'Oh.'

'It's the same thing!' she said belligerently.

'Yes, it is at that,' I agreed. 'Anyway, you found out that he isn't here.'

''Sright,' she said with a Cockney intonation, just as Perky would have said it. 'You've got sense,' she added.

I made no comment on this but said instead: 'Still, now that you are here, you might as well wait for your father, don't you think? He should soon be back and you could go home together.'

''Sright,' she said again and added, pointing to the typewriter: 'All right. Go on — work it.'

I began to work it again, and we had just finished the last page when Mr. Roy arrived. He stood over her sternly, and she looked back up at him just as sternly, and I was struck by the absurd resemblance between them. He was not in any way a handsome man and she was an unusually plain little girl, with his own indeterminate colouring, and her round eyes were like hard little coins.

'Dee, you are a very naughty girl,' he said. 'You have no business to run away like this. It is not a bit clever, and it only hurts people and makes them feel anxious.'

'I don't care,' said Dee.

He stared at her. She stared back. 'Why did you *come* down to the office?'

'I like it here. I don't like London. I like *her*.' She pointed at me. 'I want to stay here.'

'Delia, don't be silly.'

'Oh, I know I can't,' she said, 'because there isn't a bed, but I'd like to.'

'Well, we are going home now,' he told her.

'To Daneford?'

'No. Not tonight.'

'Then I'm not coming.'

'Now, Delia, that is enough. You will go to Daneford tomorrow. Say goodbye to Miss Sandison and come along now.'

'No.'

'Delia!'

'No.'

'The French say au revoir,' I said to break the deadlock between them, and it worked.

'What's that?' she asked.

'It means "until I see you again".'

'I like that,' she said and her sullen little face broke into a smile. 'Au revoir, Miss Sandison. Au revoir, Office,' and she ran through the general office calling au revoir to everyone, with her harassed father looking ridiculous as he followed hot on her heels.

'Gawd!' said Miss Slim, arriving and sinking into my second chair. 'That kid's a devil, that's what she is. If my Pa'd had anything to do with her he'd have clouted her proper, I'm telling you. I feel heart sorry for poor Mrs. Roy every time I see her — Dee, I mean. She'll not do one thing like any other kid. She's run away from two schools this year. If she was mine I'd go off my blooming rocker and that's the truth!'

'Where was she when we were down there at the weekend?' I asked.

'At Mrs. Clive's. They've got an old governess there that can manage her.'

I decided not to tell Miss Slim of my own recipe for the management of Dee.

'Wicked self-willed little beast,' Miss Slim went on, fuming.

'This contract is finished,' I said. 'Want to check it tonight?'

'Gawd, no! I've had enough. You've been quick, though. Give it here, I'll put in the safe. Thanks, chum.'

It was one of those grey, stuffy wet London evenings, and as I looked out of the steamed-up window of my bus, which was close with the smell of warm wet clothing, I felt that, like Dee, I did not like London; but I was in a worse case than Dee, for I did not like the City either. My flat, with its mass-produced gimcrack furniture, its skimpy built-in cupboards in the kitchenette, smelt as stuffy as the bus had done, and the panel electric fire in its arty wooden surround merely added a new smell, more stuffiness and no cheer.

I had intended to write letters, but, instead, I sat thinking of a little girl with whom no-one could 'do anything', a lawless little girl who ran away from schools and even from her home — a 'little beast', in Miss Slim's words who yet had been extraordinarily appealing when she stared round-eyed and said: 'I like you.' It is very flattering to be told outright by anyone that they like you; it is particularly flattering when a child tells you so outright, for children are remarkable keepers of their own counsel and conservers of their opinions.

When I had been Dee's age, I remembered, I had all sorts of private counsels and opinions which I never mentioned to anyone, not even to Tom, who of all my family, was my best friend for 'telling'. The reason for much of the privacy I could now understand was that there were many things which it was impossible to share because there were no words for them. There were no words to describe why the 'Thinking Place' among the tallest fir trees was the best place for thinking in and there were no words to describe the feeling you had when the wind blew and you swung about high in the 'Waving Tree' in your cradle-like perch in the forked branch of a silver birch in spring. The Waving Tree had got me into much trouble, for I frequently tore my clothes in its branches and there was always the question: 'Why will you not stay out of that tree no matter how often you are told?' There were no words to describe the lure of the Waving Tree when the wind blew and the rain-laden clouds rushed past; there was no way of telling how you could not resist climbing it. So you hung your head and looked sulky and behaved in general like Miss Slim's 'little beast'.

As I sat by the cheerless electric fire, thinking of my childhood and of my friend Tom, I suddenly discovered that I was crying, and that I should be crying thus caused in me a bitter shame and a sense of guilt because I did not know why I was crying. By the standards of the Reachfar code I had no right to cry, no right to be unhappy, and desperately I tried to identify the source of my misery, but, beyond the fact that the child Dee Andrews had touched in me some spring that released these tears, I could identify nothing.

It was only long afterwards that I became aware that I cried that night for the lost childhood and for the death of dreams. On the night itself, as the tears dried, I came to the practical conclusion that I had been mistaken in thinking that I would like to live by myself in a flat of my own. Hitherto, in the other posts I had held, I had lived in a household, as I had lived with Mr. Carter, and I decided that, as soon as I decently could, I would leave Andrews, Durfroy & Andrews and try to find a post where I could live with a family.

This was a reversal of my longest-held ambition. I had, for some years, wanted to try to write — I wanted to write poetry, but even in the dark deeps of my own mind I did not form these ambitious words — and it had always seemed to me that nothing foiled this ambition except the fact that I had lived all my hours, except when I slept, in the company of other people. Given a place of my own, I had been wont to think, where I could lock the door with the world and its people on the outside, I could write. It was shaming to find that instead of writing epic verse behind the locked door of my flat, all I did was to sit longing to be a child again and then crying tears of self-pity because this could never be. In my mind, I heard the voice of my dead grandmother saying: 'Oh, pull yourself together, for shame's sake!' and I could not but obey its command. I pulled myself together, decided to put a good face on things for a few more months in the City and then move on to another way of life.

I put such a good face on things and became so bright and gay around the office that, towards the end of that week, my cautious admirer Mr. Stewart took grave thought and then took what was, for him, a recklessly extravagant plunge by inviting me to dinner and a theatre on the Saturday night. I accepted the invitation for a complex of reasons, none of which was a proper reason for accepting such an invitation. I accepted because I was lonely, because it was 'nice' of him to invite me, because, perhaps, on more intimate acquaintance he might not be such a bore after all, I thought. And, of course, it was very flattering to have 'made a hit' with Mr. Stewart, who, said Miss Slim, had never shown the slightest interest in any woman before. He was also some seven years older than myself, which made his attentions more flattering still, and said Miss Slim, 'the highest paid employee in the firm and well worth thinking about'. Miss Slim used the phrase 'to think about' in only one way and with only one meaning, so that, as used by her, the phrase meant 'a man to be seriously considered by a woman with a view to matrimony'.

The upshot of my acceptance of the invitation was to complicate an already unsatisfactory situation still more. It took me many months to face the unpleasant fact that I actively disliked Mr. Stewart, and during that time I went out with him when he invited me, was bored by his conversation, embarrassed by the skinny nakedness of his mind, that was, yet, strangely lascivious. I accepted his company because it was the only male company available to me at the time and would come back to my flat wondering why I felt a little as I imagined prostitutes must feel. Young women can be extraordinarily stupid.

This was my situation, then, when, on the Tuesday morning after my first outing with Mr. Stewart, Dee walked into her father's office while I was taking dictation.

'Where have you come from?' Mr. Roy asked.

'Daneford.'

'How?'

'In the train.'

'Where did you get the money?'

'Out of Woolmer's drawer in the pantry.'

I rose to go back to my own office.

'I came to see *her*,' said Dee, pointing at me.

'What about?' her father asked.

'Nothing. Just to see her, stupid.'

'Well, you can't,' I said. 'I'm busy.'

I went out and shut the door and took myself to Miss Slim's

office, where I also shut the door. Half an hour later Mr. Roy came and found me and we took up our work again. Not a word was spoken of Dee,

On the Thursday morning she arrived again, just as before, and informed us that she had borrowed train and taxi fares from the gardener's wife, and then she turned to me: 'You can go away if you like. I'll come back. I am a persistent little brat.'

I looked at her father, feeling more than a little of a fool, and he looked back at me, obviously feeling likewise.

'Dee,' I said, 'what do you want?'

'I want you to talk to me.'

'What about?'

'Just anything. Just talking you know.'

'I see. And then?'

'Not anything. Just *be* with me and talk, you know.'

'But, Dee, I have to work here for your father. Would it do if I came and talked to you some evening?'

'*This* evening?'

'I can't get down to Daneford this evening, Dee.'

'You could get to London if I go there and wait for you. You just tell the taxi-man 112 Sloane Crescent and he takes you. Any taxi-man will.'

'All right. Ask your father if I may come this evening.'

'Why?'

'Because I won't come unless your father asks me.'

Mr. Roy solemnly invited me to Sloane Crescent that evening and I as solemnly accepted the invitation.

'All right,' Dee said then. 'I'll go back to London now. Au revoir.'

Mr. Roy tried to stop her so that he could send a member of the staff with her, but she looked at him firmly and said: 'Don't be silly. I've just come all the way from Daneford by myself.'

She let herself out of the office neatly and shut the door quietly behind her, whereupon Mr. Roy, who could preserve unruffled calm in the face of every office crisis, leaned both elbows on the table and ran a hand over his tidy hair in a distracted fashion.

'I am sorry about this, Miss Sandison,' he said at last. 'I hope you hadn't an engagement for this evening?'

'Of course not,' I said. 'Please don't worry about it, Mr. Roy. Children take these notions sometimes. She will probably tire of me very quickly.'

He sighed. He was a man of great reserve who obviously found any intimacy difficult and who would never, by his own volition, have got himself on to this footing with a member of his staff. I, too, felt awkward and embarrassed.

'She is a most difficult child,' he said, frowning, and then, after a moment, very impatiently: 'Oh well, where were we?'

CHAPTER FIVE

That evening I went with Mr. Roy direct by taxi from the office to the house in Sloane Crescent where Dee was waiting in the hall, in a big high backed chair with a book open on her knee.

'Hello, Miss Sandison,' she said.

'You see, she came,' Mr. Roy said.

Dee's eyes became indignantly round. 'She said she would. She is cussed,' she told him.

'Dee! Is Mummy in?'

'No.' She climbed down from her chair. 'Come, Miss Sandison.'

She led me upstairs to a large room that seemed to me to contain every child-amusement gadget that had ever been invented, but she picked her way neatly through it all, selected a book of poems by Walter de la Mare from a shelf, held it out to me and said: 'Read.'

'Please,' I said.

'Sorry. Please, will you read?'

'Yes, thank you,' I said

I took off my hat and gloves and sat down beside her on a sofa by the curtained window.

'Listen,' I said. 'I am not going to read for nothing.'

She looked at me and a strange light of something like scorn and disillusionment showed in her eyes, a strange look in eyes so young.

‘Father will pay you,’ she said.

‘I don’t mean that sort of something, Dee. I am going to read because of having a pleasant visit and a pleasant evening and I don’t want it spoiled by you bawling when I have to go away home to bed.’

‘I won’t make a fuss,’ she said. ‘At half-past six I’ll have my supper and my bath and then I’ll go to bed and I’ll try not to — ’

‘Not to what?’ I asked when she stopped abruptly.

Her face flushed painfully and she twisted her neat little hands together.

‘Not to what, Dee?’

‘Not to wet it,’ she said at last.

I felt a pain in my left side as if, physically, I had been stabbed.

‘Oh,’ I said after a moment, hoping that my voice had no tremor, ‘that is something not worth thinking about at all. Do you know that if you don’t think about things they very often don’t happen? I had a little dog once —’

‘What was his name?’

‘Her — it was a she dog.’

‘A bitch?’

‘Yes, but one mostly says dog instead of bitch, like saying horse when it is often a mare. Her name was Fly.’

‘Fly? Yes?’

‘And she had hairy paws and when she was small she used to wet and widdle all over the floor and get her paws wet and then she would look at the puddle and think about it. Then, one day, she did it outside on the grass instead and it all sank in and her paws didn’t get wet and there wasn’t any puddle for her to think about even, so she always did it on the grass after that.’

‘She never thinks of it now?’

‘No, not at all.’

‘That was a dog. Do *you* wet your bed?’

‘Not now, but I used to before. Everybody does, until they have better things to think about.’

‘I see. So Father doesn’t because of thinking about the office?’

‘Probably.’ A cold shiver ran up my back at the thought that

Mr. Roy might come to hear of this conversation. Having got myself into this maze of amateur child psychology, I now began to struggle wildly to get out. 'If I were you,' I said, 'I would say a poem to myself as I went to sleep — a poem that you like to think about. Is the one about "pomegranates pink said Elaine" in this book?"

'Yes. I like that one. Let's read it over and over and learn it!'

'All right.'

We read and talked until her bath-time and then she was as good as her 'cussed' word. She bathed, had her supper, cleaned her teeth and climbed into bed, and after I had heard once through 'Timothy, Elaine and Jane' she asked me to put the light out and said: 'Good night — and au revoir.'

When I came downstairs, Perky told me that Mr. and Mrs. Roy had gone out and then she offered me a drink. I accepted the whiskey and soda because it meant that I need not go back to my flat till a little later.

'Poor little soul,' Perky said then, looking down and smoothing the front of her big old-fashioned apron, 'I could manage her when she was younger, and Miss Green, that's Mrs. Clive's governess, is not bad with her now, but we are too old for her. It's only nature she would want somebody younger. But the ones that come, they haven't much patience and she's not easy and you can't blame them.'

The dreariness, the sadness, the misery closed in on me again as Perky spoke and I thought nostalgically of the sofa upstairs, the enquiring little voice, the neat little hands, the alert round eyes. I had been very happy up there for the last two hours. I put my empty glass on the table.

'I have to go, Perky.'

'All right, Miss Janet. We'll be glad to see you any evening.'

'Thank you, Perky. Good night.'

The next morning Mr. Roy was early at the office, and as soon as he arrived he called me to his inner room and telephoned to Miss Slim to take all his calls. I got a new notebook from the cupboard, thinking that we were about to embark on the draft of another of those tedious long charter agreements, and I quickly sharpened three pencils.

'Sit down, Miss Sandison,' he said. 'You won't need your notebook. I have a somewhat extraordinary proposal to put to you — it is quite without prejudice to your post here. Please understand that.'

I looked at him. He looked back at me, very much the businessman with a proposal to make.

'It is about my daughter, Delia, Miss Sandison. Would you consider acting as a sort of governess-companion to her?'

'But, Mr. Roy,' I protested, 'I know nothing about children! I am not qualified. I have no exper — '

'I did not ask about that. I simply asked you whether you would even consider such a position. I might add that the remuneration would be what you have here as my secretary but that your living expenses would be all found, at Daneford. Would you consider such a position?'

'I'd be an idiot if I wouldn't,' I said.

He smiled faintly. 'Well, now we can discuss it,' he said. 'I understand that many young ladies like yourself do not care for any position that has a flavour of the domestic about it. I wanted to clear the ground. Delia, as you know, is an extremely difficult child and is causing me a great deal of anxiety. I have entered her at two schools and she has run away from both. They were special schools — ' He flushed and began to play with a model sailing ship that sat on his table. 'She has an unfortunate physical disability — er —'

'I know. She told me about it.'

'She *told* you?'

'Yes.'

'Oh. I have had all sorts of medical opinions and I am assured that there is nothing wrong with the child either physically or mentally,' he said. 'I don't want you to go to her with the impression that I am giving way to a whim of hers. Candidly, Miss Sandison, you suit me admirably as a secretary and I shall miss you very much. I have taken this step, asking you about this, firstly for the reason that you seem to have a strange knack with the child. She told me this morning that she —' He hesitated and frowned. '— that she loved you — an expression that I have never heard her use of anyone before. It is very odd, but there it is. Secondly, I have a very difficult time' — he made a small waving motion with his hands above the surface of the table — 'ahead of me, a great deal of important business to settle, and it would be much easier if I were less worried about Delia. Your help would be a — very great personal favour to me, Miss Sandison.'

The obvious difficulty he had in speaking these last words was acutely embarrassing and I hastily said: 'I'll try it, Mr. Roy, but on a strictly temporary basis. If it is not a success, it will do Delia more harm than good — '

'That is understood. Also, if you find it too difficult, too trying, your post here remains open.'

I took a deep breath. 'Have you discussed this with Mrs. Andrews, Mr. Roy?'

'Certainly.' He looked at me as if I had been guilty of impertinence, so that I felt my face flushing. 'It was her idea in the first place that I should approach you. You see, Delia talks of little else — my wife and I have been worn down.'

'Oh.'

'There is really nothing more I can tell you, Miss Sandison — about Delia, I mean. You must come to me at any time if you want help. I do not ask you to work to any special curriculum — I do not mind if she has no lessons at all for a time. All I want is that somehow she should be controlled, made more tractable. I hope I am not asking the impossible?'

'No harm in trying,' I said banally. 'When would you like me to start?'

'I told Delia that you would join her for lunch today and tell her of your decision yourself.'

'I see. All right. But I'd have to leave the office almost now.'

'That will be all in order. We shall make some sort of arrangement for your work in the office here.'

I left the City at eleven in the forenoon on that Friday, took up my new post at noon on that day, and the next afternoon Mr. Roy, Mrs. Roy, Dee and I drove down to Daneford. There was no doubt at all that, in the Scottish phrase, Dee and I got on like a house on fire. When I thought about it, I was at a loss to understand it and it simply had to be accepted as a fact.

Not once in my first twenty-four hours with her had she tried to defy me and dig her 'cussed' little heels in. She was a model child, and very appealing too. As soon as we got into the car for Daneford, however, she and I in the back, her mother and father in front, my heart began to sink, for her plain little face folded itself up, the round eyes became hard and the mouth became a tight little button with a small vertical wrinkle at each side.

'I am looking forward to being at Daneford,' I said.

She stared straight ahead and made no reply, and for the hour and a quarter of the journey she did not speak or move, but as soon as the car stopped at the front door of the house she sprang out, held out her hand to me and said: 'Come.'

I took the hand and went with her, through the outer hall and up the staircase to the door of the room I had occupied on my former visit.

'You like this?' she asked, opening the door.

'Yes, very much. It is a beautiful room.'

'This is your room.'

'We'll see,' I said. 'You mother —'

She stamped a small foot in its neat shoe. 'It's *your* room!'

'No, thank you. I don't want a stamping-feet room.'

'I won't stamp feet!' Her voice trembled. 'I won't again. Father will make it your room.' She opened a door across the passage. 'And this is mine. Yellow for me and green for you. And that is our bathroom. And this' — she opened another door — is where we read and talk. The servants say 'school-room', but that's silly. School is grey — this is blue and white. White is for reading and blue is for talking.'

'I see. Let's take our things off and wash and have tea.'

'Up here?'

'I don't know.'

'You *must* know!' she said indignantly.

'We must see what your father and mother —'

'Must not!' She had picked up the stamping foot but put it carefully and gently back on the carpet.

'Why?'

'Because it is their house —'

'*Father's* house!'

'— your father's house,' I conceded, 'and we must find out what he would like us to do.'

'Oh, all right. And then come up here or go out?

'Yes, I should think so.'

'All right.'

She went away, pulling off her gloves, but came into the passage again as Woolmer and a gardener arrived, carrying between them my trunk. They put it into the green room.

'There,' she said with satisfaction, 'it is your room,' and she went away to wash her hands before disappearing into the 'reading and talking' room.

A little later we all had tea together round the table in the dining-room, and Dee was again folded in her strange, hostile silence. Neither her father nor I could get her to speak, and then Mrs. Roy, who had eaten one small piece of bread and butter, lit a cigarette, leaned back in her chair and said: 'You really are a most unsociable child, Dee.'

As soon as she had spoken, she tilted her lovely head towards the ceiling and sent up a long bored column of cigarette smoke, but I was conscious of that with only a fraction of my mind, for I was looking directly across the table at Dee. A gleam of open malice and hatred crossed her plain, decisive little face — a look unbelievable in anyone so young. It was gone in a second, leaving me stranded between unbelief and horror. I could not conceive that such a look could be brought to a child's face by her mother. My brain could think only of the word 'monstrous'.

As soon as tea was over, I asked that Dee and I might be excused and we left the room. As soon as the door was closed behind us, the charming little personality was back and she began to chatter like a magpie; and upstairs, while I did some unpacking in my bedroom, she arranged my shoes in a neat row, humming a little tune while she danced to and fro across the floor. As she danced, I seemed to see myself at her age, dancing down the 'strip of herbage', a moss-grown row of [illegible]nes between two fields at Reachfar. I remembered how I [illegible] inspect the bluebell bank in spring so that I might pick the very first of the harebells for a surprise present for my mother; I remembered how, in summer, I used to carry home with care a dozen of the precious, scarce little wild strawberries for my mother and I tried to imagine what was in Dee's mind instead of the gracious mother-image that had been in mine, but the very idea that a child should feel hatred for her mother was so foreign to me that my mind could not encompass it.

Dee had a good try that evening at delaying her bed-time and she succeeded up to a point, but at last she was underneath the yellow eiderdown.

'Good night now,' I said.

I did not attempt to kiss or even touch her, for I myself had not liked to be fondled as a child except by people to whom I made the first approach. Her little mouth became tight.

'Dee, what is it? Search hard for the words and tell me.'

'You will come back?' The words came out with difficulty.

'Of course! Before I go down for dinner and then again afterwards and then —'

'You promise — *cussed*?'

'Yes.'

'All right.'

When I had washed and changed, I went into her room again, and her mouth slackened into her charming infrequent smile and after dinner I went in again, but she was fast asleep. I did not go downstairs again but sat at the window of my room watching the reflection of the moon in the river and thinking over the whole situation. I had been surprised to be told that I was expected to come down for dinner every evening, for I had thought it would be routine that our meals would be served in the schoolroom. Apparently this had been so in the past, but now, Mrs. Roy said, Dee was old enough to have breakfast and lunch at table and I was to come down after her supper at night. I did not argue, not knowing the exigencies of the servant situation in the house, but there was a strangeness about it, for, quite clearly, Mrs. Roy had no more liking for me than I had for her. However, our table *à trois* tonight had been an unusual occurrence, I gathered. Most evenings I would have to dine alone, and at weekends, when my employers came down, there would usually be guests for dinner. To me it all sounded a great deal more pleasant than my bed-sitting room and kitchenette in London.

At the end of two weeks this routine was firmly established, but it was the only routine there was. Dee and I, as Perky would have put it, 'were not great ones for' routine. The only thing that we did regularly was to eat, a thing at which we were both fairly proficient. As a governess, I decided, I was a dead loss, for there was no discipline of lessons or walks, which, I vaguely understood from things I had read, were the brain and bones of the schoolroom day. Dee and I simply enjoyed ourselves, but her father seemed to be pleased to receive at his office a long letter from her written on the Sunday while he was playing squash and I was with Dee in the schoolroom writing to my father at Reachfar. Mr. Roy, too, had enough imagination to write back to her a short typewritten letter dictated to his new secretary with the initials RDA/CB at the bottom, which delighted Dee. Working on the principle that a little knowledge of any kind could do her no harm, I explained to her a simple alphabetical system of filing, so we made a folder of strong brown paper, labelled it 'Andrews, Roy D.', put the letter inside and put it in a drawer. Then a hint by telephone to Lorna Calvert brought her another letter and a new file was made for 'Calvert, Lorna (Miss)' and put into the drawer. Dee's correspondence kept her writing for far longer and with more concentration each day than she would have put into any writing or spelling lesson.

We were not entirely isolated during the week at Daneford either. Dee had no child friends, and when I attempted to enquire into this I was met with the bald statement 'I don't like other children' and a tightening of the mouth which caused me to let the matter rest until a later date. But Helen Roland came up nearly every evening to see her horses, and incidentally, she and Lorna Calvert spent all the Thursday afternoons with us (their shops' early closing day) and they were often there at weekends as well. Then, we had all four house-servants, the four gardeners and their wives, and old Riley, the groom.

During the week, on semi-duty only as it were, Woolmer wore his second-best coat and a surprisingly human aspect and would invite us to tea and a game of 'Snap' in the pantry with Fairlie, the old head gardener who was a native of Midlothian, to make a fourth sometimes, and under Fairlie's tuition we progressed from 'Snap' to a game called 'Nap', which was, I gathered, short for 'Napoleon' and at which we used to gamble like fiends, with much acrimony, for matches which, later on, Woolmer would exchange for salted nuts from the cocktail cabinet for those who had no use for matches.

After a game of this sort one wet evening, I had put Dee to bed, had surreptitiously collected the remains of her salted nuts to return to Woolmer for a future occasion, and was standing talking to him and his wife, the cook, in the passage between the pantry and the front hall. It was about eight on a winter evening and very dark.

'That's a car, Bert!' said Mrs. Woolmer suddenly, and, sure enough, a sweep of headlights sprayed over the windows of the front hall. 'Holy smoke, the madam!' said Woolmer and reached for his coat. He put on his butler's mask, went to the door which was already barred for the night and opened it. I followed him into the hall, and Mrs. Roy, mink-coated, swept in.

'Oh, there you are, Miss Sandison.'

'Good evening, Mrs. Andrews.'

'Is the master here, Woolmer?'

'No, madam.'

'Oh.' She looked nonplussed.

'I'll want dinner,' she said after a moment. 'Miss Sandison hasn't eaten yet, I suppose?'

'No, madam.'

'Dinner for the two of us then.'

Woolmer turned away to go through to the pantry, which left Mrs. Roy and me staring at one another in the dimly-lighted hall.

'Place is like a morgue!' she said.

'I know — I'd just come down.' I went to the panel of switches on the oak pillar and the lights came on in clusters on walls and ceiling.

'You have a fire in the library? Let's go in there.'

In the library, she slung the mink at a chair, the gloves, hat and bag on top of it, and went to the cocktail cupboard in the corner.

'Well,' she said, surveying the bottles, 'nobody can accuse you of being a boozer.'

'I don't care to drink by myself.'

'Well, you're not by yourself now. Gin and French?'

'Thank you.'

We sat down on either side of the big fire-place, and I found that she was surprisingly pleasant, but she was like some fashionable woman that I had met at a cocktail party, not like the mother of the child I was looking after. She did not mention Dee and I did not mention her either. She told me of her luncheon that day at some fashionable restaurant and of the people she had seen there; she told me of the dress-show she had attended in the afternoon and of the people she had seen there, and then: 'Roy had to go out of Town so I thought I'd take a run down here.'

'Just to check up,' I thought. 'You expected to find him here.'

'Good,' I said aloud because she seemed to expect some comment.

'I thought I might do it some odd night every week,' she continued. 'It makes a break for me and it must be pretty dull here for you.'

I knew that she would not care if I were dull enough to be growing green mould.

'It will be nice to see you, Mrs. Andrews,' I said, 'but I don't find it dull. We haven't had visitors today, as it happens, but Miss Calvert and Miss Roland came up yesterday.'

'How d'you like them?'

'Very much indeed.'

'I am a bit silly about my old friends — I am a loyal sort of person. I've known Lorna since I was at school. She is an awful old bag, really, with her dreadful clothes, and such a bore about her antiques, but there it is. Then she brought Helen Roland around. Helen's a pretty good bore too about her horses and so colourless it is difficult to believe, but she's harmless. Give me your glass.'

As she poured out a second drink for each of us I noticed that this was not only her second drink for the evening. When she turned back to face me, her features had the slipped-sideways look of the the slightly drunk.

'I think Miss Roland has great charm,' I said as she sat down again, and I will admit that I made the remark merely to see if it would irritate her. It did.

'Charm? Don't be stupid! She never opens her mouth. Why, look at Saturday night — we might as well have had one of her bloody horses at the dinner-table!' She went to the cupboard and added a shot of gin to her glass. 'Of course, I think virgins in the very nature of things are too dull to believe. And especially when they are over thirty. And when they get to Lorna's age, of course, they get past everything. Always being enthusiastic about the wrong things. I don't suppose they can help being virgins, of course, if nobody ever urged them.' She giggled madly at her own wit for a moment and then became drunkenly grave. 'Le's have another I'm tiddly,' she said and tried to rise to her feet, and then: 'Why the hell don't *you* mix 'em? You're not overworked!'

Not a very gracious lady at any time, I thought, and the makings of a very ugly drunk. I went to the cupboard and handed her a glass of almost neat gin.

'God, I'm bored,' she said next. 'Jew ever get bored?'

'Not often.'

'No 'magination. Thass your trouble. Like a cabbage. Lorna, Helen, the Graysons, all of them cabbages. Jus' go on from day t' day gettin' greener an' greener. Me — I wanna *live*!'

I wished she would go to sleep. I was hungry and wanted my dinner.

'An' I do! I *live*!' She shook her tawny mane and leered at me like a demented lioness. 'Don't suppose you've ever had a lover?'

I did not answer immediately.

'Or have you?' she asked, momentarily alert and strangely

vicious-looking. 'No. No. Not you. Guhnesses don't have lovers. Too mousey. I'm goin' t' bed.'

She suddenly tossed off the remains of her drink and swayed out of the room. I watched her make her way with exaggerated caution and dignity across the hall and up the staircase, and then I went through the passage to the pantry.

'Woolmer, madam won't be having dinner after all.'

'Quite, miss,' said Woolmer, and his face was as blank as a cloudless sky.

CHAPTER SIX

The next morning, Dee and I had just finished breakfast when a bell pealed in the pantry outside the dining-room.

'What's that?' Dee asked in a whisper and her frightened eyes looked in a haunted way at the ceiling.

'Your mother came down last night after you were in bed, Dee,' I told her. 'She will be ringing for her tea.'

Dee sprang out of her chair. 'I'm going riding — I forgot. I'm going with Riley — '

'All right,' I said with deliberate calm. 'Run up and change and off you go. I'll see you at lunch. Your mother is going back to town this morning.'

She smiled and said 'Au revoir', and ran out of the room.

After she had left for the stables, I went upstairs and into her yellow bedroom. She was unusually tidy for a child and seemed to take pleasure in the little routine things that she was asked to do, provided their purpose was explained to her. As a child, I myself had been taught to strip all the bedclothes from my bed each morning and hang them over a chair to air and I had asked her to do this. The chair was near the window, the yellow blankets over it and her pillow and pyjamas were on the windowsill itself. The book that she had been reading before she got up was lying by the bedside, her place in it marked with a postcard of the Tower of London that had come from Perky the day before, and, a strangely exotic touch, a large purple water lily from the tank in the corner of one of the greenhouses floated in a glass bowl of water on the little dressing-table. The plain, clean, neat room with its one exotic lily was strangely like herself — prosaic, ordered until the lily suddenly flaunted its passionate petals on the sight.

I was in the 'reading and talking' room, laying a deep dark scheme towards an arithmetic lesson — Dee would have nothing to do with figures if she could help it — when Mollie the housemaid found me.

'Madam says please to come to her bedroom, Miss Sandison.'

I made my way out of our wing, past the head of the staircase and along the long passage to the other end of the house. I knew where the bedroom was, but I had never been in it — Dee did not like that end of the house. I tapped at the door, was told to come in and did so.

It may be something of a tax on the imagination to visualise a room which was a cross between the Palm Court at some Grand Hotel and a Hollywood film set for a super-production of the life and loves of some great courtesan. The walls were a dull ivory colour, the all-over carpet and long velvet curtains a rich, dark red — the thick purplish red that I always imagine for the fabled 'wine-dark sea'. Round the walls — this was the Palm Court touch — were about a dozen gigantic mirrors in heavy carved gilt frames which wound in monstrous curlicues towards the centre of the top where was perched on each one a coy cherub, each of these about to blow a blast on a small upheld trumpet.

My mind has a habit of finding release in jingles of words, often almost meaningless, and on this occasion I seemed to hear in my brain two lines of an old Scots ballad:

> 'The coronach cries on Bennachie
> An' doon the Don an' a'—'

I blinked my astonished eyes and said aloud: 'What a — a remarkable room!'

'It is rather nice, isn't it?' came the voice from the bed. 'I had two of the old bedrooms knocked into one. Where's Dee?'

I turned towards the voice. 'She went out riding with Riley.'

'Then that's all right. As long as she isn't lurking about underfoot.'

I could hardly hear. My stunned mind and vision were now grappling with the bed which was the climax of the room. It was a sort of gilt gondola, standing on a dais a foot or so above the general floor level and its head rose in a curving gilt canopy, surmounted by two of those cherubs which were already figuring in my mind as 'coronachs', complete with trumpets, while the inner side of this canopy was padded with the wine-dark velvet of the curtains. The pillow-cases, sheets, blankets and eiderdown were all of a tawny gold colour. It all reminded me of a very bad production of *Antony and Cleopatra* which had been staged in my university days, and I fully expected to hear the flat Glasgow voice with the burr on the 'R's' of Isabella Tweedie, thinly disguised as the Serpent of Old Nile, say: 'Give me my rhobe, put on my crhown. I have immorhtal longings in me —' but I did not. My sight came into focus and I saw a face surmounted by a bulging pink rubber cap, a face that was a greasy mess of cold cream that came down over the neck to the edge of the low-cut chiffon nightdress. Around the bed, on the purple-red carpet, were a number of scraps of scarlet-stained cotton-wool. Madam was varnishing her nails.

'Oh, damnation!' she said and another sticky scrap fell to the carpet. 'Are you any use as a manicurist?'

'None at all,' I said firmly. 'I am very clumsy with my hands.'

'Oh, well.' She surveyed a long slender hand with her head held on one side. 'I suppose that'll do till I get up to Town. We got rather drunk last night, didn't we? What did we talk about?'

I was not sure whether the 'we' was being used in the royal sense or whether she really meant herself and myself. I did not enquire.

'Mostly about our love affairs,' I told her.

'So I told you about Flip, did I? I would, of course. I always think about him when I get tight.'

'My memory of last night isn't very clear either,' I lied, wondering if she meant the man Flip Orton who often came to dinner at the weekends.

'As long as you're discreet,' she said.

'Discreet? None of this is my business, Mrs. Andrews.'

'Oh, don't be so smug and stuffy! It's all right for people like you to be highly moral and respectable and all that rubbish, but some of us need more than that. And Roy is such a clod with his eternal business, business, business! It never enters his head that a woman like me has to have life — hot pulsing life all about me! It never enters his head that other men even look at me!' Her voice lost the throb of melodrama and changed to a dreamy tone. 'I've always been attractive to men — some women are and some aren't.'

She looked hard at me for a moment and seemed to consign me finally into the 'some aren't' group, and then her eyes returned to dreamy, complacent consideration of herself as she gazed at her reflection in the mirror opposite to the end of the bed while she told me in great detail of her love affair with Flip Orton.

When I had left her and had returned to my window that looked down on the river, my mind was whirling round in a many-coloured globe of vertigo. I suppose that many young women of twenty-six, in the year 1936, would not have been shocked by another woman telling them what Mrs. Roy had told me that morning, but, be that as it may, I was shocked and revolted to the bottom of my soul. It was not only that, deep in my memory, I could hear the thunderings of the Reverend Roderick Mackenzie, the minister of Achcraggan Church, against 'Cheziebel that painted her face and tired her head'; it was not only that never before had I heard of adultery between two people of my acquaintance; it was not only that the entire Reachfar code had been transgressed. The thing that shocked me most was the blatant artificiality of it all; the cheaply melodramatic gestures, the clap-trap novelette phraseology as in 'hot pulsing life'. In the midst of all the shock to my moral code, this revolt against the artificiality was uppermost.

I had been brought up in an atmosphere that was heavily

charged with what are comically known as 'the facts of life'.

For at least six months of every year the conversation at the Reachfar table had turned on sex — the lambing in the early spring, then the calving, perhaps a foaling, and then cows going to visit the bull, the stallion coming on his proud-headed round, the sow going to the boar and, every day, Falkirk, the white Wyandotte cock who was named after his home town, chasing poor Rusty, the Rhode Island red cock, away, so that he might tread all the hens himself. All this I had lived with and understood and found normal from my earliest days. What I did not understand or find normal was the mind that could find 'glamour and romance' in what seemed to me to be a dirty little hole-and-corner liaison. And I could understand still less the apparently irresistible desire to talk about it. She had not merely talked, it seemed to me, she had wallowed in it like a fat sow in a dung heap, her long fingers running up and down the smooth flesh of her arms much as a sow pushes its rump deeper and deeper into the muck that bubbles and gurgles round its belly. It seemed to me that any relationship in which true feeling was involved must be more private than this, that depth of feeling grows and thrives, as plants do, from roots of deep dark silence. And what I had heard and seen, having been heard and seen against the setting of wine-coloured velvet, gilt gondola and the coronachs simpering from the tops of the mirrors that reflected back about a dozen gondolas, each with its greasy-faced occupant, took on, as well as artificiality, an air of the ludicrous.

Philip Orton, known as 'Flip' was one of these peculiar people that are found in nearly every community that is within easy reach of a city. I knew that he went up to London by train on most weekdays, sometimes staying overnight there, sometimes coming back in the evening to the cottage in Marybourne, which he shared with his sister, a woman considerably older than himself, who bred spaniels and seemed to think of very little else. Philip Orton and his sister — Flip and Edith — were part of the 'weekend crowd' that came to Daneford and they had been there every weekend since I had come down with Dee, now that I thought of it. And I was now struck also by the thought that I had never noticed anything between Mrs. Roy and Flip. Maybe what she had claimed was true, that the affair was a complete secret. Yet I could not see how it could be when she had so recklessly got drunk in my presence and had taken it as read that she had given away her secret the night before. If, as she had said, she always talked of her love affair when she was drunk, the implication was that she had been drunk and had talked of it on other occasions, but I could not think rationally about the matter because it was something too new and fantastic in my limited experience.

At a movement behind me, I swung round on my dressing-table stool and found that she was in the room, be-pearled about the neck, mink-coated, the tawny-gold hair shining under the small model hat.

'Taking a look at yourself?' she asked. 'You could be quite attractive if you did something about all that mousey hair and took a little interest in your face. Your figure isn't bad, but you shouldn't wear these shirt blouses. They make you look like a Lesbian but you aren't. I'd know if you were.'

'Lesbian' was a word new to me and I did not know what she was talking about, but I did not have to admit this, for she went on: 'I suppose I've shocked the pants off you? I don't know why I told *you* about Flip and me. I must have got tighter than I thought last night. I've never told Lorna and she's the oldest friend I've got. Most women like me don't bother with other women, but I like old Lorna. She is very loyal and trustworthy and I think that's so important, don't you?'

The last words were an obscure threat, I felt. Mrs. Roy was regretting deeply that she had taken me into her confidence.

'Very important,' I agreed.

She studied my face for a moment, then looked into the glass and adjusted her hat by a trifle. 'You got a boy-friend?' she enquired.

'No,' I said and felt that I spoke the truth, for 'boy-friend' was not an accurate description, somehow, of my Mr. Stewart.

'What about that man Stewart from the office?' she asked.

I shook my head.

'I'd have thought you would have been interested in men,' she told me. 'I can usually tell about people in that way.' She studied me for another moment. 'I suppose you are another one like Helen Roland, cold as a frog in an ice-bound pool.' She giggled. 'D'you know that limerick?'

'No.'

She recited the lewd limerick to me and then: 'Helen's a stick really, and has absolutely no sense of humour. Well, I'd better be off.'

'Back to Town, Mrs. Andrews?'

'Yes. For lunch. You'd better call me Rose,' she said. 'Mrs. Anything always sounds so suburban and respectable. Besides, you can't talk about beds one minute and say Mrs. Andrews the next.'

I did not point out that she and not I had done all the talking about beds. 'I'll call you Janet.'

'All right.'

'Well, ta-ta for now and don't do anything I wouldn't do,' she said and went away down to her car.

As soon as she had been driven away, I retired to the library and took the dictionary from the shelf, for, for me, by far the most interesting item in our conversation had been this word 'Lesbian' which I had never heard before. The definition: 'of or pertaining to the island of Lesbos' did not seem to throw much light on the manner in which Rose had used the word or on my shirt blouses, so I obeyed the dictionary's instruction: 'See Sapphism', and turned to the letter 'S', at which point light began to break into my mind, bringing with it some resentment that an academic education like mine, which had informed me of the poet Sappho and of the rhythms and stresses of the Sapphic stanza, had equipped me so ill for the post of governess in the household of my friend Rose.

For, quite suddenly, Rose Andrews had stepped forward into the position which made me think of her, albeit ironically, as 'my friend Rose', and when I found this thought in my mind, I had the immediate reaction: 'She is no friend of mine! Why did I think of her in these words?' After a little, I came to the conclusion that I had applied this term to her because, out of all the group of people I had met since I joined the firm of Andrews, Dufroy & Andrews, Rose was the only one who had shown any real interest in myself as a personality.

The human ego is a peculiar thing and has its own terms of reference. To Mr. Roy I had been *his* secretary and was now governess to *his* child; to Mr. Stewart, I felt obscurely, I was a young woman of little intrinsic interest to him but whom it flattered him in some way to escort to restaurants and be teased about in the office; to Lorna Calvert primarily I was a young woman who had arrived providentially to look after Rose's troublesome child. Out of the group, Rose was the only one who had studied for a second the entity that was Janet Sandison; and although her study of me had been limited to a mild curiosity about my sex life, it was enough to cause that ironic response in my mind that designated her 'my friend' Rose.

I do not think that I, at that time, noticed that she had broadened my knowledge with a few careless words, more than her husband, Mr. Stewart or Lorna Calvert had done in the time that I had known them. Rose, this morning, had caused me to discover that Sapphism, what the dictionary defined as 'unnatural relations between women', existed. She had also caused me to take serious thought about the shirt blouses I wore, but, in the end, the economic factor made itself felt and I decided that I could not afford to discard six silk blouses simply because they conveyed a certain suggestion to the mind of Rose. Perhaps, without being fully aware of it, I had already come to know that the mind of Rose contained little other than thoughts of sex and was therefore over-prone to suggestion of this kind.

Rose had, this morning, taken on the character of a phenomenon that was quite new to me, and as I went about my almost non-existent duties in the house I thought about her a great deal. By the standards of the Reachfar code, I knew, I should have condemned her utterly, but there was an anomaly here. To condemn Rose utterly, I should have to sweep with righteous indignation out of her service and out of her house, but I knew that if I did this my people at Reachfar would be the first to condemn *me* for leaving a post that was even better in every way than my post as a secretary in the City had been. Besides, what my family might think quite apart, I did not want to sweep out of Daneford. I liked Dee, I liked the lovely house and garden, and Rose fascinated me with what, in my eyes, was her downright, remorseless wickedness. It gave her a demoniac glamour.

It was nearly lunch-time when Dee came back from her ride, dancing into the room, singing: 'She's gone! She's gone! The cat's away — the mice can play!'

I looked down at the child, feeling hotly angry with her.

'Delia,' I said sternly, 'you must not talk to me in that way about your mother!'

'Shizzint!' Dee said, glaring at me with ugly defiance.

'What do you mean?'

'Shizzint!' The mouth was a tight little cockleshell that opened only a crack to let the words out. 'Won't have her. Don't want her. I'll *kill* her!'

I swallowed something that was stuck in my throat and making me feel sick.

'Dee, go and change for lunch. Then, afterwards, we must take the measurements for your new bookshelf so that we can give them to the carpenter on Saturday.'

'What measurements?'

'The sizes of the books so that the shelves will fit nicely.'

'I'll soon be ready,' she said and ran off to her yellow room.

I was suddenly plunged into misery. Rose had shocked me; she had caused an uneasy breeze which threatened to break a few twigs on the tree of the Reachfar code, but Dee, with her hatred of her mother, threatened more than the tree. She was a threat to the very earth out of which it grew, the dark mysterious earth in which the primitive and natural human instincts were cradled.

In the few days between Tuesday and Friday I thought a great deal about this enmity of Dee's; but no matter how I reasoned, I could not bring it into the realm of the natural. Rose, it was true, was obviously bored with the child, and it was part of her fascinating wickedness in my eyes that she made not the slightest attempt to dissemble her boredom. In my grandmother's words, I felt that she should conceal her boredom 'for very shame'. But the boredom of Rose, I felt, was not in itself enough to account for Dee's enmity. In my experience, the mother-child tie was such a deep instinctive thing that a child would continue to love its mother even when grossly maltreated, as the Skinner children who had been at school with me in my home village had continued to love their drunken, slatternly mother.

By the weekend I had worked myself into something of a nervous state about the situation and about my own inability to deal with it, so that, on an impulse, I sought out Mr. Roy, who was alone in the library on the Saturday afternoon, with the intention of telling him that I intended to give up my post.

'Come in, Miss Jan,' he said.

Dee's form of address for me, which he had adopted, sounded incongruous on his lips, and I felt that it was more incongruous still that I should have sought this interview with him, the father of the child, instead of with the mother, but it was he, I reasoned, who had engaged me for this post, and it was to him that I should signify my intention to leave it. He sat looking at me blandly and non-committally, and I felt a surge of exasperation at this too-distant man and his over-familiar wife.

'Mr. Roy,' I said, 'I am afraid that you will have to find a proper governess for Dee.'

He frowned sharply and I knew that he was impatiently angry, as if I had interrupted some important train of thought of his by coming into this room to make a fuss about some absurd trifle.

'What on earth do you mean by a *proper* governess?' he asked snappishly.

My own exasperation quickened into anger. 'Just what I say, Mr. Roy. I mean a governess who is properly qualified as a governess, not a makeshift like me.'

'Makeshift! What nonsense is this? The child has learned more and is behaving better since you took charge of her than she has ever done before.'

'That may be so, but I am convinced that you need someone with qualifications that I haven't got.'

'You are not happy here. I suppose it is dull —' he said and stared away out of the window.

This evasion, the refusal to face the facts as I felt them to be, made me furious. 'If that were the reason for my wishing to leave I should have said so, Mr. Roy. If the child were mentally normal I should be very happy here with her!'

'Mentally normal? What on earth do you mean? How dare you say the child is abnormal?'

His face had become white and sharp with rage, but with an obvious effort he attained control of himself; the mask of a faint sneer descended over his features, and his voice, which had been shaky, was cuttingly superior when he said: 'How did you come to arrive at this ridiculous notion?'

I, however, had less control, or perhaps a hotter temper, than he had. It may even be that I was more genuinely fond of Dee and more concerned and anxious about her than he was.

'Because she hates the very sight, sound and thought of her mother!' I blazed at him. 'Are you going to tell me that any child who would like to kill her mother is normal?'

He seemed to slump in his chair; he seemed to stop breathing, even, so that my own angry panting was loud enough to fill the room.

'Her mother?' he said after a moment. 'Rose, you mean?'

'Would I mean someone else?'

He passed a hand over his forehead. 'Just a minute. Sit down.'

He looked so odd that I sank on to a chair at the other side of his big writing-table.

'I thought you knew,' he said.

'Knew what?'

'That Rose is not Dee's mother.'

'Not?' I stared at him. 'But — but how could I know?'

He looked at me, a faint smile marking his strangely closed and expressionless face. He shrugged his shoulders.

'I suppose I should have told you,' he said. 'I suppose I thought you knew already from old Slim at the office or Lorna Calvert or somebody. Oh, I don't know.'

He made an impatient waving motion of his hands above the papers spread on the table as if he wanted to protect their importance and their cleanly typewritten surfaces from all this trivial, messy business of his domestic relationships.

'I take it that the fact my present wife is not Delia's mother makes a difference to you?' he asked after a moment.

'All the difference in the world,' I told him. 'I have a stepmother myself. It is a most difficult relationship.'

'I see,' he said without interest.

He picked up a sheet of paper, read a line or two of its script with concentration, and then looked at me again with his customary distant blandness.

'My first wife died at Delia's birth,' he told me, and I felt that to tell me even this small part of his life story was distasteful to him. 'I married again three years later.' He looked down at his papers for a second and then at my face again, his expression very cold and stern now. 'Miss Sandison, I find it difficult to believe that Delia feels as you say. I think you exaggerate. Children say absurd things without realising what they mean. It is ridiculous to take the so-called feelings of a child seriously.'

My instinct was to pick up the heavy silver inkstand that sat between us and hurl it at him, at his reasonable, rational, satisfied complacency — the complacency, it seemed to me, of someone who had never felt anything and, indeed, considered all feeling rather vulgar; but before I could find words to speak he was continuing: 'But all that is beside the point. The important thing is whether you are now prepared to reconsider and continue to look after Delia.'

I was still beset by an urge to hurl the inkstand, and I do not know what I might have said in my desire to break up his cold facade had not the child's voice at that moment come from the hall outside: 'Miss Ja-an! Miss Ja-an! It's time to go down to the village!' I looked at the expressionless face on the other side of the table. 'Miss Ja-an! Where are you?'

Where was I? I did not know.

'That's Dee,' I said. 'She wants me.' I went towards the door, then turned and looked back at the man at the table. 'It's all right,' I said. 'I'm sorry I came in and interrupted you.'

'Not at all, Miss Jan,' he said, and before I had gone out of the room he had returned his entire attention to the papers on the table in front of him.

CHAPTER SEVEN

When I went to bed that night I lay for a long time regretting bitterly that I had let slip the opportunity of leaving Daneford, and with resentment I told myself that if Dee had not called out to me from the hall at the precise moment when she did I probably by now would be in a train for London, if not in prison for assault with the inkstand upon her father. My mind was now in such a muddle that I did not know what I thought or felt, and much of what I seemed to be thinking was in such strong opposition to the Reachfar code that I was almost afraid to countenance the thoughts at all.

Since the interview in the library I seemed to be seeing Mr. Roy in a new cold light, and my view of him was leading towards near-approval of Rose's cuckolding of him with Flip Orton. I knew that this near-approval was against all the tenets of the code in which I had been reared, but it seemed that the whole tree of the code had been shaken to its very roots in any case, as if it had suffered an earthquake which had rocked the very mountain-top where it stood among the Ten Commandments.

What I did not recognise on that night, what it took me some time to recognise, was that it was not the tree of the Reachfar code which had shifted position, but myself. Until now the branches of this symbolic tree had been the fibres, as it were, that held together and supported my thought processes which climbed about among them like creeping plants, finding a hold for justification of a certain decision here and sanction for a certain course of action there. But the events of this last week had taken place in a region that was beyond those safe and spreading branches, had taken place among people who had never heard of Reachfar or its code and who were beyond its shadow and admonition, and I, living among these people, now had to find some compromise, some common ground, between my way of life and theirs. It was all very frightening, but, at the same time, it had a breathless dawn-of-the-morning exhilaration.

As the days went by, with Dee and I amusing each other, while Rose, at the weekends, told me in language straight from the cinema or the few romantic novels which she had read all about her grand passion — this was the expression she used — for Flip, while Mr. Roy solemnly took exercise on horse-back or in the swimming pool or in the squash court (Mr. Roy never simply rode or swam or played a game of squash — he took exercise), I decided, as many people have done before, that it took all kinds of people to make a world and that I seemed to be the kind who, unlike Mr. Roy, lived without a plan; the kind who, unlike Rose, did not know what I wanted; the kind who, unlike my Mr. Stewart, had no ambition to get on and get rich; the kind who, unlike Lorna Calvert, had not even some vague philosophy about doing the best I could in the world. It seemed to me that I was the kind of person who lived entirely at the mercy of the people I knew, the people whom I called my 'friends'. I had come to work for Mr. Roy as his secretary because my friend Angela had suggested it; I had become Dee's governess because Dee had wanted it; and I was now staying here at Daneford because everybody seemed to want it, just in the way that I kept replying to the dull letters of a boring girl called Muriel with whom I had once worked and never wanted to see again simply because she kept on writing letters to me and I could not think of a way of making her stop.

The sort of young woman that I was at twenty-six is not capable of being unhappy or discouraged or even of thinking deeply for very long; and after lying awake for an hour or two on the night after the interview in the library, I began to sleep again in my normal way as soon as I went to bed, and during the days I went happily along, amused at the antics and anecdotes of Rose and wondering how Mr. Roy could be so clever about shipping and high finance and so silly about the people around him. And Dee was more and more a matter for pride. She no longer wet her bed, she was well advanced for her age at lessons, and, what pleased me more than anything, she was losing much of her hostility and becoming much more tractable about people, although she still had extraordinary likes and dislikes.

I supppose it was because I myself had always derived a great deal of satisfaction from observing people and wondering about them that I wanted to break down Dee's hostility, and if she and I took a bus ride to Marybourne to shop I would talk to her afterwards about the people we had seen, asking her what she thought was the nicest thing about Miss Binns at the greengrocer's and what was the nicest about the lady who had talked to us in the bus.

One day at lunch, after a trip to Helen Roland's shop to buy pencils and paper, I said: 'I do think Helen is a nice person, isn't she?'

'She's all right, I suppose,' said Dee without enthusiasm. 'At least, she's ugly.'

'Oh, Dee, Helen isn't ugly! In a quiet way she is really quite pretty.'

'Yes, I know, but ugly.'

'Dee, what do you mean by ugly?'

'Just ugly — like you and me and Lorna and Perky and everybody.'

I could think of no common factor between myself, Dee, Lorna and Perky.

'Can you explain even a little better still, Dee?'

'Oh, you know, Miss Jan! Ugly is being not all golden and creamish and attractive-to-men!'

'Oh yes, I see,' I said hastily.

The child spoke the last three words as if they were a single word, and she obviously did not know what they meant, but as she spoke them she raised a languid hand to her throat and tilted her head in an imitation of a familiar gesture of Rose's, an imitation so accurate that, in the small plain child, it had the effect of bitter satire.

I left the matter there for the moment. Dee's apparently irrational dislike of certain people was explained: all those she turned away from had blonde or golden hair, and in that same moment another small truth broke over me. All Rose's friends, the women friends she asked to Daneford because 'I am a loyal sort of person — I am just made that way', were what Dee called ugly. All of us — Helen Roland with her unassuming pale-brown hair, Lorna Calvert and I with our darker brown, and all the others of all shades of brown or grey — were, in the evenings especially, the perfect foils for the tawny-gold Rose. For a mad moment I had it in my heart to have my heavy thatch of dark-brown hair bleached to a brassy yellow out of sheer spite.

When Dee's new bookcase came, fresh and pretty in its yellow enamel paint, she and I spent a long wet day rearranging her considerable library which had over-flowed the existing bookcase into several boxes and cupboards. In the centre section of the new case, the carpenter had been requested to leave a particularly tall set of shelves to accommodate the proportions of her atlas and a number of Christmas annuals which she treasured. She fetched them from a cupboard, and I said: 'Now, *you* did this bit of measuring and it looks to me as if you've had the place made much too tall.'

'But I haven't,' she said, going back to the cupboard, 'because here is my flower book to go in and it's the biggest of all.'

I had not seen the 'flower book' before. 'May I have a look?' I asked. 'It looks very beautiful from the outside.'

'It is beautiful inside too — the pictures, I mean. Some of the poetry isn't very nice.'

I opened the leather cover, turned the first thick, gilt-edged page and read the title: 'An Alphabet of Flowers'.

'It's a yantique book,' Dee explained. 'Uncle Archie gave it to me last Christmas. He found it in a shop in Oxford where they have all yantique books. Could we go there one day, Miss Jan?'

'I should think so, perhaps.'

The book was Victorian. On each left-hand page there was a very well reproduced painting of a flower, with a large decorated initial letter of the flower's name, and on each right-hand page there were a poem and some literary references to the flower itself. It was a sentimental production, much of the reading matter very poor, but, as the discriminating Dee had said, the pictures were good and the production throughout was of a high standard. The book had all the nostalgic charm of another age.

'I think it's a lovely book,' I said, flicking over 'F' for 'Forget-me-not' and 'P' for 'Pansy – pansies are for thoughts – little pansy faces –' Under my idle fingers the page with 'R' for rose opened on my lap, with its florid picture of a spray of three deep crimson roses.

'There's a bad, bad poem there,' Dee said and went to sit down by the fire, 'a poem that makes you feel wicked.'

'If it makes you feel wicked, it is certainly a bad poem,' I said.

'You read it and see. The one called "Queen of the Garden".'

I do not think that the verse was acknowledged on the page of the book, and I have never come across it since, so I do not know the name of the writer and cannot make acknowledgement of it here. Nor can I quote it fully or quite correctly, but, some thirty years later, here is, from memory, an approximation of what I read:

'Queen of the garden bloomed a rose,
Queen of the roses round her,
Never a nasty grub that grows
Crawled on the briar that bound her.
Into her heart a canker crept,
Into her soul a sorrow.
"Queen of the garden once" she wept,
"I shall be dead tomorrow!"'

Dee was watching me carefully so I looked up and said: 'I would not say it was a very good poem. In fact, I think it is quite a bad one. But not bad enough to make one feel wicked — a poor silly rose worrying about dying. Oh, here's a good bit!

> The silken tassel of my purse
> Tear and its treasure on the garden throw! . . .

Have you ever heard of Omar the Tent-maker?'

'No. Who was he, Miss Jan?'

We were borne safely over the hurdle of the cankered rose on the swell of Fitzgerald's 'sweet song in the minor key'.

My governessing of Dee was now simpler than ever, for it was directed mostly towards the end of eradicating Rose from her thoughts as completely as possible, and during the child's waking hours at the weekends I did my best to keep her out of the house altogether. Rose made no protest about this and neither did Mr. Roy. Sometimes I wondered what his thoughts were, whether he ever tried to think forward to the end or whether he imagined that I was going to remain, growing old and grey at Daneford, until Dee was old enough to go away by herself or to get married. I often wondered about this last point myself. On the one hand, I could not imagine leaving Dee now, but, on the other hand, the cloistered life of the governess, no matter how luxurious, was not all that I wanted.

I did not take any active steps, however, to alter my way of life. When I look back to that time I find myself likening my mental laxness when I was at Daneford to the languor that, physically, overtakes someone who is lying on a warm sunlit beach with limpid waves washing near at hand. As I see it now, I went on from day to day, taking what came — and most of what came was pleasant enough – living in luxurious comfort and seldom thinking of the future. I think I had caught something of Rose's attitude to life, the attitude that nothing was more important than the style of a hat or the cut of a dress, and that the greatest hardship was to be bored or bothered about anything. Or perhaps, being a late developer, I was going through that physically and mentally lazy stage which is a frequent characteristic of adolescence. At all events, I gave everything as little thought as possible, for, now that the weakness of the Reachfar code had been exposed, thought called for definite effort, and on this sunlit beach near the limpid waters effort of any kind was repugnant.

I do not think that my attitude to life was an unusual one for people of my generation who lived through the 1930s. Indeed, I think it was fairly typical. There were the bold, intelligent far-seeing few who were aware of the implications of the Civil War in Spain and of other events in Europe, but these were the exceptions. Most of us lay about on the beach with the waters of time lapping about us, depositing all sorts of flotsam and jetsam in the nooks and crannies of our characters, unaware to a large degree of what was going on in the wider world or of the silting and erosion effects that were being worked on us or of the storm that was piling up on the horizons of our world. If there was anything unusual in my attitude at all, indeed it lay in the fact that I did, periodically, make the effort to sit up, shake the water from my eyes and brain and attempt to look around me a little and give a little thought to what I saw. Most people did not, and the people I lived among certainly did not, especially Rose. Rose was lulled and lost in a perpetual wallow in the sun-warmed sand laved by the limpid sea, like the lotus-eaters of legend, and Rose was not alone.

By Christmas-time I was more than ever the friend of Dee, and more than ever the confidante and boudoir audience of the cold-creamed Rose, and more than ever fascinated by her although at the same time frequently horrified.

Rose had a supreme self-confidence and was utterly without self-consciousness. It did not occur to her, when she made announcements about herself — except for a few remarks of sexual reference about other people, Rose invariably spoke about Rose — that her interlocutor might question the truth of what she had said, that her interlocutor might hold a quite diverse opinion. Indeed, words like 'confidante' or 'interlocutor' or even 'audience' do not accurately describe my position in relation to Rose. I think she liked me to be present when she spoke about her love-affair, partly because she did not ever like to be alone and partly because she felt the need to talk but did not want to do so without the presence of another person, because only what she called 'dotty people' talked to themselves. Nevertheless, much of her talk was not really addressed to me but to herself and was reverie, a living over again of the time she spent with Flip.

I do not want to convey the impression that Rose was a nymphomaniac. I did not then, and I do not now, believe that she was even very highly sexed, but she had a deep need of admiration, she had a childish desire to be shocking, and sex was the most daring and shocking thing she could think of; but the feature that I found most difficult to understand was that, in spite of the crudity of the 'dirty stories' she loved to tell and the lavatorial nature of the limericks with which she shocked the dinner table, in her affaire with Flip Orton she lived in her mind in the anaemic and emasculated atmosphere of the romantic novelettes which, in those days, cost fourpence at the newsagents' shops. Her forenoon reveries were spattered with expressions such as 'glamour', 'romance' and 'the bliss of being in his arms', so that the affaire took on for me a queer atmosphere of unreality. The real Rose, I felt, was the greasy-faced woman in the gondola bed whose chief interest was in the less frequently mentioned physical functions, and who, as soon as the mood of reverie was over, would say to me: 'I bet Helen Roland has hell with constipation — she looks that sort', or 'I bet that smug bitch Crawley who looked down her nose at dinner last night is as hot as hell in bed', or 'My God, how that new housemaid's breath smells!' It was as if Rose inhabited two worlds. There was the world of Rose and Flip which was filled with glamour, romance and bliss, and there was another world filled with people like Helen Roland, Mrs. Crawley and the new housemaid, people who were unglamorous enough to suffer from constipation, unromantic enough to suffer from halitosis and who had never known bliss but indulged merely in crude sexual intercourse. For this last activity Rose used an unmelodious four-letter word which is not in general use in conversation or on the written page, but this was, again, a manifestation of her need to shock. She did not use this word in relation to the activities between Flip and herself, however.

I feel that I ought to stress the fact that it was not only when she was alone with me that Rose used her unmelodious vocabulary, told her dirty stories or made her crude comments on the privacies of her acquaintance. Had this side of her been shown to me alone I should have concluded that something in me — some prudishness or priggishness — drew it forth as a natural reaction, but Rose behaved in this way with everybody in whose company I saw her, and this despite protests from Mr. Roy and the shocked faces of some guests such as Mrs. Crawley. It always happened, however, that a few guests were present who would laugh at her — Flip Orton, for one, was nearly always present at weekend dinner parties — and, of course, Daneford was one of the wealthiest and most fashionable houses in the district and had, I suppose, a certain social cachet which led to a certain sycophancy towards Rose. Frequently, though, it crossed my mind that when Mr. Roy engaged me to look after Dee he should have engaged instead a suitable person to look after Rose, who was appearing to me, the more I saw of her, to be a more and more acute case of arrested development, a development which had ceased at the age of sixteen or so.

I have remarked earlier that Rose did not protest at my arranging to keep Dee out of the house at weekends, but I should qualify that by saying that, although Rose liked Dee to go riding on Saturday forenoons, she did not like me to go with her. In her more vicious moods she would say that I was not paid to go larking off enjoying myself, and in her less vicious moods she would say that I was much better employed being company to her, Rose, than 'hanging around that spoilt brat all the time'.

On Saturday forenoons, after the long process of the reverie, the remarks about the sexual activities of her acquaintance, the bathing, the making-up and dressing were over, Rose did what she called her 'housekeeping'. This consisted in going over the account books from the grocer, the butcher and other local suppliers, for, in actual fact, the housekeeping was done by Woolmer and his wife, who was the cook. In my opinion their housekeeping accounts were both honest and economical, but Rose, no matter what her mood, questioned and grudged every pound of sugar and every bar of soap. Rose always grudged every penny that was not spent directly on Rose. It is true that she was not interested in food and ate remarkably little, but she liked to have dinner parties, and she liked her lavish table to be praised. She liked the big establishment of which she was the centre, she had to have it; but she loathed above all things to have to pay out money for its needs.

Another thing that made her extremely angry was anything in the nature of a charity appeal. The little envelope that asked for a donation to the Salvation Army threw her into a fury, and an appeal from a nationally famous orphanage would cause her to stamp round the room in a black rage and ring for the brandy and soda. *She* did not get anything for nothing, she said, and why should she be expected to give away a shilling every time somebody felt like asking for it?

I am aware that it sounds ridiculous when I say, after all I have told of her, that I still found Rose fascinating as a study and even likeable, to some extent, as a person, and I think this was because she was almost the polar opposite of myself. I do not mean to imply that, in contrast to Rose with her dirty stories and meanness about charities, I was a mealy-mouthed plaster saint who gave all I had to the poor. What I mean is something much more subtle than that — it was a question of our whole attitude to ourselves and to life in general, a question of the kind of people we basically were as a result of our upbringing and the chances of our lives.

I do not think that two women could have been more different from what Rose and I were. Rose was the only child of wealthy urban parents, while I had been born a peasant; Rose had had virtually no education and did not regret it, while I regarded my academic education as one of my most treasured experiences; Rose had all the beauty and self-confidence which I lacked; and Rose, aged forty and forty-one,

I discovered to my twenty-five and twenty-six, was married where I was not — facts which create a difference greater than most others between women.

In addition, I was what Rose called 'a dreamy poetic ditherer for God's sake; what you need is a man', while Rose was what she called 'of the earth earthy, call it dung if you like'; but, to be more accurate, I think I must add that we both slipped out of these categories and reversed our positions on one head. Rose had dreams of glamour, romance and bliss in Flip's arms, and I was utterly incapable of generating a dream of this kind about any man. At last, I can sum up, I think, the basic difference between us. On all subjects but one I probably was the poetic, dreaming ineffectual that Rose said I was, but on the one subject where Rose lost touch with the earth I was utterly prosaic. I could not have talked about any man as Rose talked about Flip Orton, least of all could I have so talked about Flip Orton. In the words of my grandmother, I would not have trusted the gentleman as far as I could kick him, but, naturally, I did not express this opinion to Rose.

It was on Saturday and Sunday mornings that Rose and I used to have our longest chats together; and having got through the housekeeping and Rose having expressed her indignation about the week's charity appeals, we would either go down to Marybourne to shop, in which case Rose would have several drinks at the King's Head, or, if the charity appeals had been unusually monstrous, she would have called for the cocktails to be brought to the library, in which case she would drink until lunch-time.

At my home there had always been a supply of whisky in the parlour cupboard and I had been accustomed to seeing it drunk all my life and at any hour of the day when the occasion was deemed to warrant it, and the attitude in my family was that a good deal more whisky would be drunk had it not been so expensive. From remarks made at Reachfar I had gathered that the price was the only limitation on whisky, and when I first came to Daneford and saw Rose drinking from eleven in the morning until one and then again from five-thirty in the evening until midnight, I believe that if I thought about it at all, I thought that she was lucky to be able to afford it. At Reachfar, however, I had never seen a member of my family drunk, and when it was borne in on me that Rose became drunk on most nights of the week, in London or at Daneford, I began to alter my attitude about whisky and alcohol in general, and I even made some small attempts to alter the attitude of Rose to it, but here, although neither poetic nor dreamy, I was utterly ineffectual.

CHAPTER EIGHT

It was early in January that I began to notice the degeneration in her and to realise that this degeneration was largely due to alcohol and the hold that it had over her. It was Saturday morning, cold and bleak out-of-doors, and Mr. Roy and Dee had started off early to go with Helen Roland on some jaunt of a horsy nature to one of the adjoining counties, when the housemaid came to tell me that my presence was required in Rose's bedroom.

When I went in, Rose was sitting at the big dressing-table with all the jars and bottles spread in front of her, the rubber cap that contained her hair on her head, a sullen look on her face.

'They gone?' she asked. Rose was not given to the minor courtesies such as bidding one good morning.

'They went about two hours ago.'

'That child will soon be as horsy as Helen Roland. Christ, I feel awful! Ring that bell and tell them to bring me a brandy and soda.'

'Have you had breakfast?'

'You know I don't eat breakfast.'

'Your fruit juice, then?'

'Hell, don't just stand there! Get me a brandy and soda!'

I rang the bell and sat down to wait till the drink arrived, while Rose started to work on her face. The cream-gold skin was coarsening, I noticed, and the flesh below her eyes and under the chin was sagging. The lips were less full, and the membrane, naked of lipstick, was corrugated with little vertical lines. After a swallow or two of brandy, and when the foundation of the face make-up had been laid, she came out of her sulky silence.

'What do you think of a man like Roy, really?'

'Think of him?' I repeated.

'Yes, think of him,' she mimicked. 'Don't try to tell me that you never think of any man!'

'I think,' I said, 'that he is a very kind and considerate employer.'

Saying this, I felt like a smug hypocrite, and I blamed Rose — as one does — for putting me into the position where I had to say what I had said which had made me feel as I felt. But Rose did not wish to be reminded, this morning, that she was talking to an employee.

She turned, rouge-pot in hand, and glared at me. 'Kind! Considerate! He's as stupid as a lump of wood! Oh, he's clever enough about cargo and all that office nonsense, I suppose, but in other ways he's a bloody fool. And all this kind considerate rubbish, that's not what a woman wants — not a woman like me, anyway. I have to have romance, colour, glamour in my life! I often wish he would jump into bed with somebody, just to prove he has it in him. Of course, he hasn't really — I found that out long ago. That monk's cell through there just suits him down to the ground.' She jerked her rubber-capped head in the direction of the room along the passage and swallowed a gulp of brandy. Then she laughed. 'You know, a little time ago I actually suspected him of having a little flutter?'

'Oh?'

'Yes. I noticed a sort of difference in him — or thought I did. Just about the time you came to work at the office, it was. I thought he'd got himself a floozie. In fact, I thought *you* were it. That's why I was so keen to have you down here as governess where I would know what was going on. I see now it was silly of me.'

'Very silly, Rose.'

'Oh, I don't know,' she said thoughtfully. She poured out

some more brandy — Woolmer should not have sent up the bottle. 'I knew that if dear Angela down in Kent liked you, you must have the makings of a lady. Angie is very fussy about whom she knows. Yes. That first weekend he brought you here — that time of the office do — I made quite a row about it, you know. I can't have Roy getting out of hand . . . You could be quite attractive if you took a little interest in your face and clothes, as I keep on telling you.'

'You must remember my position, Rose,' I said lightly. 'It would never do to have a governess around who looked like a floozie.'

'No, that's true I suppose,' she agreed gravely.

Rose, who prided herself on her sense of humour, never suspected anyone of being even slightly funny or sarcastic at her own expense. Her self-confidence was much too great for that.

'I ought to go downstairs, Rose,' I said. 'I promised Woolmer I'd help him in the cellar this morning with those new stocks Mr. Roy sent down.'

'Sit down. Woolmer is paid to attend to the cellar. I want you here and I am the most important person in this house. I can't think what Roy wants with all that hock and muck, anyway — *I* don't drink it, and all *he* drinks you could put in your eye.' She stared balefully out at the grey, bleak weather. 'God, what a day! And simply nothing to do. I'm sick of these housekeeping books and they can wait until next week.'

'What would you like to do, then?' I asked.

'It's maddening of Flip to have gone away this weekend, and here I am with a whole free Saturday. Of course, we didn't know I would be free — people are so selfish never telling their plans in advance.'

'Rose,' I said, 'have you ever thought of marrying Flip?'

It usually improved her mood and kept her from the brandy to talk of Flip.

'I've *thought* of it — who wouldn't? Dammit, I'm in *love* with him! Of course I've thought of it. Oh, God!' She rose and paced the floor, wringing her hands like an over-acting Lady Macbeth in a pink rubber cap, 'I've thought of it sometimes till I almost go mad! I've thought of it — '

'Then why don't you?' I asked.

She stared at me. 'What?'

'I feel sure,' I told her, 'that after what you have told me from time to time about Mr. Roy and yourself, if you spoke to him about it all, reasonably and quietly he would give you a divorce — '

'Divorce? Are you mad?' she shrieked, glaring at me.

'Well,' I hesitated, suddenly plunged out of my depth by her unexpected reaction, 'it isn't uncommon. People make mistaken marriages and — '

'Don't be a fool! My God, you haven't the sense you were born with!' she shouted. 'Flip's income in a year couldn't buy my hats! Of course, I have a bit of my own, but money goes nowhere these days. Love in a cottage isn't my cup of tea — I couldn't live some sordid life with one tweeny-maid in a bungalow with a lounge!' She suddenly became calmer and her tone changed. 'Besides, I couldn't do a thing like that to Roy.' Her voice sank by a tone to the key used by a second-rate actress when choosing honour before love. Rose became a martyr. 'He simply worships me — everybody knows that. Oh, he's dull beyond words and physically quite repulsive to me, but, still, he loves me and I couldn't bear to hurt him. He is my husband, after all,' she ended on a reproving note as if I and not she in her behaviour with Flip were the one of us who had overlooked this fact.

While Rose made up her face and mused aloud about the dullness of her life, I sat watching her and wondering how she and Mr. Roy had come to get married in the first place. I could not imagine him becoming intimate enough with any woman to propose marriage to her, and, somehow, the idea of Mr. Roy making love was inconceivable.

'How did you and Mr. Roy meet, Rose?' I asked.

'Oh, it was quite romantic,' she told me. 'We met on a ship in the Mediterranean, with all the moonlight and everything. Issa, the Syrian oil magnate, was on board and he and Roy were together a lot, so I knew that Roy wasn't just anybody. You know how it is on ships — you meet all sorts, and even clerks in offices have evening clothes nowadays.'

'I have never travelled in a big ship,' I said with longing, for to sail in a big ship, preferably one built on the Clyde, was one of my poetic dreams.

'It could be quite fun if so many of the people weren't always such hellish bores. Anyhow, by the time we got to Southampton Roy and I were engaged.'

She put some mascara on her eyelashes, then stared dreaming into her mirror for a little, but the dream of the moonlit Mediterranean soon evaporated and she poured some more brandy.

'Christ, what weather!' she said.

'Look here,' I asked, 'what about the wedding present for Anne Langley? Did you bring anything from Town?'

'God, no. I forgot.'

'It ought to be sent next week at the latest. Mr. Roy said to remind you.'

'Then why the hell didn't he get something himself?' She fastened her blouse and stepped into her skirt. 'I hate having to spend good money on something for that uppish little bitch. I hate weddings and all the silly claptrap that goes with them.' She bent to the mirror and took a last inspecting look at her face. 'The dress is very becoming to the girl, of course. I was a beautiful bride.'

'I know. I have seen the photographs. Listen, Rose. Would you care to drive down to Marybourne this morning? Maybe you could find something suitable in Lorna's shop.'

'That's an idea,' she said. 'And it would be something for Lorna. I like to help my friends — I am a loyal sort of person. All right. Let's do that. Go and put a coat on.'

'But there are some things I ought to do here, and if you aren't going to pay the accounts today you won't need me,' I said.

'D'you think I'm driving all that way by myself. I'd be bored to death and nobody at the end of it but that old fool Lorna and her bloody antiques. Go and get a coat!'

I fetched the coat, told Woolmer that the wine-cellar would have to wait, and we set off for Marybourne.

It was the smaller of the two cars that came round for us, and when Stoker informed Rose that Mr. Roy had taken the larger one I was afraid for a moment that she had had enough brandy to make her explode in front of the chauffeur, but she did not.

She climbed into the tonneau, I followed her, and she sat wordless, in sullen gloom, all the eight miles or so to the outskirts of Marybourne.

'The King's Head,' she said to Stoker then, and my heart sank into my boots.

Even as we crossed the hall of the hotel into the cocktail bar I began to see trouble looming ahead. The pre-lunch crowd had not gathered as yet, for which I was thankful in one way, sorry in another, and the bar was empty except for the barman. Rose sat down at a glass-topped table and ordered double dry martinis.

'That kid'll have to go to school!' she said suddenly and viciously. 'Is she still pigging it in bed?'

'No,' I said. 'She seems to be quite better and the doctor thinks — '

'It's time she went to school, then. She's simply turning into a precious little brat, that's all.'

'The doctor thinks she should have a little more time at home because — '

'To hell with the doctor! Of course, *you* don't want her to go to school — she's *your* bread and butter, after all!'

'Rose,' I said as quietly as I could, 'that is a very ugly thing to say.'

'What if it is? It's the truth, isn't it? And it's not *your* life she's making a mess of — not *your* car that's commandeered to cart her about. What are they doing away there on this horse nonsense, anyway? She should be in the schoolroom learning something. Plain as she is, God knows she'll need to learn something — she'll never find a man to keep her.' She called over her shoulder: 'Joe, bring me another!'

I was now growing angry, and I was afraid that more drink might lead to a public scene in the bar. For me to be angry and afraid at the same time is a bad combination, for my wits leave me when I am afraid, and when I am angry I need all my wits to control my temper. Just as Rose took the second gulp of the second drink, an elderly acquaintance and his wife came in, joined us at our table and ordered half-pints of beer. I was glad to see them and glad of the diversion created by their arrival.

'And what brings you ladies to town today?' Mr. Blackmore enquired in his hearty genial fashion.

'Oh, shopping,' I said as Rose made no reply.

'Spilkins have the most beautiful Bradenham this morning — I couldn't resist it,' his wife said.

Rose swallowed the last of her drink, put her glass down and rose to her feet. 'Hilda,' she said, 'where in God's name did you get that hat? It's exactly the colour of fluff under a maid's bed!'

'Goodbye, Mrs. Blackmore, Mr. Blackmore,' I said and followed Rose out of the bar.

'Let's get down to Lorna's, for God's sake!' she said to me over her shoulder.

I stopped in the middle of the hall. 'I'll wait in the car.'

'No need for that. I don't mind you knowing what I pay for the bloody vase or whatever-it-is.'

'But I mind very much about the way you are behaving today, Rose.'

'*You* mind, you cheeky little bitch?' she said, staring at me.

I was really angry now. 'That remark about Mrs. Blackmore's hat wasn't funny and it wasn't even original — it's a quotation from that cabaret man who dresses as a woman. How dim-witted do you think people are?'

I had discovered quite early in our acquaintance that a great deal of Rose's so-called humour was not original, but she had a gift for adapting comments made by cabaret artists, comedians and the like, and extracts from plays to fit situations that arose in her own drawing-room; and because she spent more time in London and went to more cabaret shows and theatres than her Marybourne acquaintances, many of these adapted comments were regarded as manifestations of her own wit. I was able to track many of her 'funny cracks', as they were called, back to their sources merely because I have been endowed with a good memory for all sorts of trivia and I had happened to hear the simile 'like fluff under a maid's bed' on the wireless.

The effect of my identification of it on Rose was out of all proportion, I thought, to its trivial nature. She was so angry that she became almost sober.

'Smart, aren't you?' she said. 'So Stewart takes you to the Café de Paris when you go to London?'

'No,' I said and looked round the hall of the King's Head, where the pre-lunch crowd was now gathering. 'Shall we get out of here?'

'Oh, lah-di-bloody-dah!' said Rose. 'Stop governessing for a little and let your hair down. What do that old cow and her bloody hat matter, anyhow? . . . All right, it *was* at the Café de Paris I heard that crack and it *was* that stinking old pansy that made it, and, say what you like, that *was* a bloody ghastly hat. Come on to Lorna's!'

I followed her down the street to Lorna's shop, of course. Rose's admission that she had plagiarised the remark from the cabaret was the apology of a child for having been naughty, and she had every confidence that the apology would put everything right. Also, I felt responsible for her. I felt it to be ridiculous that I should feel responsible for a woman much older and more experienced than myself, but I still felt responsible.

Lorna's shop was always amusing to poke about in, and Lorna knew of my liking for old paste jewellery and old china.

'Some nice old brooches and pendants you haven't seen before in that case, Janet,' she said, 'and some nice old Staffordshire bits in the back room . . . Like a glass of sherry, Rose?'

'What d'you think I came for?' Rose asked.

This was a hazard I had forgotten in the heat of the last moments at the King's Head. It was Lorna's custom sometimes to regale her valued customers with very good dry sherry out of a Waterford decanter. I accepted my glass and retired to the back room and the Staffordshire china while Lorna and Rose got down to business. Lorna came through once or twice and took away a Spode vase and a pair of china candlesticks, and I could hear Rose discussing the various items, enquiring about prices, and I heard again the chink of the sherry decanter and then came Rose's voice, cross and strident: 'These candlesticks would do, but twenty guineas is bloody ridiculous, Lorna!'

'My dear Rose, at twenty I am giving you the best price I can.'

'Oh, rubbish, after all the business Roy and I have given you and put your way!' The voice was growing louder and I could hear its drunken thickening.

'You can do better than that, you bloody old Jew. Fifteen is plenty!'

'No, Rose.' Lorna's voice was calm and firm. 'I bought them in at more than that.'

'Then you are a fool. Anyway, I don't believe you. I think it's bloody, soaking your friends like this, that's what I do!'

'My dear Rose, you don't have to buy from me, you know.'

'Oh, well, if you're going to take that line after all I've done for you, and Roy too! Not that *he'd* have done much — *I'm* the bloody fool, but I've always been loyal about my friends. But I must say I don't like being jewed out of twenty guineas just to give away to that little fool Langley, who doesn't matter a damn, just to celebrate her losing her virginity!'

'Listen, Rose,' Lorna said very quietly, 'I have been meaning to talk to you for some time. You'll have to behave a bit better. Half the district is antagonised by you and it isn't fair to Roy . . . Oh, I know Janet can hear me. That doesn't matter. She is a very good friend to you and your household —'

'She's paid for it!' Rose screamed. 'What bloody business have you and Janet to go discussing *me*.'

'We haven't been discussing you, but we are about the only people in the county who haven't. I am warning you, Rose, that you'd better pull yourself together. Your peccadilloes are not the secrets you think — not even the big one. Do you understand me?'

'Whatya mean?'

'You know perfectly well what I mean. I am referring to Flip Orton. You are mistaken in writing everybody off as a bunch of blind fools — especially Roy Andrews . . . Now, do you want these candlesticks or not?'

'Oh, wrap the bloody things up and given them to Stoker. Roy will send you a cheque.'

Lorna came through to the back room to get some tissue paper, and she stared hard into my face before she went back to the shop again.

'You're talkin' a lotta bloody rot about me an' Flip Orton.' Rose said. ''F course he's attracted to me — I've always been attractive to men — but it isn't anything. You're jus' sayin' these things t' get y'r own back'cause I called you a bloody old Jew.'

'Why I said them isn't important,' Lorna said.

'An' y're jealous,' f course. Y've always been a bit smitten on Roy.'

'Don't talk drunken rubbish, Rose.'

'You dream about him at night, Lorna?'

'Rose, you must be a bit more careful about what you say about Roy — and about everybody else too.'

'Can say wha' like. Roy loves me. 'Smine.'

'This parcel is ready. Where are Stoker and the car?'

'Somewhere. Janet'll get him. Where's she gone? Jah-net! Listen, Lorna, I su'enly go' tigh'.'

'Suddenly? You are tight too often.'

'Oh, shu' up. Leckshuring. Thass all you do — leckshur. Leckshur 'bout lechery.' She giggled. 'Thass all you do, the two of you — leckshur 'bout lechery.'

Lorna handed the parcel to me. 'Fetch the car, Janet,' she said, and as I went out into the street: 'Pull yourself together, Rose. The car is coming.'

We got her into the car with fair decency, she slept all the way back to Daneford, and I led her up to the bedroom among the coronachs in a semi-daze. I took off her hat, coat and shoes — she seemed to have lost her gloves — heaved her legs on to the gilt gondola and left her there. That was about two o'clock in the afternoon, and at five-thirty I heard her bell ring and Woolmer came up with the tray with whisky and soda. I sighed, stared out of the window and wished that Mr. Roy and Dee were back.

They arrived home about six o'clock and Dee rushed

upstairs, pink-cheeked, lively and suddenly almost pretty, it seemed to me, as she told me all about her day. She rattled on through her supper and bath and after she was in bed, recounting everything and enjoying over again every small detail, and at last she ended: 'But best of all was Helen's aunt and uncle and this place they have with simply millions of horses and foals and everything, and all the riding people coming in and out and children having riding lessons and everything, and I had a ride too just in my same clothes that I was wearing. And the town having two names like a person — don't you think that's nice a town having two names? Melton Mowbray. Father says there is a Burnham Beeches and a Stoke Poges and lots more. Could we go to Stoke Poges sometime?'

'Maybe. And maybe Sutton Valence and Wyke Regis as well.'

'How many do you know, Miss Jan?'

'Quite a few. I'll tell you tomorrow.'

When I went down for dinner, the Saturday-evening guests were beginning to arrive, and I felt that I spent my days moving from one world to another, each world almost too different from the last. But I was pleased to notice that Rose seemed to have drunk less than usual during her dressing period and was behaving very pleasantly. I hoped that Lorna's homily had had some effect.

CHAPTER NINE

In the summer of 1936 Mr. Roy went to the Continent for five weeks, partly on holiday and partly on business, but Rose did not go with him, and we saw comparatively little of her at Daneford either. Dee and I went to Dee's uncle at Frinton for the month of August, then Dee remained there for a fortnight while I went up to Reachfar on holiday and in September we returned to Daneford.

Mr. Roy and Rose now began to spend much more time at Daneford than they had done the winter before, and at first I thought that the house was going to become more of a family home and less of a rowdy weekend hotel, but this was not so. By the Christmas of 1936 I had to confess that Rose was drinking as hard as ever, harder if anything, and Mr. Roy looked very strained and preoccupied. I wondered if, by spending more time at Daneford, he was trying to estrange Rose from her rackety London set and its round of night-clubs, but his manner was always so distant and his face so closed and expressionless that it was impossible to tell what he was thinking or feeling. During the week he did not get back until the evening — if he came down at all, that is — and at weekends he was out riding or golfing all day when he was not closeted in the library at his writing-table.

It was impossible to tell, even, if he was aware of how much Rose was drinking or of how much she was degenerating. At times I thought that he noticed nothing and cared about nothing as long as he could pursue without interruption his routine of business and taking exercise, for his attitude to me was that I must get along with my business of looking after Dee and not bother him, just as his attitude to Woolmer and Mrs. Woolmer was that they must manage the household and not bother him. Maybe, I thought, his attitude to Rose was that she should just be there because he required a hostess for his house and that he had not even noticed that she was turning into an alcoholic any more than he had noticed that she had formed a liaison with Flip Orton.

I do not know why I became more and more attached to Rose. There was no logical reason for it, and it demonstrates how right Rose was when she called me a poetic dreamer when I say that in some strange way she was bound up in my mind with the dream pictures that formed when, as a child, Dominie Stevenson had told me of the Thames and had read to me 'The Lady of Shalott'. In Rose, as I knew her with my brain, there was nothing of the lyrical character of the Tennysonian lady, yet in that part of the mind that lies deeper than the brain or intellect she was fatefully linked with the Lady of Shalott. It may be that the impression remained with me of the first moment I saw her, lovely against the reflected garden, river and tree-grown island in the great looking-glass in the drawing-room; and although, when nowadays I saw Rose in actual fact, she was either wearing her pink rubber cap above a face smeared with cold cream or semi-drunk with her features sagging or sulking, the moment I was out of her presence and thought about her, the picture in my mind was of the lovely head against the background of garden, river and island.

One day in the early spring of 1937, walking in the garden with Lorna Calvert, I plucked up my courage, stepped out of my place as governess and said: 'Lorna, I am worried about Rose. She is drinking far too much.'

'I know,' Lorna said.

'Lorna, she might listen to you if you said something. That day you went for her in your shop over the candlesticks for Anne Langley — remember? — it did a bit of good.'

'I'll see what I can do,' Lorna said, and we walked a length of the terrace in silence before she went on: 'You are very good to Rose, Janet. There is no reason why you should worry about her.'

'Is there any reason why *you* should, Lorna? You worry about her far more than I do. I wonder why we do it?'

Lorna looked rueful. 'Goodness knows – especially you. My case is different. I am older than she is and I have known her since she was a child.'

'In a way, Lorna, she is still a child – she is not as mature as Dee in lots of ways.'

Lorna stopped walking and turned to face me. 'You know, I believe that is true. I had never thought of it before.'

'All this so-called sophistication she goes in for is just a sort of veneer: and all this self-confidence – I can't say what I mean, Lorna.'

'It's the self-confidence of a child that has never known insecurity,' Lorna said with an air of discovery.

'Yes, that's it! When I was about eight my mind was like Rose's – I thought that this was how the world was and that it would never be any different, and that I would be Janet Sandison as I was then for ever and ever. It is only when you grow up a little that you lose that confidence in yourself and the world and have to find a new confidence in a new self and a new world.'

'Yes,' Lorna said, 'Rose still believes the world is all hers and that it always will be.'

Lorna's voice was very sad, and I thought that she was perhaps thinking with regret, as I myself did sometimes, of the days when she was a child and everything was secure, simple in a world that was steady and unchanging, and I said: 'I think perhaps it is that child-like quality in her that is so appealing, in spite of everything.'

Lorna sighed. 'There is certainly plenty of what you call everything. I think the thing I hate most is that she is destroying her beauty. Ten years ago, Janet, she was lovely – absolutely incredibly lovely.'

'I can believe that. Even when I came to Daneford she was the most beautiful woman I had ever seen.'

We had now come back along the terrace to the front of the house, and Rose, from the drawing-room window, called down to us raucously: 'Oy, you two, stop walking up and down there like a couple of Lesbians! Come in and have a drink!' and there was a titter of laughter from the people in the room behind her.

'Oh, if only she wouldn't — everything!' Lorna said to me quietly as we went up the terrace steps, but we smiled at one another, for the same reason that the people inside had tittered at Rose's sally, because in relation to Rose there was nothing else to be done.

On a Sunday morning, about the middle of April, I was in the schoolroom alone. Dee had gone out with Helen Roland to the stables and she was going straight away afterwards to Marybourne to have lunch with Lorna and Lorna's small nephew who was staying with her. Mr. Roy had told me the evening before that he was most anxious that I should not go if Dee would go quietly without me, as it was time that she learned that I must have some time of my own. The house was very quiet, for no luncheon guests had been invited for that day and the servants were all in the kitchen wing, which was unusually silent.

Suddenly the air of the large upper floor was rent by a sound like the howl of an angry beast, which jerked me out of the schoolroom and along to the head of the staircase. The sound had come from the wine-red room along the passage and was now followed by others, less loud but quite as inhuman. Nothing like this had ever happened before. I could hear the faint tones, between the howls, of Mr. Roy's voice, which was calm and precise as ever, and then the howling turned into: 'Jah-net! Jah-net!'

I was still hesitating at the top of the stairs — my real instinct was to run down them and put all possible distance between me and the house — when Mr. Roy came out of the bedroom, looking strangely out of focus and distraught. He walked along the passage towards me cloaked, as it were, in the inhuman noise that was following him from the bedroom doorway.

'Will you go to Rose, Miss Jan?' he asked. 'Try to calm her. I shall be in the library.'

He walked in his precise neat way down the stairs and left me in the howling cavern of a passage.

When I went to the open door of the bedroom, I was almost felled by a large crystal powder bowl, which hurtled past me and hit the wall beside my head, smashed and sent a shower of strong-smelling, cream-coloured powder all over me. It was immediately followed by a large bottle of even stronger-smelling bath essence. I jumped into the room and shut the door.

'Rose,' I shouted, 'put that down!'

Rose, in the rubber cap, the cold cream on her face, hurled the heavy silver-backed hair-brush into the fireplace, where it clattered at last to rest in the marble hearth.

'Rose, what on earth is the matter?'

'The matter? Oh, Jah-net!' My name was a prolonged double howl that could have been heard in the next parish.

'Rose, stop howling like a brute beast. What is it?'

'He wants a *div-oh-rce*!'

What with the smell of the powder and bath essence, with which I was spattered and drenched, the general chaos of the room, the pink rubber cap above the greasy blowsy face that was all reflected again and again by the monstrous mirrors, I felt as if the wine-red carpet was indeed heaving and swelling like the fabled wine-dark sea. Rose was now emitting howl after howl like a coyote, and I felt for a second that the only way to hold my own and prevent myself from being deafened was to begin to howl in competition. Rose was howling in hysteria because she had been taken by surprise, and I was as much surprised as she was by this situation. So secure had she been in her self-confidence, so sure that her husband would continue to dote on her no matter how she behaved, that she had convinced me that it was so. And Mr. Roy, too, had been partly responsible for my conviction, for I had never once seen him look annoyed with Rose no matter how outrageously she behaved, and never once had I heard him make more than an indulgent laughing protest at her crudest witticisms. I believe that, in these first shocked moments, I was as indignant at the thought of divorce as Rose was.

'Rose,' I shouted, 'stop that confounded howling and tell me what has happened!'

I do not think that it was anything I said that made her stop. I think that, temporarily, she had howled until she could howl no more, and she sank down on a chair, a blowsy slattern in a gold satin robe, and began to cry.

'I want a drink,' she sobbed.

'I'll get it, but I am going down for it myself. We can't have anybody in here.'

'All right.'

I got back as quickly as I could with the tumbler full of brandy and soda.

'There, now do you want to tell me about this?'

She took a gulp from the glass. 'There's nothing to tell. He wants me to divorce him.'

'Oh. And?'

'I said I wouldn't.'

'Oh.'

'Dirty bastard!' she spat suddenly.

'Now, Rose!'

'He is! Know what he said?'

'What?'

'That if I wouldn't, *he* would divorce me-ee-ee!' and her voice rose to a hideous rending scream.

'Rose, stop that!'

She swallowed another gulp from the glass. 'The dirty low mean bastard. That last night Flip and I spent in Town — he had us followed. He knows everything. He's known for ages. What *gentleman* would treat his wife like that?'

I wanted to laugh. It was almost incredible that even Rose could say such a thing, but Rose could not only say it but think it with all her heart and mind. She went on to tell me in some detail just how little of a gentleman she considered Mr. Roy to be. And then: 'And that namby-pamby bread-and-butter little bitch! Christ, I wouldn't have minded so much if it was somebody like you he wanted, or Pipette Carstairs, or somebody with some life in them, but that horsy-smelling little snake-in-the-grass — '

'Who?'

'Don't try to tell me you didn't know, you cow!'

'But, Rose, I don't know. How could I?'

'It's Helen Roland!'

I had a few seconds of full sympathy with Rose and felt with her that 'horsy-smelling snake-in-the-grass' was an accurate description of Helen Roland.

'Christ, if I could lay my hands on her I'd strangle her! Who in the name of God would have thought of *her*?'

She rose suddenly and hurled her empty glass into the fireplace.

'Rose, there is not a bit of good throwing things and behaving like a lunatic. Mr. Roy —'

'*Mister* Roy! The little City gent that had his wife followed by detectives! Don't you go telling me —'

'Rose, try to calm down. What are you going to do?'

'What *can* I do-oo-oo?' She threw herself across the bed and began to yell again. I got up and went to the door. 'Where are you going?'

'Mr. Roy said I was to come to the library. I suppose he wants to arrange for me to leave or something.'

'You come back here this minute! Arrange! It's all arranged, didn't I tell you, by Mr. Roy Andrews of Andrews, Dufroy and Andrews, the dirty little rat! You're to stay with Dee. *He* is going to the London house. *I* am to pick up the envelope with the evidence in it — dear Helen's name, the two-timing little bitch, doesn't come into it — he went to Eastbourne with some tart — and take myself off and get a divorce. He's even given me the name of the solicitor to go to!'

I sighed. 'It seems that there is nothing that anyone can do —'

'Ow, Jah-net! Don't say that! You have to help me!'

I was away far out of my shallow depth and felt utterly impotent, but I also felt that it would help if the howling and yelling could be stopped at almost any cost. I ran downstairs to the dining-room, seized the bottle of brandy and two tumblers, and fled back to the bedroom.

'Stop howling, Rose, for pity's sake. Here, have another

drink. I'm going to have one, too, if you don't mind. I feel more than odd.'

'*You* feel odd? What the hell have you got to feel odd about. Think how *I* feel! To think that after all these years — I've been a good wife to him, entertaining the vicar and everything — what the bloody hell are you laughing at?' she broke off in a blaze.

I tried to tell myself that this was a domestic tragedy that I was involved in, that I must not laugh, but Rose was so far below the scale of tragedy that the laughter would hardly be suppressed.

'Sorry,' I said; 'it's a touch of hysteria, I think.'

She looked at me in a jaundiced way and took a large gulp of brandy and soda. 'Hysteria! I'm not hysterical, and look what's happened to *me*!' She began to sob. 'What in hell am I going to do?'

'Rose,' I said gently, 'don't you think that when the divorce is over things may sort themselves out? You and Flip —'

I was obviously on quite the wrong track. At the mention of Flip's name she threw herself across the rumpled bed and began to howl like a banshee. I filled her glass and tried a new direction.

'Where did you get this idea about Helen Roland?'

'He *told* me!'

'But why?' I paused. 'I mean — if he went to Eastbourne — '

'Why? Because he wanted me to know what a nice legal County family he and Helen were going to be! He knew it would annoy me and hurt me. You don't know your Mister Roy!'

'But' — I was very vague on the subject — 'if there's a liaison between them, can't you file a counter suit?'

'Liaison?' Rose burst into a shout of hysterical laughter. 'Where could I get the evidence, you fool? There isn't any! Dear Helen is far too high-falutin, and dear Roy is far too legal-minded, to jump into bed without a marriage certificate to hang on the wall first.' She rose and paced up and down the room a little unsteadily. 'Oh no. This is not a common-or-garden affair of two people wanting to sleep together and going and doing it. He *explained* that to me. He and Helen, he says, love and respect one another and want to build a dignified life together, he says. Christ, they'll entertain the County — Helen will be able to manage that at Daneford. You can't entertain the County in your back shop. They'll play squash and ride and have the horses to dinner, and then play billiards till they're too tired to copulate. The damned marriage will probably never be consummated. Evidence! How the hell can you get evidence for divorce against two people who have a horse between their legs all the time and not even the same horse? . . . The thing I can't take is being wiped in the eye by that niminy-piminy little bitch! I'd like to throttle her. Of course, when you think of it, she is just what Mr. Roy *would* like, the little city snob!' She sat down on the bed again. 'Gimme some more brandy. Still, I'd never have thought it of him. I wonder . . . He is at a difficult sort of age for men.' She ruminated quietly for a little between gulps of brandy. 'Maybe if I were to make up to him a bit — offer to sleep with him again — after all, any woman can lie on her back —' She had another peiod of rumination, now lapsing into drunkenness, while I, feeling nauseated, put aside my untouched drink behind the mirror of the dressing-table. 'Yes. He might be got over it. Thassa thing. I can probably work him roun'.' She lay back and stared up from the rumpled bed at the velvet of the canopy. 'But that little bitch has gotta be kept away from here!' she said, jerking to a sitting position suddenly and looking very vicious.

'That should be simple enough,' I said smoothly, feeling both mentally and physically dirty, but I wanted her to go to sleep so that I could get away by myself to gather my wits.

'Yes. Thassa thing t'do.' She lay back again and her eyes closed. After what seemed like hours, although by my watch it was about ten minutes, she emitted a drunken snore as she lay there among the tawny pillows, the grease still on her face, the rubber cap askew upon her head. Unmoved, the gilt coronachs above the mirrors held their trumpets aloft and smiled their simpering smiles as I tiptoed out of the room.

Despite the fact that Mr. Roy was waiting for me in the

library, I went back to my own room and sat looking down at the garden, the river and the little tree-grown island. I was utterly bewildered. Hitherto, I had prided myself a little on being a fairly accurate observer of people, this being my main interest, and I was now almost as furious with Mr. Roy and Helen Roland as Rose herself was. I felt that I had been cheated. Helen was so utterly unremarkable, so quiet and colourless, so much of a bore with her seeming lack of interest in anything but horses, that she had gone unnoticed by me among the people who frequented Daneford, all of whom had been dominated by the flamboyant Rose. And I felt even more indignant about the distant Mr. Roy than I did about the colourless Helen, for I felt that, in a cold remorseless way, he had used me for his own convenience. When he engaged me to look after Dee, I felt it had not been primarily because he saw in me some chance of benefit to the child, it had been because he wanted to dismiss the child from his mind in order to concentrate on getting rid of Rose. This was the 'great deal of important business to settle' that he had mentioned that day in his office when he asked me if I would look after Dee. In a muddled way I felt that he had made of me an accessory to an action of his that I felt to be unjust, although why I should think it unjust of him to divorce Rose I could not explain. Indeed, he was not divorcing her, I reminded myself — he was being generous and allowing her to divorce him — but even to remind myself of this did not convince me of his generosity.

It was a long time — years, indeed — afterwards before I discovered why I felt myself to be on Rose's side that morning and against Mr. Roy. It was because I felt that she had been human and he had not. This giving to Rose of enough rope that she might hang herself struck me, and still strikes me, as a taking advantage by a stronger intelligence of one that was weaker, which argued an inhuman lack of feeling. Surely, I felt, if he had married Rose, he must have come to know her a little; and if he did not like what he had come to know, couldn't he have remonstrated with her or have tried in some way to improve the situation? In my immature way I felt that he had not played fair. He had simply withdrawn from her, paying out the rope as he went and, in a calculating way, had waited and prepared for the day when she would hang herself, laughing at her the while, no doubt, in his tight-lipped way while she thought she was deceiving him with Flip Orton.

When I went down to the library he was as calm and urbane as if he had kept me late at the office. He indicated the tray of drinks and sandwiches that stood on a side table and he told me that he had instructed the servants not to serve lunch.

'Is Rose asleep?' he asked.

'Yes,' I told him.

'She has told you?'

'Yes.'

'I want to arrange for you and Dee to go away for a bit until Rose is ready to move out of the house.'

'Oh.'

'It would not be possible for you here, as things are.'

'Rose should not be left quite alone, Mr. Roy,' I said.

'The child is more important,' he said coldly. 'Lorna Calvert will come to Rose — a week or two at the most should see her packed up.'

I shivered involuntarily. If he had been sad or angry, it would have been better. It was the lack of any feeling of any kind in him that made me feel as cold as death. There was a telephone extension here in the library and I said: 'Could I ring Lorna up now?'

'I have arranged that. She will come back with Dee this evening. I have told them to prepare my room for her.'

'I see.'

'I am going to London tonight and I won't be coming back here for a time. The only arrangement left to be made is for you and Dee to go somewhere until Daneford is — is ready to receive you again. Have you any preference about where you go?'

'No. None at all.'

'I thought Angela's might be the best place. Or Clive's. You will be welcome at either.'

'Please arrange it to suit yourself, Mr. Roy.'

He rose to his feet. 'I am going out for a walk. Dee and Lorna should be here about five. I shall come up to the schoolroom then.'

I went up to my bedroom and sat at the window again. The early spring sun sparkled on the river and the island seemed to be hiding secrets among its trees. By what freak of feeling, by what insanity of self-delusion, had two people like Rose and Roy Andrews, of their own free will, chosen to marry one another expecting to find happiness? Why did people do any of the things they did? Why was I allowing myself to be wrapped up like a parcel by this man and sent with his child to his sister Angela or his brother Clive? Why did I not pack my things, get a taxi from Marybourne to take me to the evening train for London? Quite apart from Mr. Carter's five hundred pounds, I had quite a lot of money in the Post Office Savings Bank and I could go to a boarding-house until I found a post.

But I did not move. I continued to sit at the window, one ear half-cocked in the direction of Rose's bedroom, which was still wrapped in silence when the early spring dusk began to close in. I think I stayed there partly out of stunned inertia after the events of the morning, partly in case Rose should wake and find herself all alone, all her position as the life and soul of the Daneford 'party' in broken shards about her, for I felt in an unreasonable way that Rose, when she woke from her drunken sleep, would be like a child crying in the dark and somebody must be there to comfort her.

About six o'clock there was Dee's tap on my door, and when she poked her pig-tailed head into the room, while Mr. Roy stood in the passage behind her, she said: 'Miss Jan, Father is going to have a divorce and SHE is going away and this house is going to have the painters in and you and I are to go away to stay. Come and see Father.'

I went with them to the schoolroom, looking questioningly at Mr. Roy as I went in.

'Sit down, Miss Jan,' he said. 'We have settled everything except that this silly girl can't make up her mind between Aunt Angela's and Uncle Clive's.'

'Aunt Angela is a friend of mine, Dee, and I'd very much like to see her again,' I said.

'Don't want to go there.'

'Why not, Dee?'

'Rosemary and Susan always playing dolls' tea-parties — silly little goldiloxes!'

'Silly little *what?*' Mr. Roy asked sternly.

'G O L D I L O X E S! Goldiloxes!' she spelled out angrily. 'I hate them!'

'Now, now, Dee,' I said, 'there is no need to shout. Shall we go to Uncle Clive's, then?'

'Don't want to.'

'Now, Dee,' I said, for I had found this the best way to tackle her, 'you must be grown-up and reasonable. You have to look facts in the face and make up your mind. There *are* only two places, Aunt Angela's or Uncle Clive's —'

'Are *not* only two!' said Dee, her face very 'cussed'.

'What other is there?' I asked.

'Reachfar,' said Dee.

'Reachfar? What is that?' Mr. Roy asked.

'It is my home in Ross-shire,' I explained, very much taken aback. 'I have told Dee about it from time to time.'

'But, Delia, you cannot go inviting yourself to stay with people who do not even know you!' Mr. Roy was very stern and disapproving.

'Miss *Jan* knows me, Father, and I write to her father sometimes and he sends me postcards — four times he has sent them. I have them in my files. Sandison, Mr. Duncan, he is. And Miss Jan will invite me!'

Mr. Roy looked helpless, as only Dee could make him look. On Tuesday she and I boarded the night train for Inverness.

CHAPTER TEN

Dee and I left Daneford on the Monday evening and I saw Rose again for only a short time during the afternoon. When I went into the bedroom she was calm and sober, but when Lorna told her that I was going away with Dee she began to rave in lunatic terms against the child. When Lorna could make herself heard she remonstrated with Rose, whereupon Rose flopped over in the bed, turning her back to us, and shouted: 'Get out of here! Get the hell out of here, both of you! Women! I'm sick of the bloody sight of women!'

Lorna and I went along to my bedroom, where I began to pack my suitcase while Lorna slumped her broad hips down on to my bed. 'More clothes,' she said in a tired voice. 'I've never been so sick of the sight of clothes in my life. We are going to need a pantechnicon to take Rose's wardrobe. What a mess all this is, Janet.'

'It is, rather,' I said, going to the door. 'I'm going to ask Woolmer to bring some tea up here. You look exhausted. Put your feet up.'

When I came back into the room, I went on with my packing and said: 'You are getting the hard end of this, Lorna. What have you done about your shop?'

'My brother and his wife are down there. They have left their assistant in charge of their own place in Oxford.'

'You knew this was going to happen, Lorna?'

'Yes, but I've never known just when. Then, last week, Roy

told me. In a way I am glad that it's all over.'

Woolmer brought the tea-tray, and I felt that he too, like Lorna and all the other servants, was glad that it was all over, for I was humiliated to realise that all at Daneford except Dee and myself had seen what was coming for a long, long time.

'I did my best for Rose, Janet,' Lorna said now as the door closed again. 'From the very beginning, when I first met Roy, I told her that he was not the type to forgive. But you know Rose – that self-confidence. She said that she hadn't come to him a virgin, and that he'd thought nothing of that and that I was talking a lot of high-falutin rubbish. But I wasn't, you know. In fact, I don't think he has ever forgiven her for having a lover before himself.'

'What I have often wondered is how he ever came to marry Rose at all.'

'You would wonder, wouldn't you?' Lorna smiled ruefully. 'I don't know, of course, although I have often thought about it. I think he must have lost his head about her — anyone would have, a few years ago. She was lovely, really lovely. Then, having married her, he began to find out about her. He didn't fly off the handle or anything; he went about it in a cold, calculating way — a legal way — to prove — one can only use the words breach of contract. Roy isn't very human, Janet.'

'No, he isn't.'

'Helen Roland isn't either. They should make a perfect match. Helen will elevate Roy into real County circles — he is socially ambitious, and he will like that better than Rose's raffish friends like me.' She smiled a little. 'And, of course, Roy will restore Helen to her status as a County lady. It is all splendidly suitable,' she ended bitterly. 'People like you and I have been made fools of, Janet. We have been outplayed by Roy and Helen, but their marriage will be brilliantly suitable.'

'I suppose so. I don't really mind having been made a fool of, Lorna. I'm more interested in Rose. I suppose she will marry Flip?'

'Janet, how long have you known about Flip?'

'Almost since I first came here.'

'How did you find out?'

'Rose told me.'

'She told you?' Lorna stared at me for a moment. 'What a remarkable instinct Rose has for people sometimes. How she can pick out the ones who won't give her away!'

'Oh, that. Lorna, *can* you keep an affaire like Rose's and Flip's a secret? Wasn't she bound to be found out without anyone actually going and drawing a diagram for Mr Roy?'

'She was pretty cunning about it — so was Flip. It took Roy quite a time to get his evidence.'

'Maybe. But talking of having an instinct for people, I don't think Rose has very much, or, if she has, it is a different sort from mine. My instinct tells me that Flip Orton is an absolute stinker.'

'My instinct agrees with yours,' Lorna said.

'He seems to suit Rose, though. I suppose she will marry him.'

Lorna lit a cigarette, frowned and stared at the floor for a moment before she said: 'I doubt very much if you or I or Rose will ever see Flip Orton again, Janet. Rose doubts it, too.'

'Lorna, what do you mean?'

'Rose is not now going to be able to keep Flip in the style to which he is accustomed. I suppose Roy will give her a good settlement and she has a bit of her own, but I doubt if it will add up to a new car for Flip's next birthday.'

I sat down and stared stupidly at Lorna's plain worried face, at the myopic eyes blinking behind the thick lenses.

'Lorna, I don't understand. I just don't begin to understand about Rose. When I first came here and she told me about Flip, I thought the only thing that two people who loved one another wanted to do was to get married.' I saw Lorna smiling gently. 'Yes, Lorna, I thought it was as simple as that. I am not sure that I don't think so still. Then one day I asked Rose why she didn't get a divorce and marry Flip, and she almost ate me and said that Flip's income wouldn't buy her hats. So then I saw that she wanted to have Flip and the hats too, and it struck me as pretty immoral, but there it was. Now *you* are sitting there telling me that she feels she will never see him again because she can't give him a car for his next birthday. Do you mean to tell me that Rose has always known that it was the cars she could give him that held Flip to her?'

'Yes, I think so. The cars and the flat in Town and all the rest of it. Yes, I think she has always known it. I think she married Roy largely because of Flip.'

I was stunned. 'She told me she met Mr. Roy on a ship in the Mediterranean,' I said irrelevantly.

'So she did. She didn't mention that Flip was on the ship too? Travel is very expensive,' Lorna said.

'I don't understand. Lorna, she must love him – love him desperately?'

'Yes, I think so. Quite desperately.'

'But why? What does she see in him?'

'What do you see in Rose, Janet?' Lorna asked me gently. 'What do *I* see in her? In a way, you and I are both fond of Rose, and she has hardly ever spoken a civil word to either of us. We ought to see less in her than she sees in Flip. Flip has at least been civil to Rose,' she ended, smiling.

'But knowing all the time he would leave her if – '

'You and I have always known that Rose would cast us aside for anybody or anything that was more amusing. Sometimes I think people are all linked together in a sort of chain, Janet. You and I give a little to Rose, but she gives nothing to us. All she has she gives to Flip.'

'And Flip?' I asked. 'I don't think he gives much to anybody. Your chain ends in him – he is just a sink-hole for all the giving.'

'Maybe. Then there's Roy – he doesn't give much, but he isn't a taker either.'

'I'd rather have Rose any day,' I said. 'Lorna, what in the world will happen to her?'

'I wish I knew,' Lorna said.

Shortly after that Lorna went back to Rose's room and I did not see either of them again, except for a moment when Rose refused to say goodbye to either Dee or me; and the next forenoon, when my father met us on the platform at Inverness station, it was as if the wine-red bedroom with its mirrors and gilt coronachs were part of some long fantastic dream.

Life without Rose in it was very strange, and had I not been at Reachfar I am sure I should have missed her more than I did. The first evening at home, after Dee had gone to bed, my father, George, my uncle, Tom, our helper round the farm, my aunt and her husband, Hugh, all wanted to hear about the upheaval at Daneford, and I at once found myself in difficulties, for my sympathy lay entirely with Rose, but there was nothing that she had ever said or done that I could describe or quote to them that would not have shocked and disgusted them. By Reachfar standards there was no doubt that Rose was a wicked, immoral woman for whom hell was yawning and that Mr. Roy was a decent, upright citizen who had been sorely tried.

By the next evening, however, my family's interest had centred itself on Dee.

'She is an awful clever little craitur,' Tom said. 'In a way she minds me on Janet herself at that age — kind of enquiring about everything and not what you would call a specially bonnie bairn and the plaits in her hair and a-all.'

'The little coat she has would have bought Janet's clothes for a year at that age,' my aunt said. 'Oh, well, poor little craitur and them with their divorces and everything.'

My aunt was completely fascinated by the subject of the divorce, so foreign was it to the way of life that she knew that it was as if the society gossip column of a newspaper had come alive in the Reachfar kitchen.

'Och,' George said, 'their divorces and capers will make no difference to the bairn as long as she is here if nobody speaks about it and she's not reminded of it. She'll be far too busy to be thinking about the like o' that.'

He was right of course. George is usually right. Dee was so busy about Reachfar that she had time only to run into the house for her meals and run out again. I do not know what she did all day, probably the things that I myself did at her age — like fishing for newts in the quarry pond and climbing trees — and she certainly picked a lot of wild flowers which stood in rows of vases and jam-jars on every windowsill in the house. And, of course, she fed the baby chickens and the baby pigs, who squealed round their fat muddy slut of a mother, and she rode on the plough horses, the current Dick and Betsy, her legs 'doing the splits' across their broad backs.

'What I like about Reachfar,' she announced one evening, 'is that everything goes on for ever 'n ever. When Miss Jan was here, the horses were Dick and Betsy and Dulcie, and they are *still* Dick and Betsy and Dulcie when *I* am here although it's years and years after and they are really different horses. When can I go to see Dominie Stevenson's school, please?' This was different. Men do not go on for ever and ever, and Dominie Stevenson had died of old age and drink about two years ago. My father faces facts.

'The old Dominie isn't there now, lassie,' my father said. 'He died two years ago.'

'Oh. He was old?'

'Yes, very old.'

'Then that is all right. His school is still there?'

'Yes. It is Mr. Campbell's school now.'

'When can I go to see it?'

We arranged that on Friday, which was still known as 'market day' although nowadays it merely meant that some of us went down to Achcraggan to buy the groceries, I would take Dee to see the village school.

We arrived at the gate in the red sandstone wall, where the ferns and weeds grew in every niche, just as the children came pouring out into the playground for their afternoon break, and apparently the season of the skipping rope was early this year, for, in a moment, it seemed that every little girl was doing something with a rope while every little boy had urgent business with a pocketful of marbles. Young red-haired Mr. Campbell appeared on the steps of the schoolroom and drew his pipe from the pocket of his tweed coat. I went over to him, Dee holding my hand, through the maze of skipping ropes which stopped turning as the little girls looked at us, and I introduced myself and Dee and told him why we had come. He was only a little older than myself; obviously Achcraggan School was his first charge as headmaster and he was delighted to show it to us.

'There you are then, Dee,' I said. 'Like to go in?'

But her eyes were fixed on the girls with the ropes.

'Mary!' Mr. Campbell called and a little red-haired girl, very much her father's daughter, came running towards us. 'My girl Mary,' the young man said. 'Mary, this is Delia Andrews, all the way from London for a holiday.'

The children looked at one another in silence for a moment.

'Can you skip?' Mary then enquired solemnly.

'Only by myself,' said Dee.

'Och, big rope is easy!' said Mary. 'Come on!'

Within five minutes Dee was skipping her turn with about eight others.

All too soon Mr. Campbell looked at his wrist-watch, then reached inside the door and picked up the big old brass bell from its shelf.

'It's Friday!' I said hastily. 'Give them another five minutes!'

I spent the five minutes explaining that Dee had been a nervous child who was only getting over a strong enmity to other children and that she seemed more at ease today than I had ever seen her; but at the end of ten minutes, of course, the bell had to be rung. The children coiled up their ropes, picked up their marbles and ran into their appointed places in their lines, leaving the one small figure, all alone, in the middle of the playground. It was the saddest thing, I thought, that I had ever seen and I had to brush tears from my eyes as I looked at her.

'Come, Delia!' said Mr. Campbell suddenly. 'Run along beside Mary!'

A beatific smile broke over her face; she stood rooted to the ground for a moment and then ran to push her way into the line. They filed in orderly fashion into the school, and Mr. Campbell turned to me.

'There's only an hour to go,' he said to me as if apologising for what he had done. 'You can wait for her?' I nodded. 'Just come into the house and sit with my wife, then. The kids are going to have — '

'The poetry lesson,' I said.

'How did you know?'
'It always was.'
'It is better not to tax them too much on the last day of the week,' he said. 'Come along into the house and get a cup of tea.'
I sat happily in the pleasant sitting-room of the schoolhouse with Mrs. Campbell, who was nursing a baby on her lap while a four-year-old boy built bricks into a little wooden waggon in the middle of the floor. Dee's hour of school passed very quickly and she and Mary came in hand-in-hand after the bell had rung for the end of the week.
'Miss Jan, it is a *beautiful* school! And it was Horatius at the Bridge and I could say a verse too. And then we had a story.'
'That's fine. Mrs. Campbell, this is Delia Andrews.'
'How d'you do?' Dee shook hands. 'Is that baby a boy or a girl?'
'A girl. Her name is Isobel.'
'It is the newest one I have ever seen.'
'Is it? She is three months old. Would you like to hold her for a moment?'
As if dazed, Dee looked at me, then back at the baby. 'Yes, please.'
'Sit down on this stool, then,' said Mrs. Campbell and put the infant into her arms. 'That's the girl. That's right. Keep that arm steady under her little head.'
All too soon for Dee, my father and my aunt came for us and it was time to leave.
'May I come to school tomorrow, please, sir?' Dee asked Mr. Campbell, and I noticed that already she had the correct form of address for the schoolmaster, who looked round at us all with that air of helplessness that Dee could so often induce.
'Mr. Campbell doesn't have school on Saturdays,' I said.
'Well, when he *does* have it, then,' she persisted.
'This is not the right school for you, Dee,' my father said. 'You have to go to school at home in England.'
Her mouth tightened; the stamping foot tensed to the ready.
'Don't want to. I like this school. It is a red school, not grey.'
'There are red schools in England too,' I told her. 'Come

now, we have to go home to Reachfar.'

'If I am staying at Reachfar, I can come to school,' Dee said. '*You* came to this school when you stayed at Reachfar.'

'How long are you to be here?' Mr. Campbell asked.

'Only two more weeks or so,' I told him.

'Let her come, Reachfar,' he said to my father. 'It will be all right.'

'Where is Dee able to walk all this way every day?' my aunt asked, horrified.

'Miss Jan walked!' Dee said and brought the helpless look to my aunt's face too.

'Dang it!' said my father. 'It canna harm the bairn to let her come, Janet. It's very good of you, Mr. Campbell.'

'Not at all,' the young man said. 'Delia, you will be here at nine o'clock on Monday morning. Don't be late, remember.'

Late? Dee had the house in an uproar long before daylight on Monday morning. From the lumber-ridden depths of the west attic, during the weekend, a leather satchel of mine that was at least fifteen years old was extracted, cleaned and had a pencil and rubber put inside. A piece of rope was obtained from the barn, and my uncle and Hugh carved a pair of skipping-rope handles out of the leg of an old chair. On Monday morning, the rope, a packet of sandwiches and an apple were put into the satchel, and before the clock struck seven Dee was off to school.

'Janet,' my aunt said in haunted tones as the small figure disappeared over the brow of the hill, 'what in the world will we do if anything comes over her?'

I made no reply because I did not know the answer.

But nothing came over Dee except that she fell into the Reachfar Burn on the way home and came into the house soaked to the skin, one hair-ribbon missing, one pigtail completely frayed out and the hair solid with mud. She was utterly and completely happy, happier than I had ever seen her, and my family were so pleased to see her safely home that they would not have cared had she been stark naked and painted blue.

At this time, historically speaking, what Tom called a

'comical-looking wee craitur of a mannie' in Germany, whose name was Adolf Hitler, was causing a lot of young men to be marched about in orderly squads, halting periodically to raise their right arms and shout: 'Heil Hitler!' and a new word was coming into common English usage, namely the verb 'to condition'. People would tell you darkly that Hitler was 'conditioning' the young men of Germany, and more darkly still that his Storm Troops had 'conditioned minds'. People spoke of this as if it were something completely new under the sun, but for my part I felt that Hitler would have done well to come to Reachfar as an au pair pupil of my family and find out a little about the advanced technique of conditioning minds, for my family are past masters at it. Not that they would have admitted to having anything in common with Hitler, mind you. Like most people at that time, they thought of him as a figure of fun and called a particularly aggressive little bantam cock 'Adolf' as a fitting comment on both the bantam and the Fuhrer.

After Dee had been at Achcraggan School for a week and had announced by letter to her father that she was now at school and would not be home for several years, and her father had written a rather sharp letter to me and I had written back to him to explain what had happened, I said to my family: 'Look here, this is all very well, but this kid has to be persuaded to go home soon, and go to a proper school as chosen by her father.'

'Och, the poor bairn!' said Tom. 'She is fine where she is and doing grand at her sums an' a-all.'

'I never was much of a hand for the school myself and I wouldn't care at a-all for one where a person had to be stopping day and night' — George.

'What prison sort of a place will they put her to at all?'— Hugh.

'And the food at these boarding schools . . . '— my aunt.

'That's right enough, Janet,' said my father. 'She will have to go to her own kind of school.'

The rest of my family looked at him as if he were one of the murderous treacherous Campbells, with his hands still bloody from the massacre of Glencoe.

'She ran off from two of them English boarding-schools

already, you was telling us,' said Tom.

'That's just the point!' I shouted, before they could all come in again with a second round of objections. 'She has got to be persuaded to go to a boarding-school and *not* run away.'

'Oh,' said my family, collectively, seeing that boarding-school for Dee was inevitable.

From then on poor little Dee had not a chance. The campaign started that very evening over the supper table. 'I mind once,' Tom said to George, 'Sir Torquil telling me about the boarding-school he went to as a boy and all the boys was wearing tall hats a-all the time like people will be doing at a funeral, George.'

'My, do ye tell me that, Tom?' George enquired. 'It is myself that would like fine to be at a school with a tall hat on me a-all day.' Dee began to giggle. 'Would I not look fine with a tall hat on me? Maybe you will go to a school like that down in England some day, Dee.'

'I couldn't, George, silly! That's Eton — it's only boys go there.'

Gradually, as day followed day and meal followed meal, Dee's school arose, almost a solid edifice, from the centre of the Reachfar kitchen table. It started by being a 'red' school, and then it had to be near the sea, like Achcraggan School, but George and Tom convinced her that it was desirable that it should be 'a bittie bigger than Achcraggan School with a nice puckle trees about it.' At the end of two weeks George and Tom were sitting at the kitchen table on a Sunday afternoon, helping Dee to write to her father describing the kind of boarding-school that she wished him to find for her, and when the envelope was sealed, addressed and stamped she took it back and wrote along the top of it: 'Personal and Terrible Urgent.' My family are not clever with the brilliance of a cutting diamond that makes its mark with a scream and a shower of sparks, but they are masters of the technique of the smooth, barely perceptible drip-flow-drip-flow that can wear away a stone.

As I observed my family at work on Dee, conditioning her mind to the idea that boarding-school was the most desirable of things, I had a curious sensation that time had slipped out of joint by some eighteen years, giving me the opportunity to observe, at twenty-six years old, myself at eight years old in the process of being 'brought up' by my family, except that Dee had it more easy than I had had, I felt, for the great force that was my grandmother was no longer here. In my memory of the actual process there were, repeated again and again, the words of that grandmother: 'She is far too determined — she has far too much mind of her own.' And, because these words had been so often spoken of me by the voice of authority, I had come to believe them true and to think that I had, indeed, a mind of my own. It was disconcerting to discover, as I watched Dee's mind being moulded and changed before my eyes, that any mind of my own that I might possess could have been developed only in the last six years or so and that for the first twenty years of my life my mind, far from being my own, had been made almost entirely into what my family wished it to be.

They had imposed on me a set of standards and attitudes, and at the same time had eradicated in me the desire to question them or consider the merits of any other set, just as now they were imposing on the mind of Dee the utter desirability of going to boarding-school and the moral impossibility of considering any other future. They were five adult minds, of a shrewd and wily type, pitted against the mind of one small child; they could not do other than carry the day. But was it just? I was haunted by an uneasy uncertainty.

My 'common sense', that quality so valued by my grandmother and my family in general, told me that they must be justified, that the child must go to school, and go there in a happy and receptive frame of mind if possible, and that my family seemed to be achieving this end when all other attempts had failed; but to what extent was this conditioning of a mind justifiable? I was haunted by the feeling that my family was doing on a small, relatively unimportant scale exactly what Hitler was doing in Germany and that both were tainted by some obscure but mortal sin.

Never in my life until now had I questioned the basic morality of my family, the justice of its standards or the essential 'rightness' of its judgements, and even now the inner questioning induced in me a feeling of disloyalty, and disloyalty itself was a mortal sin against the Reachfar code. Nevertheless, as I watched them at work on Dee, the inner questioning went on until I discovered suddenly that the mould which they had built round my own mind had cracked and fallen away, as the puddle clay can be broken away from around a cooled iron casting, but that, unlike the cooled casting, my mind had not completely set before the breaking of the mould. Instead of standing in firm peaks of 'morality', or lying in flat plains of 'common sense', or having neatly shaped patterns of 'conventional behaviour', my mind had collapsed on the removal of the mould into a rubbly, shivering, disorderly heap of odds and ends of memories among which a few ideas grovelled about in obscure blind purposelessness, like some half-dead creatures that had been imprisoned for years and were at last free to grope, by barest instinct, towards the light.

It was early in June, in the end, before Dee and I returned to Daneford — Dee, by this time, clamouring to get away to her boarding-school. Mr. Roy met us at the station in London on our return and hardly recognised his own daughter. She had contracted a Highland accent, together with a good deal of the idiom, for I, in spite of years spent in other countries, still lapse into it when I go home, so that she had heard no other speech. She had grown, and in one way she had matured, although in another way she had become more of a child. In the taxi, between Euston and Sloane Crescent, she told her father that it was imperative that she should go to school the very next day.

'But why such a hurry?' he asked.

'Father, I have to go to school to get education to be earning a puckle pennies when I'm big!'

I was maliciously pleased to see him look really startled when I glanced sidewise at him to observe the effect of this extract from Reachfar philosophy couched in the idiom of George and Tom.

'Have you found my school yet?' she pursued.

'I think so. You and Miss Jan and I will go one day to see it.'

'See it? But when do I *go* to it?'

'Not until the autumn. There are holidays until then.'

'Ach, Father!' she said disgustedly. 'It is myself that has a good mind to go right back to Reachfar!'

'I have a plan for the holidays,' he told her.

'What?'

'Would you like to see Canada?'

'Canada, Father?'

'Uncle Clive and I have to go on business, and Aunt Elsie and the boys are coming too.'

'And I can come?'

'Yes.'

'And Miss Jan?'

'No,' I said.

'Why not?'

'Because I don't want to,' I said, giving the one reason that Dee could always understand.

'Why don't you?'

'Because I have things to do in London.'

'I think that's silly,' said Dee, 'but a person has to please themselves of coorse,' and it might have been the voice of Tom that spoke to us.

'She will lose the accent,' I said to her father.

'Oh yes. School will soon put that right,' he said in a satisfied way.

Dee did not accept straight away and without protest that she would go to Canada, come back and go to school, and that I would find another post and no longer be with her all the time. She did her best to persuade me to come to Canada, and she worked out an ingenious scheme whereby I would be taken on to teach the poetry lessons at her school; but when, in the taxi, she had given voice in the Reachfar idiom to the idea 'a person has to please themselves of course', she had laid a foundation for part of her own design for living. She had seen and accepted the point that Rose had never seen until that dreadful morning in the gold and red bedroom. Until then, the world and everyone in it had, for Rose, existed to please Rose, and the discovery that this was not so had been a severe shock. At least, I thought, no matter what happens to Dee, she will not reach the age of forty under that particular misapprehension.

During this last month before the departure for Canada we spent less time at Daneford and more at the London house, for Dee had to be re-outfitted, having outgrown all the clothes she had not ruined in the Reachfar trees or in the Reachfar Burn. She and I, walking in the parks or visiting museums or galleries, decided that London was not such a bad place after all, but when, one evening after she had gone to bed, Mr. Roy told me that my place at the office would be open for me as soon as I liked, I heard myself say: 'Your present secretary suits you, doesn't she?'

'Very well,' he said, 'but she knew that her post with me was temporary. And I have arranged for her to go to Sykes in the Cargo Department.'

'I — I really don't want to come back, Mr. Roy.'

'I am sorry to hear that. Why not?'

'I am probably very foolish,' I told him, 'but I would rather work for a lower salary if I could avoid that awful bus or tube business every morning and evening. There is something – something destroying about it.'

'Oh, come, Miss Jan!' His tone was indulgent. He might as well have called me a fool and have done with it. 'Thousands of us do it every day.'

'I don't find that an effective reason for me to do it,' I told him, as I would never have done before the mould that once was round my mind had broken away.

'You are extremely foolish, Miss Jan,' he said, and his voice was quite cross. 'The money is in the City. You have ability and could go a long way.'

'What's the use of going a long way in a direction that you don't really want to go?' I asked.

He did not attempt to answer me but merely made an impatient noise.

'Don't bother about me any more, Mr. Roy,' I told him. 'I want a job and I'll find something.'

'Well, anything I can do — introductions, references and so on –'

'Thank you. I may take you up on that when the time comes.'

When the time came I found another post easily enough. I have always found the mechanics of earning enough to live on a simple matter — it is when I leave off doing the earning and start doing the living that the complications set in for me.

CHAPTER ELEVEN

Only about two years had passed since I first saw Daneford, Rose and Dee, but when I look back it seems to me that the young woman who found a new post in London, putting Andrews, Dufroy & Andrews behind her, was someone very different from the young woman who Miss Slim piloted to lunch on her first day in the City. I think I can best describe the difference by saying that, on that first day, there had still existed for me a group of people known vaguely as 'the grown-ups', who were quite different in every way from myself, and especially were they different in that the world held no uncertainties for them. Now, two years later, I began to feel that, without being aware of it, I had crossed the dividing barrier and had myself entered that grown-up world, and I was finding that to be a citizen of this world did not imply the state of certainty and security which I had thought was its main condition. It was only now that I saw that Mr. Roy and Rose, Helen Roland and Lorna Calvert no more had the key to certainty and security than I had; looking further back, I saw that Angela Carter and my former employers Mr. and Mrs. Whiteley-Rollin were as much at the mercy of the winds of circumstance as I was. Looking back further still, I saw now that those omnipotent, omniscient gods of my childhood, my family at Reachfar, must often have been as puzzled by life as any of the rest of us, but these last seemed to have maintained a steadier course than most other people I had known, and it was on realising this that I rediscovered the Reachfar code.

That old tree of the many branches might shake and rock, and sometimes, even, drop a twig or two in a stormy wind, but it remained a tree, something to cling to, and it was immeasurably better than no tree at all. And I found that it could be pruned to the climate of the moment, that its obsolete and decayed twigs could be cut away, but that a strong, serviceable bulwark against the winds of the world still remained.

Mr. Roy and Dee went away on their trip to Canada, and when they came back Dee went to her school in Devon. I heard from her spasmodically for a year or two, but eventually her letters stopped coming and I made no effort to keep in touch with her. I felt that Mr. Roy regarded Dee's going to school and my leaving his employment as the closure of a chapter which he wished to put behind him and forget, and life was too full for me to look upon this closure with any great regret.

I do not remember that I gave much thought to Rose. When she left Daneford she dropped into the social whirlpool of London, a different pool from the more mundane one in which I swam, and itwas unlikely that I would run across her. The divorce went quietly through, and in a short time Helen Roland and Mr. Roy were married. Shortly after this event I met Miss Slim on the street by chance one day and we had lunch together. Naturally the marriage was her main topic of conversation.

'Quiet wedding, of course. Register office and only Mr. and Mrs. Clive and one or two of the family. Not like when he married the first Mrs. Roy.'

'Don't you mean the second Mrs. Roy?' I asked, for I have a long hard Highland memory, and those early days when I was harrowed by Dee's attitude to the woman whom I thought was her mother still rankled.

'Gawd, that's right!' said Miss Slim. 'I'd forgotten about the first one — she was just like this one, dull and quiet and not much to look at. *Three* of them — quite the film star, isn't he? Of course, there's only the one divorce.'

'Where is Mrs. Rose now?' I asked.

'Somewhere Knightsbridge way, I think. You've never happened to run across her?'

'No.'

'Last time I went up west to do some shopping I was taking a look down Bond Street. I met her — just outside Asprey's it was.'

'Oh?'

'She's changed.' Miss Slim's voice was sad, nostalgically sad.

'She's got fat and wasn't a bit smart. When I think of how she used to be! Remember her that day in the flame satin swimming costume?'

'I remember.'

'I wonder how much Mr. Roy allows her? She divorced *him* after all. By law, he should have to give her quite a bit.'

'I suppose so.'

'Well, she didn't look it.' Miss Slim was silent for a little and then: 'I've worked for the firm all my life and I am still loyal to the firm and Mr. Clive; but to tell you the truth, I've never felt the same about Mr. Roy since that divorce. It was an effin' shame, that's what it was. There he is — you would think he was as cold as a cod on a slab — and him going on like that so that poor Mrs. Roy had to divorce him. You can say what you like, it's neither right nor decent. Broke her heart, that's what he did, if you ask me! That's what she looked like, all down in the mouth, and broken-hearted, and not a word to say for herself, as if she didn't care any more for any damn' thing. It makes me so that I just can't *take* to this new wife of his, somehow. At the last outing I was just looking at her and wondering what he could see in her after the last Mrs. Roy. Very lah-di-dah, she is, but no glamour, no personality, nothing to look at. After you've *seen* her, you can't even remember her.'

'She has a lot of charm, Lily. I got to know her a bit when I was down there with Dee.'

'Well, I must say I prefer Mrs. Roy's — Rose's — type myself. You couldn't forget you'd seen *her*. Did you as much good as going to a dress show or the pictures or something. I like people that have some personality, something to take you out of yourself.'

I did not try to disillusion Miss Slim about her view of Rose as the ill-used wife, or try to justify Mr. Roy in her eyes, for I think that a harmless illusion cannot hurt anyone, and Mr. Roy was not the man to be worried by Miss Slim's poor opinion of him, even had he been aware of it.

'Talking of personality,' she said next, 'you have turned into a bit of something yourself.'

'What in the world do you mean, Lily?'

'Just what I said, chum. I've noticed it every time I've seen you since you went to Daneford. When you first came to work at the office you were just a nice quiet clever kid, but being down there with Mrs. Roy so much has brought you out. I'm not surprised really. It must be like a tonic to be in her company a lot — when she was like what she used to be like, that is.'

'Oh, rubbish, Lily!'

When Miss Slim and I parted that day I was in what Tom would call 'a mood of insultment'. I was indignant at the very thought that a sojourn with Rose could be said to have a tonic effect on anyone, especially on me. I went back to my own place, threw down my hat, gloves and handbag and began to slap books and magazines around my living-room in a pet. Then, angrily, I began to go back over, to take stock, as it were, of the two years that I had spent at Daneford, two years which I had now put behind me as time that the locusts had eaten, time in which I had accomplished nothing, a time of disintegration.

Mr. Roy had been, for him, fulsomely grateful for 'the improvement' in Dee and for what I had done for her, but these opinions of his carried no conviction for me, for I had an instinctive awareness that my influence on the child had been of the very slightest and that I had not in any way changed the direction in which she would go. All my presence had done for her was to ease her path a little by imbuing her, indeed, with a little of my own low cunning, so that she learned to go her own way tactfully instead of bluntly, so that she learned to walk warily and with grace around, instead of trying to ride roughshod over the obstacles that stood in her way. I had not worked much of a change in Dee, nor had I made of her what Mr. Roy called 'a normal person', a phrase that he often used but whose meaning always remained obscure to me. If anything, Dee was now even more of a renegade from her father's 'normal thing' than she had been when I first met her — the only difference was that now she was debonair instead of tatterdemalion in outward mental appearance.

Memory of my two years spent at Daneford did not centre round Dee, with whom I had spent most time, or round her father, who was the author of my presence there, or round Lorna Calvert, whom I had liked, but round Rose, who, by the standards of the Reachfar code, was the least worthy of consideration of all the people I had met there. And I remembered Rose with affection, with more affection than I remembered any of the others, even Dee. Although I thought about this for a long time, trying to explain it to myself, I came to no conclusion. It was a complete anomaly because the memory pictures I had of Rose were either of Rose greasy-faced and sulky in the pink rubber cap or of Rose drunk and lewd-voiced, telling her latest dirty story; but in spite of these pictures, a warmth hung about her in my mind, a warmth that glowed, a pinkish light that made me think of Miss Slim's word: 'glamour'. In spite of the memory of the drunk or greasy-faced reality, the glamour was there.

All this thinking I was doing after my lunch with Miss Slim took place on a Saturday afternoon, for in this new post of mine my weekends were free from Friday evenings until Monday mornings. While thinking, after I had got over my fit of the pet, I went about washing stockings and gloves and mending underclothes and doing those other small jobs that women do. About seven o'clock, Alan Stewart — yes, that same Mr. Stewart of Andrews, Dufroy & Andrews — would arrive to take me out to dinner.

Young women of my class and upbringing in the 1930s were in a curious position. I have mentioned all this before, but it cannot be emphasised too much as part of the female human situation of those years, nor is it possible to over-emphasise the stress that was laid on the desirability of our 'standing on our own feet', 'earning our living' and 'being independent', and yet the young woman who approached nearer and nearer to thirty years of age, standing on her own feet, earning her living and being independent — or, in other words, remaining unmarried — began to gather about her, in people's eyes and minds, an aura of failure. Tradition died hard. Marriage was still the most desirable of all fates. It was all very, very muddling.

Even before I had gone to Daneford, I had realised that in relation to myself Mr. Stewart was a bore, and, what was even worse, had in him a curious poverty of mind that made something in myself shrivel and wither; but these things that were felt only by me did not affect his appearance in the eyes of the world at large as a most eligible parti, and I was allowing the eyes of the world to influence my own sight to a greater and greater degree in this matter.

Rose, who believed in marriage as an institution that brought a woman free food, clothing and shelter for the rest of her life (given a little luck), had told me frequently that Mr. Stewart could afford quite a high standard in these things. Mr. Roy, who believed in marriage as a more respectable state for a woman than any other — it was what he termed 'the normal thing' — had a high opinion of Mr Stewart's ability to conform to the pattern of the conventional husband. Miss Slim, the companionable soul, felt that if I accepted Mr. Stewart I would have a companion for the rest of my life, a very desirable end, for 'he is a very steady chap, always has been', she said. And finally, when I had been at Reachfar with Dee, my family had on several occasions made remarks to the effect that I seemed to have a way with children and that it was a pity that I had none of my own to look after. All this and probably several other things had culminated in the fact that when I returned to London I dined three times with Alan Stewart, and on the third evening accepted a proposal of marriage so that, now, as I washed my stockings in my small bathroom and cogitated the while, my half-hoop of small diamonds reposed on the glass shelf in front of and level with my nose. 'Hideous damn' thing,' I told myself, looking at it. Ever since my childhood I have talked to myself when I am alone. 'Next time I'll get something more pleasant to look at.'

I had squeezed the surplus water out of the stockings and was hanging them over the towel rail before it struck me that I had given words to a thought that was, to say the least of it, unconventional.

'Next time?' I stared at my face in the small mirror. 'What did I mean?'

I do not remember anything more in detail until some hours later, when Alan was standing, in white tie and tails, with a red carnation in his button-hole, in the middle of my small living-room while I turned off lights and checked to see that I had my keys in my handbag.

'It's a pity,' he said with heavy gallantry, 'that brides can't wear black. It suits you better than anything.'

I looked down at my long black velvet skirt, then clicked the clasp of the bag and turned round. 'It isn't that they can't,' I said; 'it is that they don't as a rule.'

'Comes to the same thing,' he said.

'It doesn't, you know.'

'Oh, forget it! We'll be late.'

I did not say anything more, but I did not 'forget it', for it seemed to sum up much of the difference that was between Alan's mind and my own.

This was Alan's big night, the night on which I was to be presented to his family, who had gathered in London for that purpose and which consisted of his widowed mother, who had come down from Scotland to stay with her daughter Kitty, who lived at Ealing where her husband Kenneth worked in a bank, while we were to be joined by Alan's other sister, Betty, who was down from Glasgow on holiday with her accountant-husband, Bill. After a silent taxi ride, during which I could feel Alan putting my silence down in a pleased way — as if it were a credit entry in a ledger — to shyness at the important moment before me, we alighted at the door of a large grey hotel in Bloomsbury, which seemed to me to have the aspect of a female prison. At two shabby tables, drawn together in a corner of the large, brownish-grey lounge that faded away into the dusty distance, the family awaited us, and there seemed to me to be a mile of worn carpet between the entrance and the point where the party was seated.

It has always been a source of annoyance to me that the clearest telepathic impressions I have received in the course of my life have been of a type whose very nature has precluded my checking their accuracy by direct reference to their sources. It was so now. As Alan and I began to walk from the door to those two distant tables, I could hear the words as if they were being spoken aloud: 'Oh dear, what has Alan gone and done? She is not our sort at all! Oh dear!' and by the time we were standing by the tables all five people there were in an uneasy flutter. This was my bad luck. Had the inspired producer of a lavish film chosen from millions of candidates three women designed solely to throw me into high and absurd relief, he could not have found three women better equipped to do it than Mrs. Stewart, Kitty and Betty. I am not and never was a beautiful woman. I am about five feet nine inches tall, have a normally proportioned body, and, brought up as I was, in an old-fashioned way and largely by my grandmother, I was trained to move, walk and sit in a way that she thought proper, and this, combined with a thick growth of dark brown hair that had never been cut or professionally dressed, gave me, with my height, an appearance that was unusual when small blonde women seemed to be fashionable and therefore preponderant in number. When, therefore, I stood like a pillar of black velvet to be greeted by the fluttering mauve chiffon of Mrs. Stewart and the georgette frills of Kitty and Betty, I felt, and no doubt looked, like a giraffe bending over to exchange civilities with a group of fluffy kittens. Probably my mind saw them through a horror lens of exaggeration, but I am still sure, at this moment, that the combined height of those three women was no more than fourteen feet.

There ensued hours, literally four hours, of everybody putting everybody at ease. I have read somewhere that the hallmark of an accomplished hostess is the ability to put at their ease the most ill-assorted guests at her table, and this may or may not be so. At this table in this hotel in Bloomsbury, however, Cupid, I gathered from Mrs. Stewart, was the host, and I remembered with bitterness from my reading of mythology that Cupid was reputed to be physically blind. I now came to the conclusion that his mental perceptions and powers of discrimination were also extremely limited.

My 'intended', as Betty jovially called Alan, was now inducing in me a hysterical desire to giggle, for something in his demeanour was reminding me of the time in the 1920s when George and Tom went to one of the many 'Big House' sales that were taking place in our district in Ross-shire at that time. They came home, late on a summer evening, in the high spirits that a holiday and an unusual amount of whisky could induce in them, with, at their feet in the trap, a rather moth-eaten-looking peacock, which they proceeded to turn loose in the sloping cobbled yard of Reachfar. It might have been the dying light of the long tiring day, it might have been the dying fumes of the whisky, it might have been the cold, bleak gleam in the eye of my grandmother, but, as the bird trailed his ragged tail-feathers disconsolately across the cobbles and the hen-droppings, George turned to Tom and said in a wondering voice: 'Man, Tom, I didna think it would look as foolish-like as this when we got it home, did *you*, now?'

Mrs. Stewart, who stressed the fact that she was giving the party, ordered drinks; and after a hushed colloquy with a broken-down waiter, which gave to the proceedings a strange atmosphere of secret sin, glasses of a pinkish-brown, slightly glutinous liquid, containing a cherry impaled on a tooth-pick, appeared. When these had been drunk, either Ken or Bill said in a reckless way that this was a celebration after all and a second round was ordered, whereupon everybody seemed to me to become very uninhibited. This applied especially to Kitty and Betty, and as Betty raised her glass for the second time she looked round at her family with an air of: 'We came here to look this woman over, so, dash it, let's *look* her over!' and then turned to me and said: 'I must say you don't *look* much like a Highland lassie!'

This was one of these unfortunate remarks which are intended to be complimentary but which have no value because they give away the fact that the speaker has made the remark from a background of total ignorance. Nobody, I have been told repeatedly, could be more typical of my race and background than I am; but as the conversation went on, it became obvious that Betty and all her family seemed to be working from the premise that all Highland lassies sat at spinning wheels crooning melodies (with English words by Kennedy-Frazer) beside peat fires. 'I am Highland all right, although no longer a lassie,' I said, doing my best, but this struck a wrong note too, for another of the facts that Betty, Kitty and Mrs. Stewart did not face was that women get older.

'People are just as old as they feel, I always say,' said Mrs. Stewart with an air of high originality, and I, feeling that a thousand ages in my sight would be like this evening gone, agreed with her fervently.

The move to the dining-room was made and I felt more and more trapped in a situation of papier mâché falsity that was illumined by an oddly furtive light. There was an air of being on the spree, of having a night out which was yet cramped by the desire that the other diners in the room should have the impression that the Stewarts lived habitually like this, dining, in evening dress, in restaurants every evening. Being a Saturday night, it was 'Gala Night' in the hotel, which meant that towards the end of dinner a few musicians appeared in a weary way on a platform in a corner near which there was a small floor space unencumbered by tables. I looked round at the distant dusty spaces and back at the two purple asters that drooped in a vase on our table, and suddenly knew that I was feeling shamefully and violently sick, with a desperate urge to vomit. When, at long last, Mrs Stewart and the 'girls', as Kitty and Betty were jointly known, rose with coy remarks about powdering of noses, I retired with them to the cloakroom feeling very shaky indeed. I might have recovered, for the cloakroom was more airy than the dust-distances of the food-smelling dining-room, but that, as soon as we were inside, Betty sat down and took off one of the satin shoes she was wearing. 'They're new,' she explained and showed the back of her heel where blood stained her stocking.

'Oh dear! Take your stocking off and put some powder on it,' her mother said.

Betty did as she was told and exposed a foot that was tortured out of all resemblance to a human foot — toes crumpled and sprouting a large corn on each, the great toe folded over the adjacent one in a grotesque fashion that made my gorge rise. I dashed headlong into the lavatory and was wretchedly, violently and extremely noisily very sick indeed. That distorted foot seemed to symbolise the entire evening.

When I emerged there was no concealing what had happened, even if they had all been stone-deaf, for my skin was greenish-white above my black velvet, and water streamed from my eyes and nose. I was aware of looking probably more revolting than Betty's misshapen foot, but I did not care. I saw before me, wide open, the way of escape, although before escape could become actual there was a prolonged discussion among the whole family in the draughty hall.

'I'll be perfectly all right,' I kept saying, 'but I had better go home. I am sorry to spoil the evening.'

'Of course you must go home, dear,' Mrs. Stewart clucked. I suppose she was quite a kind old woman. 'Alan will take you right away and we'll all meet another night. Ken, did you think that fish was all right? I thought there was something funny about it myself. Kitty, are you feeling all right? Kitty has a very sensitive inside — can't *look* at strawberries. Are they getting a taxi, Alan?'

'It wasn't the food, Mother,' said Alan with the authority of the eldest born child and the only son. 'It was an excellent dinner. It was probably the drinks. You see, Janet never drinks anything as a rule.'

I was so overcome at this that I do not think I uttered another word to the Stewart family. The taxi arrived, we got in and set out for my flat. I sat staring out at the Saturday-night crowds under the Saturday-night lights, which, in London, always seem to be more gay than the other lights of other evenings, as if even the electric units were burning the remains of their week's wages in an extra orgy of spending. What Alan had said about me to his mother was not true, which, in itself, did not matter to me a great deal. Alan could lie to his mother about anything he chose, I supposed. What mattered to me was that he wished it were true that I 'never drank anything as a rule' and that, as my 'intended', one of his intentions was, without even his own awareness of the intention, to make it true. To Alan, I was not I, Janet Sandison, at all. I was a Highland lassie, love-lilting in a cloud of peat reek beside my spinning wheel, awaiting the love and the moulding of Alan Stewart, who had made good as a chartered accountant in the City of London.

When the taxi stopped at the door of the house-converted-into-flats where I lived, I turned to him and said: 'Don't get out. Please hurry straight back to the hotel and tell your mother how sorry I am about this. I'll be all right.'

I allowed myself to be kissed, I descended to the pavement, and the taxi drove away, but I did not go into the house. Instead, I went walking tap-tap-tap-tap on my high heels down the damply glistening pavement to the Thames and stood looking over the embankment wall at the reflections of the lights in the black water.

I do not remember what I thought about — I do not think I was capable of any coherent thought. I had a vague consciousness of being trapped, trapped in some web of circumstance and convention. I think I knew that I had no real desire to marry Alan Stewart; I think that at this stage I was even aware that I actively disliked him, but yet my life seemed to be oriented towards this marriage in a way that was inescapable. My family expected the marriage to take place; all my friends, such as Miss Slim, accepted it as an imminent event, and Alan's family, obviously, was resigned to it. And, of course, it was the sensible, reasonable thing for me, a woman of twenty-seven with no fortune, face or prospects, to do. And there would be a fuss with my family if I cast aside yet one more suitor. And there would even be a mischievous fillip in going through with it if only to annoy that smug mother of Alan's, who obviously hated the idea of another woman coming between her and her only son. My mind was a muddle of a million threads of thought, all criss-crossed and tangled and full of a turgid movement, black and oily as the dark water of the Thames beyond the wall, with the reflections of the lights coming and going in it, intangible, unsteady, eternally elusive of the grasp.

As I turned away from the river to go home, still with the conviction that I was trapped beyond release on this course on which I was set, a public-house at the street corner, which was enjoying a fashionable vogue, opened its door and disgorged on to the pavement five giggling people — three men and two women — just as I passed. Foremost among the group was Rose, whom I had not seen for over a year. She was not drunk but merely exhilarated, and she recognised me at once in the lights from the windows beside the pavement.

'Blow me down!' she bellowed with her life-and-soul-of-the-party good fellowship which her entourage applauded with renewed giggles and titters. 'If it isn't me old boozin' buddy, Janet! And got up regardless!'

'Hello, Rose,' I said weakly.

I wanted to get away, for I knew from experience that Rose in this hearty hail-fellow mood was at the stage when one more drink would curdle her temper and I felt that I had had my share of social strain for one evening, but she seized me in a matey way by the upper arm.

'Let's all go back in and have one more little drinkie with me old chum!' she said.

Her party, none of whom I had met before, were only too willing to comply, and one of the men pushed open the door of the bar.

'Where's the boy-friend?' Rose enquired in ringing tones and looked vaguely up and down the pavement. 'At the loo?'

Her entourage tittered again, and 'Oh, shut up, Rose!' I said and, taking the line of least resistance, walked towards the open door.

'Drinks on me,' said Rose when we were inside and jammed against the wall in the corner. 'Ernie, go get them. Janet, what'll you have?'

When Ernie returned with the drinks, Rose's exuberance died down a little and I was relieved to notice that she seemed to be growing sleepy, which was the alternative reaction to the curdling of the temper, but with the first swallow of the new drink she awoke suddenly and gazed round at us all with portentous solemnity. 'Funny thing,' she said. 'I get divorced and she gets married. There's one born every minute.' This was greeted by her claque with a wild outburst of laughter and comments to one another about the brilliance of Rose's wit. 'She's doing very well for herself,' she told them when the laughter died down. 'Stewart's his name. In the City. It's him I asked was he at the loo.' Like a professional comedian, she waited for the titter that she deemed this sally to deserve, and, having received it, she went on: 'Silly of me actually. Stewart doesn't go to the loo — too refined.' While her audience responded to this with renewed and louder laughter, she turned to me and poked me roguishly in the ribs. 'Can just see him on the wedding night, old girl,' she said, 'getting out of bed in the middle of the big do to make sure the door's locked!'

With this, she gave a shriek of laughter like a demented cockatoo, drained her drink at a gulp and said: 'Let's all go back to my place! I'm sick of this pub!'

I found it easy to slip away from them outside, for they were all more drunk than I had thought, and I made my way quickly back to my flat. I do not remember what I thought about, but I remember what I did. I found a small box and some cotton-wool. I took off my half-hoop of diamonds and I made up a small parcel with a short letter enclosed, and I stuck sixpence in stamps on it and went out and posted it in the pillar-box at the end of the street.

All the next day, which was Sunday, I answered neither telephone nor doorbell, but my ex-intended got me on the telephone on Monday morning. He was very, very indignant, but when he began to rebuke me for my carelessness in mailing the ring through the unregistered post I hung up the receiver. It was like shedding from my shoulders an unbearable load, and it was difficult to believe that the shedding was so easy of accomplishment.

CHAPTER TWELVE

Between 1937 and 1951 many things happened to many people, but the main thing that happened to me that is relevant to this story is that in 1947 I married, and about two years later my husband and I went to St. Jago, which is an island in the Caribbean, and in 1951 we came home to Britain on leave. At the end of November of that year, Twice — Twice is my husband, whose name is Alexander Alexander — and I had come down from Reachfar to London to spend a last two weeks shopping and eating British food prior to sailing from Avonmouth for St. Jago, and when I use the word 'shopping' I ought to explain that I was buying things like linen and towels for our household, and Christmas gifts for our friends, while Twice, who is an engineer, was seeing to the shipping of plant, equipment and tools for the various people in the island who had commissioned him to act here in Britain on their behalf. We did not, therefore, see each other except in the evenings during these last two weeks, and, not being a dawdling shopper, I was soon left with time on my hands.

Fifteen years had now elapsed since I left Daneford, and six years of war had intervened, a six years that broke many contacts; but one of my contacts that had withstood all the years was that between me and Angela Carter, although for a long time it had been no more than the gossamer thread of cards exchanged at Christmas.

One grey afternoon, while I was sitting in the lounge of our hotel waiting for Twice to come back, a wedding reception was being held and I caught a glimpse of the covey of bridesmaids who were carrying bouquets of the tawny-golden roses which had always decorated the drawing-room at Daneford on party nights. As the group of giggling young women disappeared up the stairs, I found myself thinking of Rose, and from her my mind went to Dee, Mr. Roy, Lorna, Helen Roland, all round the Daneford group, and from there back to old Mr. Carter and Angela. Why, I thought, don't I ring up my friend Angela? And so I did, and the next afternoon she came to the hotel to have tea with me.

Angela, who was not a great deal older than myself, was now a smart, blonde little matron, her complexion still fresh and good, her smile as pretty as ever, but she seemed to me to be much smaller than I remembered. This, I think, this memory of her as a bigger woman, was based on the illusion that, when I worked for Mr. Carter, because she was the mistress of the house, I saw her with the eyes of the mind as Authority and part of the grown-up world and therefore as larger than myself. It was disconcerting for a moment, on meeting her again, to discover that she was about half my own size and weight.

'You look exactly the same, Janet,' she told me. 'I would have recognised you anywhere.'

'People tell me that I change very litle,' I said. 'It must be the Reachfar rock in me.'

Over tea we talked of the time I had spent in Kent long ago, and of old Mr. Carter, and of the daily crises in the library, but it was Angela who said: 'It was all splendid training for you. Of course, we didn't know at that time that you were going to be part of Roy's do with Rose. Lord, what a horror she was!'

Maybe, as they say, time is a great healer, or maybe, as they also say, distance lends enchantment to the view, but, no matter what they say, I was not prepared to go along with any nastiness about Rose. I do not know why this should have been, but I felt it was all very well for my friend Angela to sit there in her mink coat and her pretty hat, with all the security of her husband and three successful grown-up children behind her, and prepare to be nasty about my friend Rose. I know more about Rose than she does, I thought. She took good care to keep well out of the way when Mr. Roy was getting rid of Rose, I thought. But for Rose, I might be married to that terrible Alan Stewart instead of to Twice, I thought.

'Rose wasn't all that bad actually,' I said. 'I got along very well with her.'

'You must be about the only person who did,' Angela told me a little huffily.

I changed the subject. 'Where is Dee and how is she?' I asked. 'She wrote to me for a year or so and then it all dropped off.'

As a change of subject, this was not a tremendous success, for Angela's pretty satisfied face developed a little dissatisfied wrinkle between the brows.

'We've had the most appalling time with that girl,' she said.

'Oh? In what way?'

'My dear, in every possible way.'

'But how?'

'Oh, it wasn't the girl's fault, I suppose, and yet a lot of it was. I've never met a more difficult creature. I think it was partly that Canadian education.'

'Canadian?'

'Yes. Roy sent her to Canada, to a school near Toronto, in 1939, you know, and she didn't come back till '45; and, my dear, you should have heard her accent and have seen her clothes! And then, she is as plain as a pikestaff. She wasn't at Daneford for a week before she and Helen were at loggerheads — '

'What about?'

'My dear, how do *I* know? But she calls Helen Helen-the-Horse!'

Angela's voice was shocked and indignant, but, in spite of that, I giggled, and she glanced at me and went on: 'I suppose Helen is pretty horse-crazy, but honestly, Janet, Dee was impossible. Then Roy asked me if I would have her and see to her clothes and take her about with my two. Rosemary was twenty and Susan nineteen at the time — '

'And Dee would be eighteen, wouldn't she?'

'Yes, and about the plainest, most awkward thing you can imagine. Really awful.'

Now, I was forty-one at this time, and down the years I had put a great deal of thought and effort into trying to bring myself up to be a rational, reasonable woman, but it was being borne in on me that this meeting I was having with my dear old friend Angela was putting a sore tax on all my rationality and reasonableness. I had sprung to the defence of Rose, and now, over Dee, I found myself looking at Angela and thinking: 'You are one self-satisfied little smug-pug, with your handsome son and your two pretty daughters who have made successful marriages — one of them even having got herself a title, as you told me a moment ago. But Dee used to call these daughters of yours the "Goldiloxes", and she was darned right at that, and she is probably darned right still!'

'She was with us for six months,' Angela was saying, 'and it was one long scene. My nerves were in shreds at the end.'

'But what were the scenes about?'

'Everything. She didn't want to do this, she didn't want to go there, she wouldn't wear that dress, she didn't like so-and-so. And she had simply no idea of how to behave and didn't seem to want to learn.'

'But what *did* she want?' I asked.

'Go into the city! Into the firm!' said Angela, her blue eyes round with horror.

'But why not? She was her father's daughter. She was intelligent. Why shouldn't she go into the firm?'

'My dear Janet, none of us girls have *ever* gone into the firm!' said Angela.

I had never before seen the slightest resemblance between her and her brother Mr. Roy, but I saw it now. Here was the rigid mind which had been brought up to the creed of the 'normal thing', and the normal thing for 'us girls' of the Andrews family was a fine ignorance of where the family money came from, an early introduction into society and an early and successful marriage if at all possible. Rosemary and Susan, the Goldiloxes, were the normal thing and Dee was not.

'But, Angela,' I said, 'Dee is of a different generation from yours and mine.'

'It is not a question of generation, Janet. Rosemary and Susan had none of these queer ideas.'

I felt like saying that they had never had Dee's intelligence either, but instead I said: 'Rosemary and Susan had a different upbringing from Dee. She had a very difficult childhood, Angela.'

'I know that. That was all that terrible Rose's fault.'

'It wasn't entirely the fault of Rose — ' I began.

'Then whose? Roy wasn't to blame — he was devoted to the child. No father could have done more!'

Why, I wondered, am I sitting here with this woman, arguing like this? Why did I ask her here at all? I wish she would go away. I wish Twice were back. I wish we were off to the West Indies!

'And what is Dee doing now?' I asked.

'Oh, she seems to have settled down and come to her senses at last, thank Heaven.'

'So Mr. Roy let her join the firm?'

'How did you know that?'

I laughed. 'I know — or used to know — Dee.'

'Well, actually, he didn't really want to let her join the firm, but he had to in the end. You have no idea what we all went through, all because of old Uncle Archie.'

'Uncle Archie?' I had only a vague memory of the old gentleman whom I had met only once, who had been the donor of the 'yantique' Alphabet of Flowers to Dee. 'What did Uncle Archie have to do with it?'

'My dear, he died in 1949 and left every penny to Dee. He left her everything — his London house, the river cottage at Marybourne, everything — not a sou to any of my three or Clive's boys or anyone. She set up house all by herself in Knightsbridge; started going to classes at the School of Economics; got into the most frightful set of people — you've no idea. She got mixed up in some political riot or demonstration or something in Hyde Park and was taken to *prison*. Poor Roy was driven nearly crazy. And then she announced that she was going to work for Carleton Grayson —'

'Carleton Grayson?' I stuttered, laughter bulging in my chest as I remembered this competitor firm to Andrews, Dufroy & Andrews. 'Carleton Grayson?'

'Yes. Can you imagine it? The appalling disloyalty of it! And it made Clive and Roy look such fools that — '

The bulge in my chest was too much for me and I gave way to a raucous shout of laughter.

'What is so amusing?' Angela asked.

'I'm sorry, Angela, but to an outsider like me it really is funny, you know. And so typical of Dee.'

'It may be typical, but I shouldn't think it could be funny,' Angela said, 'even to an outsider'; and I felt that she gave to the last word the meaning that it carried in the social class to which she belonged. She began to gather her handbag and gloves together. 'I really must go. It has been so nice to see you again, Janet.'

But her voice had a hollow ring. It would soon be Christmas, I thought, but probably we would not be exchanging cards this year.

'But before you go,' I said, 'I take it that Dee did not actually join Carleton Grayson?'

'Of course not! She went into our own firm.'

'And how is she doing in it?'

'Oh, well enough, I suppose, but she got engaged last month, thank goodness, and that should see the end of this City nonsense. Marriage should settle her down.' Angela rose and began to pull on her gloves. 'He is considerably older than she is, which is probably a good thing in her case.'

I could not think of anything to say. I felt that this engagment was an anticlimax to Dee's grand fling at defying Mr. Roy, the Andrews family and their whole tradition of the normal thing.

'It's not much of a match,' Angela went on, 'but it's more than I, for one, expected — to see her engaged at all. He has been with the firm for a long time — a very reliable man. Roy and Clive are thinking of bringing him on to the Board. Maybe you remember him. Alan Stewart his name is.'

Angela held out her neatly gloved hand to wish me goodbye. She might have been a mule who had kicked me in the solar plexus.

'Alan Stewart?' I said. 'Yes. Yes, he was with the firm when I was there. Yes, I remember him.'

'I really must fly. Goodbye, Janet. I hope you have a good trip out to St. Jago.'

I sank down on to the sofa and watched her disappear round the revolving door.

I was still staring at the door when Twice came in, and as I blinked at him he said: 'What's happened? Seen a ghost?'

'A whole clan of them,' I told him. 'A whole clan of Macabers, as Tom would call them, including one very nasty spectral one called Alan Stewart. Would you buy me a drink? Maybe even two drinks?'

'I warned you that you shouldn't go raking up that murky past of yours. Let's drink up in the bedroom if you can walk that far. It'll be quieter.'

Twice listened with patience and interest to my story of my afternoon with Angela. Twice is a person of few intimacies. In the course of his business and work he makes a vast number of acquaintances and, in general, gets along very well with people, but he seldom gets on to the plane of intimacy with anyone, partly, I think, because he himself is very reserved in nature, and partly because people are not a hobby with him as they are with me. Twice, I believe, is more deeply interested in engineering, which is his profession, and social history and music, which are his spare-time amusements, than he is in the quirks and foibles of the people around him, but nevertheless he is always very interested when I recount to him my muddled observations about people, and he is more than patient, I must grant, with the muddles, mental and social, that I get myself into as a result of my excursions into other people's minds and lives.

'Being over forty and coming back to this country on leave after a time abroad like this is very, very muddling,' I complained at last. 'That Angela! I used to think she was the nicest person, and she's not at all, really. She is just a smug, middle-class, self-satisfied poop!'

'The one I am interested in,' Twice said, 'is this poop Stewart. I've learned a certain amount about some of the men in your life but very little about this one. But now that we have got him out into the open, let's hear about him. What sort of a bloke was he? Or rather *is* he?'

'Now, he was a *proper* poop! and I bet you he still is. And this thing about him going to marry Dee! It's disgusting. Why, it's — it's almost incest!'

'Flash, don't be ridiculous. He may be twice her age, but lots of young women like older men.'

'It feels like incest to *me*!' I protested angrily. 'And as for liking him, Dee Andrews must be off her head!'

'But *you* must have liked him once! Dammit, you were engaged to him!'

Our voices were rising, as, in those days, our voices tended to do when Twice and I had what we called a quiet discussion about anything.

'I did *not* like him!' I said, and I could feel my face flushing with anger, embarrassment, and I do not know what other compound of feeling. 'He had a mind like a skeleton in a lewd position! And he was vain and ambitious and mean and told dirty stories, and he had an awful old mother as mean-minded as himself that he spoke about as if she were the Virgin Mary! I *hated* him!'

'Then why did you think of marrying him?'

'I *didn't* think of it!'

'But you said you were engaged to him?'

'Oh, lord yes, I was engaged to him. But I didn't think about *marrying* him. Dash it, it's when I began to think about being married to him that I broke off the engagement!'

Twice looked at me very earnestly for a moment and then said: 'Look, let's have that second drink.' He rose from the bed where he had been sitting and poured the drinks out. 'Now, listen, don't go losing your temper, but I am in a little bit of a muddle about all this. Let's take it in stages. (A) You got engaged to him. (B) Then you thought about being married to him. (C) Then you broke off the engagment. Is that right?'

'Yes,' I snapped.

'It seems sort of illogical to me.'

'Young women of twenty-five aren't logical! Oh, you wouldn't understand, Twice. You've never been a young woman of twenty-five.'

'I have never been a steam turbine either, but I can see how one works if somebody shows me a diagram.'

'Young women aren't steam turbines!' I snapped at him again and then I felt annoyed with myself for being so angry because I could not really trace the source of the anger. 'In fact, young women of twenty-five are pure hell,' I told him, 'or, anyway, *I* was. But I won't admit that it was all my fault. Oh, the devil with it! Why are we squabbling about all this, anyway? In another two weeks we'll be at sea, and I won't be sending Christmas wishes to Angela Carter this year.'

'We're not squabbling although you have got up rather a head of steam. I was just interested in this Stewart. I think that's natural enough. You know, sometimes I feel a bit resentful of all those years you have lived that I know so little about. I have never heard of this Miss Slim you mentioned before, for instance.'

Twice is good for me, I think. I began to feel more reasonable.

'People, for me, have what you might call contexts,' I told him. 'Basically, I am tremendously egotistical and selfish, I think. I never think of people except in relation to myself and as part of the furniture of certain periods in my life. If somebody like Miss Slim belongs, as Miss Slim did, to a period that I didn't enjoy very much, I seem to have the knack of burying the period and Miss Slim with it, if you see what I mean. It's the same thing that I am inclined to do with old Jean, my stepmother. It was ages, if you remember, before you discovered that she even existed. It isn't that I mean to hide things, Twice. It simply happens . . . And I have told you about Dee often enough.'

'Yes, but why? Isn't she part of the context too?'

'No, not the Miss Slim, Mr. Roy, Alan Stewart context. I

took Dee up to Reachfar, and it is there that I always remember her, and maybe that's why.'

'You have told me quite a bit about Rose on and off, too. It is Mr. Stewart who emerges as the submerged quantity,' Twice said. 'What did kill the great romance? How did it all end?'

'Persistent, aren't you? I doubt if I can see the thing clearly even at this distance of time. But you are hitting a very sore nail on the quick with that word "romance". The romance idea was the curse of the lives of young women in my day, and I shouldn't be surprised if it isn't still a curse, after listening to Angela today.'

'What do you mean by the "romance idea"?'

'This fluffy, woolly, sickly pre-conditioning of young women to fall in love, as they call it, with the first eligible man who looks at them. It's all right for you to laugh — they don't do it to men. But for young women it is pure hell. You've heard me raving on this subject plenty of times, Twice. I sometimes think it is a mania with me; but honestly, when I look back on all the uncertainty and puzzlement and frustration and heartache of those years and think how they were all aggravated by society and its romance-idea I could spit with rage. What a waste of time and energy it all was! As if the process of growing adult isn't difficult enough without wondering if you should marry this man and secure your economic future, or marry that man and have fun, or just sleep with the other one and see how you like it, thus throwing your bonnet over the windmill for good. Human relationships are difficult enough to achieve without society and your family and economic circumstances causing extra pressures; and when I think of Alan Stewart and what Rose saved me from, I should thank her for evermore on my bended knees and fasting.'

'Rose? What had she to do with you and Stewart?'

'If it hadn't been for Rose,' I said, 'I'd probably have married the poop and wouldn't be sitting here now. I'd probably be either on the streets or in the mad-house.' And I told him of that evening long ago and the meeting in the bar on the Embankment. 'And that's the story of Alan Stewart,' I ended. 'Do you wonder if I kept it buried deep and long? I can feel myself squirming and going all red inside with shame even now. It's all so awful. There I was, smugly despising Rose for trying to hang on to Mr. Roy and all he could give her and refusing to be aware that I myself was contemplating marrying Alan Stewart for precisely the same reasons. It makes me crawl with disgust at myself . . . But there is a queer thing. None of us seem to be able to see straight for ourselves although we are all very good at seeing straight for other people. Rose's love-life, for want of a better word, with Flip Orton was about the phoniest thing in the world. Her whole vocabulary about it was phoney — full of phrases like "hot, pulsing life"; and then there was this awful bedroom like a lush film set. And anyone with half an eye could see that Flip was interested in Rose only because of her wealth. Rose really knew it, I think, but she wouldn't let herself know it, just as I wouldn't let myself know about Alan Stewart, and Rose smothered what she didn't want to see or know in a lot of romantic claptrap. But she could bend an eye like a gimlet on the affairs of other people and see right through to their very core. After all, she hardly knew Alan Stewart, you would have said, but she hit off his whole horrid character in that one sentence that night in the pub. Mind you, she only said what she did to raise a laugh from this claque of hers, but she hit the mark.'

'It was an extraordinarily cruel thing to say,' Twice commented.

'Rose was often cruel. I think she enjoyed being cruel, but it was mostly that she would do anything or say anything to draw attention to herself and raise a laugh. She had to be the life and soul of the party, and if a few people got hurt in the process it didn't matter much. I wonder what has become of her?'

'You didn't ask Angela?'

'I would have done if she hadn't been so nasty about her right at the start. Dash it, I wish I had never laid eyes on Angela today, Twice!'

'Oh, forget it. There's no harm done.'

'It's a mistake to go raking up the past. One can't go back – not that one wants to. It has just brought forward all the old frustrated, dissatisfied, puzzled, helpless feeling that belonged to that time. Then there is this trouble about Dee. I have a stupid feeling of responsibility for her and what happens to her.'

'Oh, come; an engagement to marry is not usually regarded as trouble; and as for your responsibility for her, that's purely silly.'

'I suppose it is, and yet there it is. It takes so little to influence the course of a life, and at that time, when I was governessing Dee, I was completely without direction myself. I just went on from day to day doing what seemed to be the expedient thing — '

'But don't we all? Most of the time, anyway?'

'I suppose we do.' I found it difficult to express what was in my mind. 'But at that time I was simply drifting about, and Mr. Roy — he *used* me as an expedient, an expedient to get Dee out of his hair while he got on with the business of divorcing Rose. Because that is all it was, taking me on as her governess. I don't think he cared a hoot what sort of person I was. All he cared about was that I might keep her quiet. It's – it's like giving gin to a sick baby to keep it quiet while you go to the pictures!'

'Flash, that's hardly a fair comparison. It seems to me that Andrews did the best he could. After all, the kid was better when you left her than when you went to her, wasn't she?'

'That is just what I wonder,' I told him. 'The point is that she seems to be in a good-going mess right now, and I wish that I didn't feel that I've had a hand in it.'

'But, darling, she's *not* in a mess! Apparently her family are quite pleased with everything.'

'Well, *I* call it a mess!' I said angrily.

We left the subject of Dee and talked of other things, but the memory of the child who had clicked the lid of the inkwell haunted the back of my brain, seemed to be just under the blanket of my sleep that night and was in the forefront of my mind when I awoke the next morning. And, of course, while I sat up in bed drinking tea and staring gloomily at the opposite wall, Twice noticed my mood and began to ask me questions again. In the end, we nearly came to a quarrel when Twice said: 'I think you are being utterly unreasonable and silly about this, Flash. If I didn't know you so well, do you know what I'd say?'

'What?'

'That you are simply being dog-in-the-manger about this child and this man Stewart. You didn't want him for yourself, but you don't want *her* to have him either.'

'Twice Alexander! How dare you — '

'You calm down,' he told me, 'and come to your senses. You haven't seen the girl since she was a child fifteen years ago. She comes of this solid, traditional, middle-class City family on both sides. She sowed a few wild oats for a few years — all right. But she has probably found her feet in the solid tradition she belongs to and is making a sensible marriage of the kind that people of her sort do make and she is probably doing it with her eyes wide open. People who belong to that tradition, who have aunts like Angela and fathers like your Mr. Roy, don't toss their bonnets over the windmill and run away to the West Indies with penniless engineers the way you did. Now, let's give Rose, Stewart, Dee and all the rest of them decent burial and get on with the business in hand. What are you going to do today?'

'Nothing much. I am having my hair washed in the afternoon, but I'll be back about five . . . Twice, don't let's quarrel.'

'I'm not quarrelling, my pet. I am sorry you ever saw this Angela, though. I'm sorry because it is all my fault, really. It's miserable for you, hanging around this place waiting for me all day.'

'It isn't your fault. But I promise you not to rake up any more Angelas. I tell you what I'll do. I'll go out and look for an exhibition of pictures and spend the morning educating myself. That should keep me out of trouble.'

'I wonder,' Twice said. 'Oh well, one can only hope.'

But it was he who got us into the rest of the trouble, and serve him right, as I told him several times, after being so sane and rational and reasoning with me.

That day I spent the whole forenoon looking at pictures, having coffee and looking at more pictures. Then I had lunch alone, wrote some letters and went out to have my hair washed, and when I came back to the hotel about four-thirty I found Twice entertaining a young woman for tea. When I came into the lounge, Twice, who was facing the door, saw me and stood up, and the young woman stood up too and turned to look at me. 'Miss Jan!' she said as I came forward. 'I'd have known you anywhere!'

It was only her version of my name that told me who she was. I would never have recognised Dee Andrews. She was very little taller than she had been as a child of nine, but somehow she did not belong to the class of women that is described as 'petite'. She was not fat, but there was about her a sturdiness and a lack of fragility that the word 'petite' connotes for me. And she was extraordinarily colourless. Her hair was of the same mid-brown, cut in the way that the coiffeurs at that time called 'windswept', but which, in fact, so often looked merely untidy, and in Dee's case it looked slightly unbrushed and generally unkempt as well. Her skin was sallow, her eyes an indeterminate hazel. She was, as Angela had said, uncompromisingly plain. It was only after a moment or two that I began to notice something of the old Dee in her and this was the neatness of movement. The small hand that had clicked the lid of the inkwell long ago handled her teaspoon with the same neat precision, and the small feet which used to tense to the stamping ready were now crossed on the carpet with the same firm control and air of determination.

'It was Miss Slim who told me where to find you,' she said when we were all sitting down.

I felt uncomfortable and irritated, because I had not wanted this meeting, and this irritation at once focused itself on the fat memory of Miss Slim. *She*, I thought, was the one who got me into that horrible outing to Daneford long ago when I did not want to go! With my mind transmitting confused curses in the imagined direction of Miss Slim, I smiled at Dee and said: 'Miss Slim? How did *she* know?'

Dee laughed. 'Miss Slim always knows everything, Miss

Jan. Surely you remember that? She had been on the phone to Aunt Angela this morning, actually.'

'Oh, I see.'

'I think it's a bit mean you getting in touch with Aunt Angela after all this time and not with me.'

'Aunt Angela did send me the odd Christmas card,' I reminded her.

'Oh, I know.' She looked thoughtful for a moment. 'I was the one who fell away,' she said then. 'I fell away from a lot of things, with the war and being in Canada and everything. And, of course, Aunt Angela always remembers about Christmas and birthdays and things. She's that sort.' She dismissed Aunt Angela for the moment. 'I've often thought of writing to Reachfar. I knew your family would forward my letter, but I never did it.'

'Oh well, never mind. Here you are now.'

I felt very false and hollow, as if the ground between us were shaky and insecure. 'Tell me what you have been doing all these fifteen years.'

'Oh, nothing much,' she said, looking down into her teacup, but then suddenly she looked up at me and her round eyes had the hard copper-coin glint of long ago. 'Anyway,' she said, 'I've no doubt you have had a fairly comprehensive summary of me and my doings after tea with Aunt Angela yesterday.'

I glanced across the table at Twice; Dee's glance followed mine, and, looking from one of us to the other, she said: 'That's partly why I came here this afternoon. I didn't want you to sail away with the idea that I am a complete monster.'

'You are not fair to your aunt, Dee,' I said. 'She did not give me the impression that you were a monster. Actually, she couldn't have done even if she had tried. Monsters begin to show their monstrosity even when they are only eight years old, so I wouldn't be convinced that you had turned into one.'

'Then you are different from the family,' Dee told me. 'But, anyway, it doesn't matter now. They have calmed down; they are beginning to accept one as one is and, of course, I've done the right thing by getting engaged at long last. Not that I did it to please the family, though!' she broke in on her own speech defiantly. 'I did it because it suits me, and it suits them too, which is a blessing in a way.'

'Aunt Angela told me that you were engaged,' I said, and at that moment Dee happened to raise her left hand from her lap to the table-top to accept a cigarette that Twice was offering her. On the ring finger I saw, with my eyes popping, the half-hoop of diamonds that I, fifteen years ago, had apostrophised as it lay on the bathroom shelf while I washed my stockings and which I had later consigned so carelessly to the unregistered post. I did not know whether I wanted to laugh or to burst into tears; my sight was blurred and my ears were buzzing, but Twice's voice broke through the blur and buzz, sounding urgent and slightly strident, as he made the remark of a kind very foreign to him: 'And what a very pretty ring!'

I glanced quickly at him; my brain cleared a little and I said: 'Yes, isn't it?'

Dee looked down at the ring on her neat small hand. 'It belonged to Alan's mother. He was very devoted to her. Miss Jan, I suppose you knew Alan long ago? When you worked at the office, before you came to Daneford?'

'Oh yes,' I said. 'I knew him a little. He was chief accountant then.'

'He is secretary to the company now. He was appointed when old Mr. Pink died. What a pity he's not here! He'd have loved to meet you again.'

'He is out of Town?' Twice asked.

'He went over to Holland at the beginning of the week and he is going on to Hamburg and then the Baltic. He will be gone for about three weeks. When do you sail?'

'In about ten days,' I said, and hoped that my paean of gratitude was not echoing in my voice. 'Tell me,' I went on quickly, 'do you know what happened to old Lorna Calvert?'

'Lorna? Lorna is about the best friend I've got, Miss Jan. She is a splendid person. She and I have often talked about you . . . Look here, what are you two doing at the weekend?'

'Why?'

'Why don't you let me drive you down to see Lorna?'

'That's awfully nice of you, Dee.'

'She'd be *so* thrilled!' She turned to Twice. 'Mr Alexander, do let's do it. Lorna would love to meet you. She is terribly fond of Miss Jan.'

'If Janet would like it,' Twice said, 'I am more than willing. London at the weekend is about the end, and our car has been shipped. We are like a couple of stranded refugees, as I told you, with having to put off our sailing like this . . . Flash, would you like to visit your friend Lorna on Saturday or Sunday?'

'Very much,' I said. 'Is she still at Marybourne, Dee?'

'Yes, but not at her shop any more. She had to give that up during the war.'

'I know,' I said. 'I was near Marybourne in the war and tried to look her up once, but nobody seemed to know where she had gone.'

'Oh, my gosh, Miss Jan, of course you don't know anything about any of this!'

'Any of what?'

'Lorna's at Uncle Archie's cottage on the river. He left it to me when he died. She's looking after Rose!'

'Rose?' Unable to believe my ears, I stared frowning at Dee, who stared back at me and then burst into a fit of giggles.

'Do you mean Rose — your father's — Rose that was at — '

'Father's ex-wife, yes,' said Dee.

'How did that come about?'

Dee had another burst of giggling and turned to Twice. 'You said when we were talking that you couldn't imagine Miss Jan as a governess. Can you imagine it now? How did that come about?' she mimicked, with which Twice joined her in laughing at me. After a moment, her decisive, plain little face became sober and she said: 'I'll tell you how it came about, Miss Jan.' But then she turned to Twice: 'I hope all this isn't a bore for you, Mr. Alexander. I am afraid it is, though. Two people talking about the past are always a bore.'

'This doesn't bore me. You see, it's partly Janet's past,' Twice told her, smiling at her.

'I like you enormously!' she said to him suddenly. As she spoke, her entire face seemed to change, as if she had removed a mask, and her eyes shone and her neat, even little white teeth sparkled in a brilliant smile. Momentarily, she was very appealing as the child of the reading and talking room emerged through the screen between past and present, but in a second the flash was gone and the hard mask of the young woman was back in place as she turned back to me, repeating: 'I'll tell you how it came about. When I came back from Canada in 1945 I ran into Lorna on the street one day when I was with Helen.' She turned to Twice. 'Helen is my father's present wife, Mr. Alexander. She is a real bitch.'

'Dee,' I said, 'that will do.'

'Look, Miss Jan, there's no good you going on as if I were still in the nursery,' said Dee, and to my fury I saw Twice suppress a grin. 'I am a big grown-up girl now and I know a bitch when I see one. Helen is very much the County down around Daneford, and — well, anyway, she was a bitch to Lorna in the street that day and she was a bitch *about* her afterwards. The thing I can't understand about grown-up people — the ones in my family, anyway — is that they seem to think that anyone younger than they are is automatically an idiot. And they are such liars! Helen seemed to think I didn't *know* about Lorna being an old friend of hers who was kind to her and brought her to Daneford and introduced her to Father and everything in the first place. What did she think I was doing all the time when she used to come up every weekend and ride with Father and me? Did she think I was blind? . . . So I just told her what I thought of her for being a bitch to Lorna like that.'

'And what *did* you think of her?' Twice asked.

'I thought she was just a snobbish disloyal bitch and I said so, and I don't believe in just saying things, so I found out where Lorna lived and went to see her as well.'

'I see,' I said.

'What do you see?'

'I see that you would do any damn' thing practically if it would annoy Helen.'

Dee giggled. 'You've probably got something there. But it wasn't *only* to annoy Helen, Miss Jan. Honestly, it wasn't. I have always liked Lorna, and she was always kind to me when I was small.' I smiled at her. I had to, for her plain little face was full now of an earnest honesty that went to my heart. 'All right, Dee, I believe you. So you went to see Lorna — '

'Yes, in an awful dreary flat in Earl's Court, and she had Rose there, and Rose was sick, and they didn't have enough money or anything. Miss Jan, it was ghastly!'

'But, Dee, Rose was quite wealthy!'

'I know, but it seems that she has spent it all.'

'And what was the matter with Rose?'

'Heart disease. It's worse now. She can't get better. But her mind has gone a bit queer now and that makes things easier for Lorna in a way.'

'So you brought them to Uncle Archie's cottage at Marybourne?' I asked.

'No. Not then. I couldn't because I didn't have the cottage then, but I helped them as much as I could and went to see them quite often because it cheered Lorna up. Then Uncle Archie died and left me the cottage, and that made everything much easier. They have no rent to pay, and their money is quite enough now, and they are as happy as can be. But, Miss Jan, you and Mr. Alexander *will* come down at the weekend, won't you?'

'Yes, I think we will. Dee, *why* have you done all this for Lorna and Rose?'

She glanced round the room and then down at her neat little hands.

'I like Lorna for being — for being such a *friend* to Rose. But I suppose I did it mostly to annoy Father and Helen.'

'But why?'

'Why not? They have annoyed *me* quite a lot one way and another. I don't see why grown-up people should have the right to annoy one just because one is young. And all this thing of bullying one and knowing what is best for one. How *can* they know when they don't even know *one*?'

'Don't talk rot, Dee,' I said. 'Older people are bound to be a little wiser than young ones, generally speaking.'

Even as I said this, I became aware that I was now indeed

inside that 'grown-up' world that, with its views and instructions, made so much trouble for the young.

'I am not speaking generally,' said Dee firmly. 'I am speaking about me and my older ones. When I came back from Canada, where *they* made me go, they didn't know one thing about me, and they weren't prepared to try to learn either.'

'Well, I gather that they have been taught a little by now,' said Twice. 'Would you ladies care for a little drink?'

In the end Dee spent the whole evening with us and did not leave the hotel until nearly midnight, having arranged to call for us the next morning and drive us down to Marybourne to spend the weekend at the cottage.

'I hope this isn't going to be a bore of a weekend for you, darling,' I said to Twice when we were going to bed. 'We seem to have got entangled with my past after all.'

'Nothing could be a bore to me if that little Dee is involved in it,' Twice said. 'I think she is the most attractive and engaging little piece I have ever seen.' He frowned hideously at his own reflection in the looking-glass. 'Look here, your past aside, what sort of cove *is* this poop Stewart?'

I stared at him. 'What do you mean, Twice? I mean, why are you asking?'

'Well, I wouldn't like that little girl to get in a mess.'

'I don't think you need worry, really. She seems to be fairly adept at looking after herself and going her own way, doesn't she?'

'But is she and does she? She doesn't seem to me to have much way that is really her own. All she is doing is to run counter to her family whenever she can, and that isn't quite the same thing as going her own way, you know.' He sat down on the edge of the bed, took off his shoes and socks, wriggled his toes and stared at them. 'I'll tell you what I think is a queer thing — her not knowing *you* were engaged to Stewart once.'

'And I'll tell you another thing that is uglier than queer,' I said. 'At least it is to me. That ring she is wearing, that was Stewart's mother's to whom he was so devoted, was bought at a shop in Regent Street in 1936 and presented split new to *me*, and Stewart's dear old mum never laid eyes on it until she saw it on my finger in that hotel in Bloomsbury.'

'Flash! Are you sure?'

'Of course I'm sure! I spent a lot of time one way and another looking at that ring, wondering what the hell I was doing wearing it.'

'So that's why you gasped like a hooked cod at tea?'

'Wouldn't you have felt like a hooked cod? I have never looked upon myself as the romantic sort, but I thought the resurrection of the ring, complete with sentimental legend about old mum, was a bit much even for the parsimonious Stewart.'

'He is parsimonious, is he?'

'Yes. Or at least he used to be, in a furtive, secretive sort of way. I mean, he would always tip a waiter or spend the odd bob that it was the correct thing to spend, but I always had the feeling that he hated doing it.'

'I know the sort of Scotsman you mean,' Twice said. 'What is he like to look at? Good-looking?'

'Darling, how do I know now? I haven't seen him for fifteen years!'

I was impatient with the very thought of Alan Stewart, and growing irritated because Twice was showing every sign of getting his extraordinarily persistent teeth into this subject of Dee's engagement. Also, I could not understand the reason for his interest in the engagement, in Dee or in any of it. 'He was tall and thin and dark and quite well built,' I told him as I took the pins out of my hair. 'I should think he would have worn quite well. He had thin sharpish features — a typical accountant or banker type, you know, a *City* type. A bit like that man Fellowes in Anderson, Drew's office.'

I went through to the bathroom, brushed my teeth and washed my face, but when I came back to the bedroom Twice was still sitting there, and he said: 'I still think it's queer that neither her father nor her aunt nor anybody have told her that he was engaged to *you* once.'

'But, Twice, they didn't know I was engaged to him. It was after I left Daneford and was up here in London working for

Sir Richard that Stewart and I got engaged. And I was moving in quite a different set. Even Miss Slim didn't know about it. It was through old Mr. Rollin that I got the job with Sir Richard, and I left the whole Daneford set behind. I have told you I was pretty sick of them by the time the divorce and all that was over. Stewart was just a sort of hangover — and hangover is just the word too!'

'That little Dee is too good for some parsimonious hangover in a city suit!' said Twice.

'Darling, what's got into you? It is as if Dee Andrews has completely bewitched you!'

'She has, in a way, Flash.' Twice, still sitting there bare-footed on the edge of the bed, looked up at me. 'I've never met anyone quite like her before. She seems to me to be a sort of original. It is difficult to describe what I mean — she has a different air about her from other girls of her age and it gives her a fascination.'

'I half understand what you mean. She has always had that different air. I like her myself in a besotted, almost-against-my-will sort of way, but I always have. And, after all, she belonged to me more than to anybody for over a year.'

Twice stared down at his wriggling toes. 'She is so very appealing. She is so sort of honest and courageous, and she has absolutely nothing on her side in the way of prettiness or anything.'

'What did you talk about before I got back?' I asked.

'You mostly. And Reachfar. And she said a thing that struck me, quite early on. She was telling me about you and Daneford and so on; and when I said I couldn't imagine you as a governess, she said: "Miss Jan didn't governess me much. She was more of a friend. But it was from her that I learned a thing that I think is terribly important. Miss Jan taught me that truth is the most important thing in the world and that it is quite hard to find sometimes."' He smiled at me and looked down at his toes again. 'It struck me, somehow, the way she said it. You see, Flash, you are a very true sort of person and you seem to have given her that side of yourself. Maybe that is why I fell for her so heavily.' He got up and began to undress, but after a moment he was frowning at his own reflection in the glass again. 'And that's why I don't like the sound of this Stewart with his parsimony and phoney stories about second-hand rings. He sounds like one big phoney to me, and that little girl is no phoney. And I'll tell you another thing!' He stuck his chin out at me belligerently. 'If he's seven years older than you, he's seven years and six weeks older than *I* am, and *I* wouldn't want to marry that little girl!'

'All right,' I said. 'No need to blow your top! In any case, I'd prefer that you stay married to *me*!'

'You know what I think?' he asked with his chin sticking out further than ever.

'No what?'

'I think this Stewart of yours is just a proper dirty old man!'

'He is not my Stewart, thank heaven,' I said. 'And I am almost certain he is a most improper dirty old man, for he was a very, very dirty young one.'

'I think it's absolutely disgusting!' said Twice. 'Why, it makes me feel — giving her a second-hand ring and phoney story — it makes me feel sick in my stomach. Why, it's — it's — it's like — like —'

'The word you are searching for,' I said, 'is incest. For goodness' sake, Twice, get undressed and come to bed. It's after midnight!'

CHAPTER THIRTEEN

By nine o'clock the next morning I had placed a ban on the name and personality of Alan Stewart as a topic of conversation, for Twice, in the grip of an enthusiasm or an indignation, much as I love him, can wear the nerves to shreds; but when Dee arrived about ten with her car all his indignation melted away like snow before a sunlit wind as they chattered to one another while loading our bags into the boot. Twice shut down the lid and ran a broad caressing hand over the coachwork. 'What a beauty!' he said then, standing back on the pavement and looking with his head on one side at the Daimler. 'You are a spoiled darling, Dee.'

'Could you be bothered to drive her, Mr. Alexander?' Dee asked him. 'Then Miss Jan and I can gossip all the way.'

'As a governess,' I informed the ambient air, 'I was always a great one for tact. When taking engineers to the country in your Daimlers, I always said to my charges, always offer to let them drive, for they make rottenly nervous passengers anyway.'

'I *wasn't* being tactful!' said Dee, and down came a small brogued foot with a crack on the pavement. 'I would *like* him to drive for me!'

I stared down at the neat brown shoe, for that sharp crack had disoriented me for a moment as if the equivalent of an earthquake in time had happened.

'My goodness — ' I began when I had recovered myself, but as I looked at her I saw that her round eyes were swimming in tears. She turned away.

'I am sorry,' she said. 'I am behaving badly.' She opened the door of the car. 'Shall we all sit in front? There is plenty of room.'

Twice's eyes were fixed on my face and I felt myself flushing.

'Dee,' I said, 'I am sorry I said that, but I was only teasing Twice, you know. He will love to drive this car of yours. You couldn't offer him anything he would like more.'

'Twice?' she said in a questioning voice, looking from me to him over the top of the car door. 'Oh.' She smiled faintly. 'I thought — Oh, it doesn't matter.'

'Yes, it does,' Twice said. 'What did you think, Dee?'

She swallowed convulsively. 'It's all silly.' She ran the tip of her forefinger along the top of the door, watching it travel as she had watched the lid of the inkwell click down long ago. 'Aunt Angela and — and people are always going on about tact and men and things.'

'But I am not a man-and-things,' Twice said, 'so you don't have to be tactful with me. I am just a simple sort of cove who likes good cars and likes to drive them, and has a wife with a tongue like a shrew.'

She smiled at him, a curiously intimate smile that made me feel isolated from them for a moment, although not unhappily so.

'You are very nice to me, Mr. Alexander,' she said.

'You'd better call me Twice,' he said. 'Everybody does.'

'I like it, but why do they?'

'Nobody did until Janet did. It is just the petty economical governessy sort of thing she would think of. My name is Alexander Alexander and she grudges having to repeat herself.'

Dee, standing beside him, looked at me and gave a small chuckle at my expense. It was like the signing of an alliance between them, that chuckle.

'You get in at the other side, Miss Jan,' she said. 'I'll sit in the middle,' and she climbed into the car and slid under the steering-wheel.

As once before on a car journey over this road, I sat thinking very hard about Dee, but she was not silent this time, as she had been on that day when we drove to Daneford with her father and Rose. This time she and Twice talked all the way and I was the silent one, although my cogitations were of the unproductive sort that did not get me anywhere. But that sudden little outburst of Dee's on the pavement outside the hotel and the vulnerability indicated by the ensuing tears had worried me. She was not, it seemed, the hard-shelled, self-possessed little miss that she had appeared to be the night before, but I had got no further than this when we arrived at the cottage and Lorna came out to the gate to meet us.

Lorna had changed very little; her hair was grey, that was all. And she still had her air of benign good nature as her myopic eyes blinked behind her glasses.

'Where's Rose?' I asked when we were inside.

'Upstairs,' said Lorna. 'She doesn't get up until about four in the afternoon, and she may be later today, having to dress specially smartly,' and she gave a significant twinkling glance at Twice. 'I don't know how much Dee has told you, but the great thing is to let nothing surprise you. Sometimes she is all right; other times she is pretty queer; and, anyway, you never know from one moment to the next.'

'How is her actual health?' I asked.

'Not good. Her heart is very rocky. According to the doctors she shouldn't be alive at all, but she is, and I can *not* keep her off the bottle. But she seems to be quite indestructible . . . Throw your coats anywhere and we'll have a cup of tea in a minute. You must all be half-frozen.'

'Rose will probably be down for tea today with Twice being here,' Dee said.

'She is not having tea just now,' Lorna told her gravely. 'She says it's ruining her figure . . . Twice — that's what I am going to call you — sit here. It's very kind of you to get mixed up in this hen-party. Otherwise I wouldn't see Janet.'

'And I wouldn't see you,' said Twice. 'I like hen-parties with the right sort of hens.'

Lorna put her head on one side, smiled at him and then said solemnly: 'If you say these gallant things you are in for a wonderful time with our Rose!' and Dee giggled with a light-hearted enjoyment that I had not heard in her since I had met her again.

'Miss Jan,' she said then, 'I have a surprise for you. I kept it specially.'

'Oh? What?'

'Come with me to the kitchen and I'll show you.'

I followed her along the passage into the kitchen, where an old man, wearing a stiff celluloid collar, a crimson muffler, a thick grey suit and a bowler hat, was sitting in a comfortable chair beside the stove, but before Dee could speak to him a white-haired little old lady came bustling through from the scullery. It was Perky. She must have been well over eighty now, but she was as spry as ever, and when Dee said: 'I bet you don't know who this is, Perky!' her bright old eyes sparkled, her pink cheeks became pinker and she said: 'Oh yes I do, Miss Dee. That's Miss Janet, that is! I'm ever so pleased to see you, Miss Janet.'

When I had greeted her, she turned like a sprightly little teetotum towards the static old man in the chair and said: 'And this is Alfred, Miss Janet. Alf, I've told you time and time again about Miss Janet.'

''Sright,' Alf confirmed, shaking my hand.

As I think I have said before, I like old people and I was entranced by Alf. I made all sorts of conversation with him while Dee talked to Perky in the scullery, but he ventured no remark except various shades and gradations of ''Sright', although he looked pleased all the time and seemed to be enjoying our chat.

'Who,' I asked Dee when we went upstairs to wash, 'is Alf?'

'Miss Jan, you *must* remember Alf!'

'Remember him? I have never seen him in my life before!'

Dee sat down on the edge of the bath and stared at me. 'I suppose it *is* possible,' she said after a moment.

'What?'

'That you never saw him.'

'I assure you that I have never seen him before. Who is he?'

'It is so queer that you could have lived with me for about two years and not know about Alf. I have always thought you knew everything there was to know about me, Miss Jan. It's so queer that Alf could be in my life and you not even know about him.'

'Who is he?' I repeated.

'Perky's admirer. Alf sitting in the kitchen at Sloane Crescent with his muffler and bowler hat on is about the earliest thing I remember. He lives down here with her now.'

'So she is married? You might have told me, Dee!'

'Oh no, she isn't married to Alf. It's so odd to think you don't know. Oh no. Perky wouldn't marry him — not ever. She wouldn't lower herself, she always said.'

'Lower herself?'

'Yes. He was in the fruit and vegetable business — had his own barrow and everything, but Perky would have none of it. It wasn't respectable, she said. Then after the '14-18' war he turned himself into a bricklayer to try to please her, but she said that wasn't respectable either. Bricklayers were jerry-builders, she said, and it just wasn't respectable. All this happened before I was born, but I know all about it — I thought everybody did. So then he went back into the fruit and vegetable business.'

'Isn't he respectable now that he has retired?'

'No. Perky says he will never be respectable now. She likes him, but he just isn't respectable, but now that she is living down here in the country she feels it is better to have a man about the house. He can hardly walk, she waits on him hand and foot; he isn't respectable, but he is a man about the house. Miss Jan' — Dee looked at me very gravely — 'people are really awfully queer, aren't they? Especially women?'

'Men can be pretty queer too,' I said.

'Men get more chances to please themselves about things, somehow. Women seem to get pushed around a lot more. You have to be as old as Perky to be able to do what you like if you are a woman. If you are young, you can't have a man about the house unless you are married to him,' she told me with a smile.

'You can,' I said, 'but it isn't usually done.'

'No. It's not what Father calls the Normal Thing.'

'Mind you, all women don't get pushed around, Dee. Nobody ever pushed Rose around. It was Rose who always did the pushing, and I gather that she is still doing it.'

'Flip Orton pushed her around,' Dee argued. 'He took

nearly everything she had and then ran off to the States. I think men are bloody.'

'No, just not respectable,' I said.

''Sright,' said Dee, in exact imitation of Alf. 'Miss Jan, Twice isn't bloody. I've never met a man like Twice before. He's got none of that horrid thing of looking down at one in a soppy indulgent way as if one were a dear, silly little woman.'

'If he had, he couldn't be living with me. He is only about five foot eleven, and if he tried to look down in a soppy way at me I'd reach up and brain him.' Dee giggled and I went on: 'But, seriously, Dee, I think the nicest people are the ones who don't make a sort of fetish of being men or women and are content just to be people. I always like best the ones who are not too conscious of the difference between the sexes. Women like the Goldiloxes and Rose are a frightful bore, really, in their different ways. I gather that the Goldiloxes have turned into dear silly little women who like to be looked down at and indulged and have a silly little world of their own which is quite apart from the world of men. And then Rose, fifteen years ago, regarded the world of men as something she made forays into like a pirate or a freebooter.'

'She still does,' Dee said.

'But the world is different now – girls are not brought up to be silly little dears or marauding femmes fatales like Rose.'

'Girls are still supposed to be silly little dears in our family, Miss Jan. Even Helen the Horse, Father treats her like a silly little dear.'

'Your family is very conservative, Dee. I think being a shipping family has something to do with it, perhaps. Shipping has a lot of hangovers from the past in spite of all its modern developments, like Bills of Lading for the Caribbean still talking about the Spanish Main. It is very difficult for things and people to shake off the past. Sometimes I feel as if my past is spreading out behind me like a peacock's tail that I have to drag along and the people in it are the eyes on the feathers.'

'There are some pretty squint eyes among them then, like Rose and me.'

'Rose, yes, perhaps, but what is so squint about you?'

She frowned, looking down at her hands. 'Oh, nothing much, I suppose. But I wish you and Twice didn't live so far away.' She looked up and smiled at me. 'It would be nice to come and talk to you when I get to feeling — squint.'

'Do you feel squint a lot of the time?' I asked.

'Not when I am by myself. It's other people that make me feel it, people like Aunt Angela and the people at the office. You can see them thinking that I must be queer to work at the office when I don't have to. Miss Jan, I often think that I simply loathe other people!'

'I've often thought the world would be marvellous if there was nobody in it except oneself,' I said. 'All the trouble I have ever got into has been because of other people, but all the nicer things that have happened to me have been because of other people too — like meeting Twice. I met him through a ghastly woman called Muriel — '

'I remember her!' Dee said. 'Oh, I don't mean that I ever met her, but when the letters came you used to say: "Oh dear, here's another dreary from my friend Muriel."!'

'Well, there you are. She was as dreary as could be, but when I find myself hating people and being bored with them, I always remind myself that if I had never known Muriel I would probably never have met Twice.'

'But if only people would let one be what one *is*!'

'Look here,' I told her, 'if you know exactly what you are, you are pretty lucky and about the only person in the world who does. I am forty-one now and I keep on finding out new things about myself all the time.'

'What sort of things?'

'Well, I thought for years that I liked your Aunt Angela, and now I find that I don't at all.'

'She is all right except that she's so silly and that's probably because people made her like that. People do make you into things.'

'Only as far as you let them do it, Dee.'

'I say, you two!' Lorna's voice called. 'Come and have some tea!'

We had a comfortable forenoon meal round the fire while Twice and I answered Lorna's questions about St. Jago, and then, while Twice and Dee drove up to the village to the shops for Lorna's requirements for the house, Lorna and I sat on, smoking and talking.

I had always liked Lorna, but I had not known her at all intimately, and it seemed that it was only now that her life and character were coming into their true perspective for me. It was only now that I discovered that Lorna's life was, in the main, one of those many women's lives devoted to thankless service to other people. The only short interval that had been her own was the few years in the thirties when she had had her little antique shop. Before that she had nursed, until they died, first her father and then her mother; during the war, which had put an end to her antique shop, she had served with the Red Cross until the death of her brother's wife, whereupon she had gone to keep his house and rear his young family. No sooner was his youngest child at school than he married again and Lorna found herself homeless.

'I was too old to start in antiques again,' she told me 'but something always comes along. Rose needed me, and then Dee came along for both of us. Dee is a good child, Janet. Roy has never understood her, but then Roy has never understood anybody much, poor thing. And I'm so happy about this engagement of hers.'

I avoided the topic of the engagement. 'I don't suppose you ever see Mr. Roy?' I asked.

'Goodness, no! I suppose he hates us being here so near to Daneford, so he will think himself into believing that we don't exist.' She laughed and got up. 'Excuse me a moment, Janet. I'm just going up to see that Rose is all right.'

She was gone for only a few moments, and when she came back she said: 'Poor Twice! Rose is up and getting all set to give him the full treatment. I told her he was out, and she said to let her know when he came back. I don't know whether she has taken in the fact that you are here or not. She seemed to, last night, when I told her you were coming. But today she has mentioned nobody but Mr. Alexander.'

'I don't know how you cope, Lorna. You must get to feeling dippy yourself, don't you?'

'Maybe I *am* dippy, but I'm not aware of it,' she laughed,

her old comfortable husky laugh. 'Poor Rose! Although why I should call her poor I don't know. She is as happy as a sandboy.'

She sat looking into the fire for a moment, blinking in a puzzled way behind her glasses.

'Janet,' she said then, 'why is it that one can't help liking Rose in spite of — everything?' She laughed. 'I often remember how you described her goings-on that day at Daneford long ago as "everything". You have always liked her, haven't you, in spite of the hell's delight with her in the Daneford days?'

'It wasn't a question of liking her,' I said, trying to be accurate, 'so much as of being fascinated by her at first, but I got to like her later. When I came to Daneford, Lorna, I hadn't met very many people, and certainly never anybody like Rose. Rose used to say in those days that I was a poetic dreamer who was all brains and no sense, and she was pretty well right because Rose herself got mixed up in my mind with romantic dreams about the Thames and the Lady of Shalott and a lot of stuff like that. She caused a sort of battle between what Twice calls the Reachfar in me — Reachfar is my home in Ross — which is my core of hard sense and what Twice also calls my Celtic Twilight, which is my poetic dreamy side. According to the Reachfar side of me, hell was gaping for Rose because she was guilty of every sin in the calendar. Yet, there she was to look at, the lovely Rose, beautiful as a romantic dream and the Celtic Twilight would get the upper hand. Then, as my Reachfar side saw her, she *lived* in a dream, a dream of bliss with Flip Orton when it was sticking out a mile that he was an absolute stinker. Then, I think that ghastly bedroom at Daneford came into it, with all those mirrors with the gilt coronachs — '

'The what?'

'Those cherubs with the trumpets. They got to be known in my mind as coronachs. A coronach is really a funeral dirge but the Highland people believed that a supernatural coronach cried on the wind to foretell death or disaster. From the first moment I saw those cherubs, I thought of them as coronachs. Anyway, there was Rose among the coronachs and the mirrors, so that I never knew whether I was seeing her or a reflection of her, and then I got to feeling that she herself wasn't sure whether she was real or only a reflection in one of the mirrors. That was the Lady of Shalott theme again. It is awfully hard to explain, Lorna, but in the end I came to feel that Rose never saw herself as she really was, that what she saw was a sort of reflection of herself that she had conjured up. That made me feel that she really couldn't look after herself and that I was sort of responsible for her, and I think one tends to get fond of people one feels like that about ... It is ridiculous to say it, when one remembers her language and how she carried on that dreadful Sunday when Mr. Roy told her about the divorce, but, to me that day, it was as if Rose's mirror had cracked from side to side like the Lady of Shalott's.'

'It *was* like that for her,' Lorna said. 'I think it was that day that her mind cracked too. She knew that day that Flip would leave her. Oh, I know she lived in London for years and drank and racketed about until she got ill and was supposed to be sane enough, but I think it was on that Sunday that her mind began to go. She just could never accept that all the fun of Flip and Daneford and everything was all over. I think you are right when you say that she never saw herself as she really was – what she saw was some wonderful mirror image of her own making. She is the same still, only more so, as you will see.'

'Yet she was extraordinarily acute in those days at seeing other people as they really were — everybody except Flip Orton, that is. But about herself she was absolutely comic. "I am always loyal to my old friends —"' I quoted.

'Yes, a very loyal person, just made that way,' Lorna ended for me. 'And you knew the minute you turned your back she would be saying you were a Lesbian or a pervert. She still says the loyal thing, by the way. Still, it is mostly because of Rose that you and I are sitting here right now, Janet, and I must say it is very pleasant. It *is* good of you and Twice to have come.'

'Oh, rot! Apart from liking you and Dee, I owe Rose a great deal. She helped me an awful lot with my belated process of growing up and finding out a little about myself. Not that Rose meant to be helpful, but when I saw how she was deluding herself it made me take a closer look at *myself*.'

'You can bet your boots that Rose never meant to be helpful,' Lorna said with a rueful smile. 'Rose was never interested in helping anybody except Rose, and still isn't.'

'It just shows you that people do things whether they mean to or not,' I said. 'I often think that the whole concept of human free will is absolute bunk . . . Listen, what happened to all those mirrors and coronachs and that gilt gondola of a bed at Daneford? Is Helen the Horse, as Dee calls her, sleeping in it?'

'I shouldn't really think so,' Lorna said, 'but of course I wouldn't know. I don't take tea at Daneford now.'

When Dee and Twice came back from their little shopping expedition I could feel the intimacy between them come into the house with them, a sort of laughing comradeship.

'We are not really back yet,' Dee told us. 'We've just brought the fish because Perky wanted it early and we're going off again.'

When they had gone out and the car had driven away, Lorna said: 'Those two seem to get on very well. I've seldom seen Dee so lively and like her age. As a rule she either behaves like an old City man of eighty or a badly brought-up child of fourteen. She has given poor Roy the devil's own time of it.'

'So I gather. I had tea with Angela Carter, her aunt, in London. I find myself — although I don't know much of all that went on — taking Dee's part, Lorna. It seems to me that she has been pushed hither and yon all her life to suit other people's convenience.'

'The way I see it,' Lorna said, 'she has had all the inconveniences and pressures that a family can bring to bear without ever being really part of a family.'

'You couldn't be more right.'

'Roy is an absolute stick, always has been. If he had given in at the start, when she came back from Canada, and let her go into the firm, there wouldn't have been any of this nonsense. But he simply stone-walled — kept saying a woman's place was in the home. Actually saying it, you know. Apart from its being absolute nonsense these days, there was the fact that the poor child hadn't got a home and never had. I gather from everybody that Daneford is more of a stable now. Roy and I had the most frightful scene in Earl's Court, you know, when he found out that Dee was coming to visit Rose and me. I behaved like a perfect fishwife, and I am not a bit ashamed of myself, either.'

'Good for you, Lorna! I wish I'd been there!'

'I couldn't have done it if anyone else had been there. It was when he referred to our place as "this squalor" that I lost my temper.'

'Mr. Roy always felt that what the rest of us recognise as life was mere squalor,' I said, 'as if he walked upon a disinfected pavement a foot or two above the level of the gutter where the rest of us wallowed along.'

'Dee is like him in lots of ways, Janet, but not in that particular way, thank God. She has inherited his cleverness without all his coldness. Her getting along with your Twice like this is typical. Her intelligence is very mature in some ways. Her fiancé, Alan Stewart, is twice her age, you know. But you probably know him, don't you? He's been with Andrews, Dufroy & Andrews all his life, more or less.'

'Yes, I used to know him a bit.'

'I'm delighted about the engagement. I think he is just the thing for Dee — very calm and steady and balanced.'

Yes, I thought, Alan Stewart is ever so calm and steady and balanced, and just about to juggle himself on to the Board of one of the soundest firms in the City of London, but I did not say this to Lorna. Aloud I said: 'Dee's intelligence may be mature, Lorna, but I wonder just how balanced she is emotionally?'

'Oh, she is too much like Roy to be subject to emotional swings and roundabouts,' Lorna said comfortably.

I was not convinced, remembering the sudden stamp of the foot and sudden tears of that morning, but I did not argue the matter and Lorna continued: 'She is a cold-blooded and calculating little thing in lots of ways and she is the first to admit it. She put Rose and me into this house, for instance, but she quite frankly told me that her main reason for doing it was to discomfit her father and keep the place aired!'

Again, I did not argue with Lorna or tell her of the passion of indignation that Dee had displayed about the poverty and misery of the flat in Earl's Court.

'There is a lot of Roy in her,' Lorna went on. 'Indeed, this engagement of hers to Alan Stewart makes me think more of a political move within the firm than of a young girl getting married, just as Roy's marriage to Helen was a political move on his part into the County and on Helen's part a political move back into the real status of her family.'

'If Dee is the political sort,' I said, 'she and Alan Stewart should get along very well together and go a long way.'

'I say,' Lorna said suddenly, 'wasn't he a bit of a flame of yours at one time? The time of that party at Daneford when the boy played the piano and Rose got so cross?'

'Oh, that?' I said airily. 'That was only office nonsense, as Rose would have called it. He wasn't much my type — I'm not the political sort.'

I flattered myself that I carried this off quite well, but I was relieved to hear the outer door open and Twice and Dee chattering in the hall.

We had a late lunch, for which Rose did not come down but told Lorna that she would rest so as to be at her best in the evening, and after a quiet hour or two Dee and Twice went off in the car again with an air of mystery, but they returned after only a short time, Dee carrying a sheaf of long-stemmed pinky-golden roses which she presented to Lorna.

'Lorna,' she said, 'these are from Twice for *you*.'

'Oh, how lovely! But, Twice, you shouldn't have done it – they're such a price just now, but, goodness, they *are* beautiful!'

She took the flowers and stood looking down at them, and she seemed to be very much moved by the small gift. There had been very few flowers in her life, I felt.

'Thank you,' she said after a moment and laid the roses gently on the table. 'Thank you, Twice. I must go and get vases and bring in the drinks and see how Perky and Alf are getting on with the supper.'

But before she could move, the door of the room suddenly flew open and Rose stood there, one hand high against the wall, the other on her hip, posed like a model in a shiny magazine. She was an extraordinary sight. Even Twice, who can make up his mind not to be astonished and whose mind, unlike mine, usually does what he tells it, was considerably and visibly shaken for a split second. Her hair looked like a maltreated bundle of springy, brilliant brass wire; her face was plastered with make-up of the deep ochre shade which she had always favoured but which now fought a losing battle against the blueish tints in her skin and lips; flesh hung in folds about her face and body; her swollen ankles bulged over her high-heeled shoes; and she was encased in a tight woollen dress of brilliant lime green. She looked at me, looked at Twice, favoured him with a smile of ghastly coquetry, then looked back at me and said: 'I know *you* – you're Janet Sandison. How are you, you old cow?'

'I'm very well, Rose. This is my husband, Twice Alexander.'

'Twice!' She went towards him, took his hand and gazed into his eyes. 'Twice, what a cute name! Oh!' Her eyes fell upon the roses which lay on the table. 'You brought these for me?' She turned back to Twice, the flowers held close to her painted face. It was a dreadful sight. 'That was very, very sweet of you, darling.'

I felt that hours were passing while I stood there staring at this apparition simpering round the incongruous sheaf of delicate pink and gold flowers. Both Dee and Lorna had told me of the change in Rose, had tried to warn me what to expect, but nothing could have prepared me for this. We all – except Rose – seemed to be suspended in a vacuum. Twice, horribly embarrassed at being the target for this travesty of coquetry, was utterly speechless; Dee looked vaguely guilty and ashamed; Lorna stood looking at Rose as an over-fond, over-indulgent mother might look at her ill-brought-up child, while I simply stood rooted to the carpet, staring.

'Well,' said Rose, her bloated face taking on a petulant look over the flowers, 'isn't there a drink in the house, Lorna, for heaven's sake? Janet, don't just stand there – can't you see I want some vases?' She turned back to Twice and the petulance vanished. 'They *are* lovely, darling,' she said.

She gave the roses one more cuddle, cast them a little roughly on the table, swayed to the fireplace, took a cigarette from a box and leaned provocatively towards Twice for a light.

Lorna picked up her roses, and I followed her to the kitchen, but as I shut the door I saw that Dee had gone to stand by the fireplace, looking protectively at Twice as if prepared to defend his honour with the poker if need be.

'Lorna,' I said when we were safely in the little pantry off the kitchen, 'that's appalling! Is she always like that?'

'With men? Yes,' said Lorna and began unconcernedly to arrange her flowers. 'I tried to warn Twice, but one can never really warn people. But he'll soon get the hang of it. All she wants is a little admiration and he won't have to act very much. She is convinced that all men are crazy about her. Janet, the drinks are in that cupboard over there. There's a bottle of whisky with a little red mark on the corner of the label – that's for Rose; it's coloured water, really, so don't give it to anybody else. I usually put her on to it at about her third round – she doesn't know the difference by then. The great thing is not to let *her* get at the bottles.' I fetched a tray and began to bring out the bottles and glasses.

'This visit, especially with Twice in the party, is going to do her all the good in the world,' Lorna went on. 'We don't get many people. She embarrasses the men and offends the women, but you've got more sense than to be offended. You see, it is difficult to make some people believe that she isn't entirely responsible, especially the women. The sort of remarks she makes to women and about women don't sound as if her brain had gone – they are always too near the mark.'

She drew back from her flowers, put her head on one side, admiring them. 'Aren't they nearly too beautiful? Those goldy ones make me think of Rose as she used to be.'

'Lorna, don't, for pity's sake!'

She did not seem to hear me. 'I think she still sees herself like that, you know,' she continued in her gentle voice. 'This – this mental decay – it is as if her mind had become stuck at a certain point in time, at the point when she was at the peak of her beauty and success, at the time when she was at Daneford, with Flip seemingly adoring and Roy on a string. Sometimes she thinks she is still up there at Daneford and that this is my old cottage where she used to visit me sometimes . . . We'd better go through there with the drinks . . . Anyway, Janet, just take things as they come and don't let her worry you. She orders Dee and me about as if we were housemaids, and she will probably do the same with you. Just try to cope.'

'Don't worry, chum,' I said. 'I am not going to quarrel with Rose at this stage.'

In procession, Lorna with two vases of flowers and I with the tray of drinks, we went back to the sitting-room, where Rose turned off the smile she was bending on Twice to scowl at us and say: 'My God! How long do you two women need to find some drink and a few glasses? . . . Twice, darling, have a little drinkie. What will it be?'

The whole evening had a nightmare quality, but when at last Rose almost fell asleep where she sat, and Lorna, luring her with a glass of fluid out of the marked bottle, led her upstairs to bed, first I, then Dee, and lastly Twice, broke down into the relief of semi-hysterical laughter.

'Goodness, Twice,' Dee giggled, 'you were marvellous!'

'It's dreadful to laugh like this,' I gasped out, 'but I can't help it. That bit about the grocer's boy leering at her nearly killed me.'

'It seems to me that to laugh is all one can do,' Twice said. 'Dee, I wonder if I could have another small drink? The bit that kept getting me was the I-am-always-loyal-to-my-friends gag, Flash. You have quoted it so often, and there it was, larger and more hypocritical than I had ever imagined.' Lorna came into the room. 'Janet,' she said sternly, 'Rose says that I am to give you a month's notice. She says you are nothing but a hanger-on; that Dee must go to school at once; and that you seem to think that men visit this house simply to entertain *you*!'

This led to a renewed burst of laughter, and then Lorna said: 'I can't thank you enough for this visit. I really can't. She is better than she has been for weeks, and she's had only two real drinks tonight and they were quite small.'

'She seemed as tight as a tick to me,' Dee said.

'She is, Dee, but that isn't alcohol. That's Twice!' said Lorna.

Very shortly, we all went up to bed, in preparation for a long hard day on the morrow, as Twice put it.

The house had two little projecting wings at the back on either side of a narrow courtyard, and Dee's room was in one wing and ours in the other.

'If you hear movements in the night, don't worry,' Lorna told us. 'Rose's room is off mine, and she can't get out without being followed,' and with a roguish wink at Twice she went away.

'Miss Jan,' said Dee, 'would you like to come and see my room?'

I had the feeling that I had had with Perky at Daneford long ago, that Dee very much wanted me to 'come and see' her room, so I went with her along the landing. She shut the door and stood with her back against it.

'I just wanted to tell you,' she said in a low voice, 'how terribly much I like Twice.'

'That is very nice of you, Dee.'

'You don't mind?'

'Of course not. Why should I mind?'

'If I had somebody who belonged to me as much as he belongs to you, *I* would mind,' she said.

'I don't think you would, Dee. Not really.'

'I wanted you to know. I'd hate you to mind, but I'd rather know if you minded.'

'But I don't mind, and I am not going to start minding, and if I have to say the word mind much oftener I'll get it on my mind and go out of my mind.'

She smiled. 'I wish you weren't going away to St. Jago just when I have found you again and we are having such fun.'

'It is rather a pity,' I said, but in one way I was being insincere. I should have liked to see more of Dee, but I did not want to see anything of Alan Stewart. 'What were you and Twice laughing about on the stairs?' I asked.

'He was telling me about the time you threw the pie-dish at him and it went through the window.'

'Oh, he was, was he? I bet you he didn't tell you why I threw the pie-dish.'

'No. Why did you?'

'I don't actually remember at the moment, but that's not the point. The point is that the story was incomplete – he was only telling you one side of it — the side that suited him, the dishonest so-and-so.'

'He's not dishonest! He is the honestest man I have ever met!' She caught at herself and added in a quieter voice: 'Stories are always one-sided and incomplete, anyway. That's partly why everything is always such a muddle.'

'But *is* everything a muddle, Dee? I should have thought you were in less of a muddle than most.'

She looked at me for a moment, hesitated on the brink of speech and then turned away.

'Oh, I'm all right,' she said, opened her case which was on a stool at the end of her bed and took out her pyjamas and dressing-gown.

'It is time we were all in bed,' I said awkwardly. 'We none of us have the stamina of Rose.'

'No . . . Good night, Miss Jan.'

I left her and went back across the landing to my own room, but I was suddenly unhappy with a miserable sense of having been inadequate for the wrong reason, inadequate because I had been selfishly unwilling to try to help, and so, of course, although I had been yawning more than anyone when we left the sitting-room, I now had no inclination to sleep or even to go to bed. Twice, already in bed, watched me dawdling about the room, staring out of the window at the dark river, picking up my hair brush and putting it down again, and eventually he said: 'What's up, Flash?'

'I'm worried about that kid.'

'Who? Dee?'

'Hush! Her window is just across the courtyard there and it's open.' I drew the curtains across the window of the room.

'What's the matter with her?'

'I don't know. There is nothing definite. But I don't like all this stuff people are handing me about her being a cold, calculating little piece. It just doesn't ring right. It reminds me of the time she came to the office and said: "I am a persistent little brat." She only said it and believed it and lived up to it because other people had kept telling her repeatedly that she was a persistent little brat.'

'And so she is,' Twice said.

'I know, but I can't explain what I mean. It is as if she had picked out a line for herself, a line of cool calculating efficiency, as if she has built up a legend and now everything is part of it, her character, her engagement to Stewart, everything. Yet, at the same time, she knows deep down that it is all a legend, that it's all false, like Rose seeing a reflection of herself all the time and knowing all the time that it was false and yet not admitting it.'

'Look, Flash, the truth is that you don't like this engagement to Stewart. All right. I'm not blaming you. I don't like it myself, and you knew the bloke and I didn't. But what can one do?'

'I suppose you are right. There is nothing one can do; and, anyway, what business has one to do anything?' I got undressed and brushed my hair. 'Gosh, Twice, I'm glad I am no longer that age, anyhow! I wouldn't be twenty-four again for all the gilt-edged securities in the City of London!'

'Nor me neither forbye and besides,' said Twice in the idiom of Tom. 'Gosh, it's warm in this room!' He threw the eiderdown down to the bottom of the bed.

'Thames valley fug,' I said and opened the window still wider. 'But keep that eiderdown within reach. There will be a cold mist from the river in the small hours. I spent many a December in this climate during the war without any of Daneford's central heating . . . Darling, thank you for coping with Rose, by the way.'

'Not at all — it was a pleasure, but, as I have said before, you have some very odd friends.'

'I will admit that Rose tonight startled even me,' I told him.

'Oh, well, tomorrow is another day,' he said and picked up his book.

CHAPTER FOURTEEN

The next morning, in spite of the muggy warmth of the night before, it was cold, clear and frosty, and Twice and I were sent by Dee and Lorna to take a walk along the river bank while they prepared the lunch and Perky and Alf went to church. Rose, of course, was in bed, creaming her face and varnishing her nails and generally preparing for further conquest from lunch-time onwards.

'The best thing will be to take her for a drive in the afternoon, Lorna says, that is if she gets up and doesn't change her mind,' I told Twice as we turned off the road by the bridge and on to the tow-path by the water's edge. 'We could have tea at Maidenhead. There is a hotel where Lorna knows the people and she and Dee have taken Rose there before . . . Are you hating all this, darling?'

'Lord, no! I mean, as long as one knows she is really crazy it is all right. But, you know, if a bloke met her in a pub it would be pretty frightening. What I mean is that, in a way, she doesn't *look* all that crazy. I mean – oh, I don't know what I mean. All I can say is once again, that you have some damn' queer friends, my pet.'

'I'm sorry I got us into this, Twice.'

'Don't be. It is a lot better than a foggy weekend in London, anyway. You know, I've never really seen the Thames in its country parts before. It is extraordinarily beautiful, isn't it?'

The bare willow fronds, fringed with white hoar frost, trailed in the dark grey water that slid so quietly and agelessly by.

'I think the Thames is more beautiful in winter than in summer,' I said. 'I like it all cold and quiet, with no punts about. I spent nearly the whole war about seven miles up-river from here. Monica and I did a lot of walking along these tow-paths; but the Thames always makes me think of Rose, somehow.'

'Good gracious, why?'

'I don't know. The first morning I spent at Daneford I came down for a walk by the river. There is a little island further along here — a sort of Lady of Shalott's island. I had just met Rose. She was very beautiful, but I didn't like her. It was all a sort of muddle of poetry and beauty on one side and Rose being beautiful and yet not liking her on the other. Anyway, Rose and the river became tangled up in my mind. Young women go through the devil, Twice. That's why I am sort of bothered about Dee although one can't do anything. She is developing a sort of crush on you, by the way.'

'No,' he said. 'It isn't a crush. She isn't sloppy-minded enough for that sort of thing. I like that kid, Flash, but I can't think of her as a young woman. She has much more the mind of a boy. That's why I say it isn't what one calls a crush any more than what I feel about her could be described as a crush. It is an open-eyed sort of thing with quite a lot of respect for one another in it. She and I could easily quarrel like hell.'

'Don't, if you can help it.'

'I don't intend to on this short acquaintance. What I mean is that she and I could have an honest, nothing-barred relationship of the kind that working colleagues can have. But I don't think I could bear her to play the fool or do anything silly. I would be too mad at her if she betrayed her intelligence. I wouldn't be able to keep quiet.'

'It is probably just as well that we are on our way out to St. Jago,' I said. 'This whole situation is fraught with trouble . . . And there is the island. The Lady of Shalott is working at her web in front of her mirror just in among those trees there. I think we should turn back now. I wasn't sure last night, Twice, but now I think I am glad that we came down here. It is like laying some ghosts out of my past. I don't mean Rose and all that, but the ghosts that lurk in one's mind, the ghosts of what I myself did and thought and puzzled over. I seem to know now, more finally than before, that I shall never be twenty-five again, and it isn't a bad thing to be quite, quite certain.'

'You are quite nice at forty-one.'

'You save that for this afternoon,' I told him. 'You will need it all for Rose.'

And he did. Rose came down for lunch in a very sprightly mood, gowned in pale yellow and wearing a saucy little hat made of feathers which, when she tossed her brassy head and shrieked with merriment at some of her own sallies, made her look like a crazy cockatoo. She had, however, forgotten that she had dismissed me from her service the night before, and, after introducing Twice to me, informed him that I would not be with her much longer as Dee was going away to school soon.

'The child should have been at school long ago,' she told him confidentially across the corner of the table, 'but I hate getting rid of people who have worked for me. I am always loyal, sometimes in a silly way, but I am just made that way.'

When lunch was over, we set off for the afternoon drive as planned, Rose and Twice in the front of the car, Lorna, Dee and I in the back, and Rose behaving as if the three of us were not there and, indeed, did not exist at all. It was all very macabre, in a way that is difficult to describe. Rose, you see, would have given no impression of being a mental case had one been a stranger who knew nothing of her past history, and I was beginning to see how exact was Lorna's analysis that Rose's mind had 'become stuck at a certain point in time'. Even to me she was less like a mentally deranged woman than like a very solid and fleshy ghost from the past, a past not far enough away to be romantically interesting but only distant enough to be outmoded and embarrassing.

Her wit, for lack of a more accurate word, had always been dependent on the risqué, not to say the coarse; and the repartée, for which she had been known, had depended on an up-to-the-minute knowledge of the cliché of the moment. But the moment of her zenith had been about 1933, before I even met her, and at that moment she had become arrested. I had not realised until this afternoon that the up-to-the-minute cliché of some eighteen years ago takes on with time an unbelievable silliness and that what was risqué in 1933 has the chestnut flavour of an old music-hall joke in 1951. And then the coarse remains the coarse in any age. I spent a most uncomfortably embarrassed afternoon, and I think this was true of all of us except Rose, who, when we arrived back at the cottage about six o'clock, was in high fettle.

She swept into the little sitting-room, where Lorna was rousing up the banked fire, as if it were the big drawing-room of Daneford, cast her fur coat at the nearest chair with a sweeping gesture, drew Twice towards her by the arm and led him to the fireplace. From this vantage point, she looked round at the rest of us in a scornful way, glanced at Twice with roguish intimacy and said: 'Here I am, surrounded by women as usual. Why do I let it happen? I ask you, am I the sort of woman people would take for a Lesbian?'

This was the sort of remark that, in 1935 or so, when sexual divagation was seldomed mentioned, used to cause half-salacious, half-embarrassed titters among her acquaintance, but now, at the end of this long hard day in 1951, it fell extremely flat. Not one of us could raise the expected giggle of appreciation, and she at once became petulant. The heavy flesh about her chin sagged further, her brows lowered.

'Lorna, go and get the drinks!' she ordered. 'What are you here for? And you two, go and help her!' She turned to smile at Twice. 'Sit down, darling, and we'll have a quiet little tiddley together.'

Twice glanced at Lorna and me and gave us an almost imperceptible dismissive jerk of his head, followed by a fleeting grin before he went to sit down on the sofa that Rose was patting in an intimate way. Lorna and I left the room, Dee following us unwillingly, and as I shut the door she sat down firmly on a chair in the hall.

'I'll stay here and listen to what goes on,' she said.

'Quite a good idea,' Lorna agreed, and she and I went to the kitchen.

'Madam has had a lovely day, Perky,' Lorna said, 'but she is a little over-excited. Send supper in as soon as you can and remember to put the hall clock to half-past eight before you ring the bell.'

'Yes, Miss Lorna. Now move yourself, Alf, do, can't you see I'm in a 'urry?' Perky bustled to the cooker, which was nowhere near Alf, with her pan of potatoes. 'It's the gentleman, Miss Janet,' she told me gravely. 'Madam does love the gentlemen, always did, but they are not good for her, never were.' Having put on her potatoes to cook, she placed her hands on her round hips and looked up at me from her bright eyes. 'Still, Mr. Roy didn't ought to have done to her what he did. I've known Mr. Roy since he was a baby, but I still say it, Miss Janet. Mr. Roy turned hard. Very hard.'

''Sright,' said Alf.

'I'm ever so glad Miss Dee has seen you again,' Perky said. 'All the good in the world it will do her, Miss Janet.'

''Sright.'

'Miss Dee told me you met Mrs. Hubert — her Auntie Angela – in Town, Miss Janet. I am sure she said a lot of hard things about Miss Dee, but don't you believe them. Miss Dee is a good little girl and always was.'

''Sright.'

'Better bring the drinks,' said Dee, pushing her head round the door. 'I think Twice is getting hard pressed.'

'Come on!' said Lorna to me, seizing the tray, and we scuttled out while Perky shook the potato pan violently as if that would make it boil more quickly.

In the sitting-room, Rose and Twice were side by side on the sofa, very close together, and when I came round to a chair opposite to them I saw that Rose had a large photograph album open on her knees.

'And here I am as a bride,' she was saying, showing Twice one of the many photographs of which there had been such numbers at Daneford and in the London house.

'Absolutely lovely!' said Twice.

'Give her this,' Lorna hissed at me, 'and try to get that album away from her.'

'Here you are, Rose. Have a little tiddley!' I said, feeling very hollow. 'I'll take the album, shall I?'

'You bloody won't!' she snapped, and tried at one and the same time to grab the drink and hold on to the large book, with the result that some whisky splashed over it before it slid to the floor.

'All right, Rose,' I said, and Twice, bending, picked up the album and placed it on the sofa between them.

At this little gesture of attention she at once became good-humoured again, rolled her eyes roguishly at him and began to swallow her drink, and then in a genial way she said: 'Come along, girls!' and indicated that Lorna, Dee and I were to sit down.

Before we had well begun our drinks, of course, Rose was handing her empty glass to Lorna, who went to the tray and refilled it, mainly from the marked bottle, I noticed, and as Rose finished this second drink there came the tinkle of the bell from across the hall.

'That's dinner,' said Lorna, rising.

'Hell, let them wait,' said Rose. 'I want another drink.'

'Rose, dear, it's half-past eight — '

'I don't give a damn if it's half-past ten! What do I pay them for?' I felt that we might be back in Daneford in 1936. She held out her glass with a heavy lurching gesture and the heavy leaves of the album flicked over where it lay on the sprung sofa. 'Get me another drink, I tell you!'

With a small sigh, Lorna went to the tray again and came back with the refilled glass.

'Well, here's to — ing!' said Rose and took a large gulp. Then she leaned over the album to pat Twice in an intimate way on the thigh.

I saw a sudden change come over her as if, in some inexplicable way, her baggy flesh were melting before my eyes. Her arms and shoulders seemed to become a rigid framework and the bone structure of her face seemed to protrude through the excessive flesh. It was as if the round skull with the pelt of brassy hair and the bloated face were sharpening to take on the pointed outline of the head of a snake. In the moment that I noticed that she was looking down at the photograph album, Lorna reached over the back of the sofa, seized it and put it, closed, on the table by the drinks tray. The rigidity went out of Rose's body; the puffiness flowed in about her face again; her body sagged heavily and, raising her glass, she drank off its entire contents. Then, weightily, she struggled to her feet, Twice helping her. Standing there, with him beside her, she looked at us three women. The foolish, complacent, flirtatious look, that dreadful travesty of the expression of the successful beauty, had left her face, leaving it flabby and dead except for the eyes, which glittered with a hard sane malice. She fixed them on me.

'So you didn't marry Stewart after all! You found this one instead!' She waved a hand at Twice and turned to Dee. 'And this poor ugly brat — ' She stopped, stared at Dee for a moment, then stared at me and burst into a raucous roar of laughter. 'My God! Stewart! She's going to marry old Stewart, the only man who ever looked at her, and *he's* only taking her to get a partnership in the firm!' Before any of us could move, she had drawn a harsh breath and, pushing her bloated face within inches of Dee's, she half-shouted: 'Old Stewart's on the up and up! He used to get engaged to governesses, but now its heiresses!' She lurched towards the table. 'Gimme a drink! I'm going to bed! To hell with the lot of you!'

Lorna quickly picked up the marked bottle and filled a tumbler with the brown fluid. Rose grabbed it from her hand and made for the door, with Lorna trying to follow her.

'Lemme alone!' she said savagely. 'Going up by m'self! I'm sick of the sight of you bloody women!'

She swayed out of the room, and Lorna shut the door. Across the shattered air I looked straight into Dee's face; her round eyes stared back at me and I felt sick.

'But what happened?' Twice asked.

Lorna picked up the album, opened it and held it out to us. From the buff-coloured page, the handsome supercilious face of Flip Orton looked at us.

'It doesn't always happen,' Lorna said. 'In fact, quite seldom.'

She put the book away in a drawer. 'I've thought of destroying the album, but sometimes her own photographs keep her happy for hours and she often spends a long time mooning over the pictures of Flip . . . Sit down, all of you. I'll just tell Perky to leave the supper in the oven and we'll all have a peaceful drink. We need it.'

'I'll go, Lorna,' Dee said and went out.

'Lorna, I'm terribly sorry,' Twice said. 'Everything seemed to be going so well.'

Lorna smiled. 'My dear Twice, don't worry. She will be as large as life tomorrow. Since you are leaving early, you won't see her, but you can take my word for it. You have been marvellous with her. It's a pity she had to spoil it for you with one of her moments of truth.'

'Moments of truth?' I repeated.

'That's what I call them,' said Lorna, smiling. 'That's what it is when you think of it. It is reality breaking through and Rose doesn't like reality. It makes her extremely rude, as you saw . . . Come along, don't let's be miserable on your last evening. I've loved this visit and I can't bear to have it spoiled.'

'Lorna,' I said, 'the visit is spoiled all right. Didn't you hear what she said?'

'My dear Janet, you mustn't be upset by the things she says. I simply don't listen.'

'Lorna, you didn't grasp the thing! *I* was engaged to Alan Stewart once! I didn't want Dee to know. Do you think she took it in?' I knew very well that Dee had taken it in.

'Dee took it in all right,' said Twice.

'Perky's keeping the supper, Lorna,' Dee said, coming back into the room. 'Miss Jan, did Rose mean that Alan was once engaged to *you*?'

I looked up at her. Her plain little face was quite calm, with a half-amused quirk about the eyes, very different from the staring naked mask it had been a few moments before.

'Yes, Dee,' I said, 'he was, but that was a long time ago. We – we decided it wouldn't work.'

Lorna and Twice had moved first towards the drinks tray and were now making for the door. Dee turned her head towards them.

'You needn't go having buckets of tact,' she said, 'I knew Alan knew Miss Jan, and I knew he had been engaged before, but I didn't know it was *to* Miss Jan, that's all. After all, it would be odd if Alan got to the age he is without ever having looked at anyone else, wouldn't it?'

'Very odd, Dee,' Twice said.

'I do think you might have told me, Miss Jan!' she said. 'Why didn't you?'

I felt as if I were being put in my place by a very poised, self-assured person of three times my age.

'I don't really know why,' I half-stammered.

'Come to that, why didn't you tell *me*?' Twice asked, coming in with all the assistance in his power, which was considerable, for it made me smile in appreciation of his quick wits.

'No woman likes it to be known that she was jilted in her youth,' I said. 'Well, not exactly jilted — that isn't fair to Alan. But I simply wasn't right for him and things — well, they just sort of fell through,' I ended weakly.

'Well, never mind. You fell upon Twice and that is very nice,' said Dee. 'Lorna, I think we could all have one peaceful drink, don't you? The trouble with Rose is that she gives one no time to have a drink oneself with always having to have her glass refilled and then creating a drama.'

All this was very smooth, and from then on the evening continued to be smooth — too smooth, I felt — and I wondered whether the strangely brittle atmosphere was entirely imagined by myself. We had one drink, had supper and came back to the sitting-room, and over the coffee I was positively grateful when Rose's voice bawled lustily down the stairs: 'Lorna, where the hell are you, you old cow? Bring me up a drink!'

'*There* we are,' said Lorna with satisfaction and went to the marked bottle.

Leaving the door open, she went upstairs with the tumbler, and Rose's voice came floating down to us: 'That was a nice man Janet Sandison brought for drinks tonight, but of course he'll never stick to her. My God, she *is* dull, isn't she?'

Twice, Dee and I were still giggling together when Lorna came downstairs.

'What did I tell you?' she said. 'Everything in the garden is lovely.'

We all went to bed early, for which I was thankful, and I wondered whether I was the only one who felt shattered by what Lorna called our day with 'Rose in Wanderland', but I was grateful that Twice agreed that everything had gone a little too far and a little too fast.

'Heavens, what a sinister moment that was!' he said as he rolled into bed. 'It all just goes to show that truth will out.'

'You know,' I said, 'I was the one that made a skeleton in a cupboard out of Alan Stewart. One is so silly in one's mind. I kept on thinking that because he was a lewd sort of skeleton to me he must look the same to Dee if she knew he was in my cupboard, but he isn't in my cupboard any more. He's in Dee's, and to her he doesn't look like a skeleton at all.'

'No, he doesn't. But I don't like him any better than I ever did.'

'Neither do I. But then, one doesn't have to. Dee is the one and she seems to like him all right.'

'I have a feeling that he is not going to go unquestioned about his whirl with her Miss Jan, though. She is, after all, a persistent little brat. Let me know if your ears start to burn just about a week after we land in St. Jago, will you?'

I giggled. 'I'd love to see the smugness melting off his face when she drags my rattling skeleton out of his cupboard!'

'Open that window a bit more before you get into bed. This frost, fog, or whatever it is, feels like a horse blanket.'

I opened the window wide, listened for a moment to the faint sound of water falling over the weir and got into bed.

I did not know when I awoke whether I had been asleep for five minutes or five hours, and I did not know what had awakened me, but I lay dead still, in a tense uneasiness, listening. The weir was only a few yards from the end of the garden, and all I could hear, at first, was the steady, soothing flow of the water, but after about a minute — or it may have been less — I heard again the sound which I now knew to be the one that had awakened me. It was not loud, but it was eerie, monotonous, not quite human and queerly rhythmic. In the pitch darkness it was very frightening.

'DAH-da-da, DAH-da, DAH-da-DAH, DAH-dada, DAH-da, DAH, DAH!' It went on for a little time, then stopped, and there was no sound but the peaceful flow of the water over the weir. Then it began again in the same eerie, monotonous chanting rhythm. I jumped when Twice's voice whispered from the bed across the room.

'Flash, you are awake?'
'Yes. What's that noise?'
'It's been going on for quite a while. Rose, I suppose.'
'Doesn't sound like Rose,' I whispered back.
Twice came over through the darkness to my bed, which was nearer to the window. 'Hush, there it goes again. It's coming from outside!' He went to the window, putting his head through between the drawn curtains. After a moment, he came back and switched on the lamp beside my bed. I shivered.

'It's the most inhuman yet human sort of noise,' I whispered.

'It's like *your* voice when you talk in your sleep.'

'Dee!' I said, and now I jumped out of bed and went behind the curtains to the open window.

Twice joined me, and we stood in the bay behind the curtains, looking out into the murky grey darkness and listening, but the chant had come to an end again, and once more there was only the sound of the water over the weir. We were about to turn away and go back to bed when there came a pathetic little wail that ended on a sob, and then the eerie monotonous: DAH-da-da-DAH-da-DAH-da-DAH — '

'I'm going along to that child's room,' I said to Twice. 'Something is wrong with her!'

'Quietly, then. Don't let's startle her.'

In our overcoats, for it was bitterly cold now, we crept across the landing and I put my hand on the door-knob, turned it gently and eased the door open. We could hear the words now, high-pitched and uncanny:

'Queen of the garden bloomed a rose,
Queen of the roses round her —'

Dee, intoning her little verse from the 'yantique' book, was sound asleep, with her face to the wall, when Twice turned on the little fountain-pen torch inside the curve of his hand. On the table beside the bed lay her pen and a sheet of paper, and on top of the writing-paper lay her half-hoop of diamonds. In the little circle of light from the torch I read the words: 'Dear

Alan, I am sending back this ring. I am very sorry, but — '

I did not read any more, but indicated the sheet of paper to Twice and bent over the bed. There was a wet patch on the pillow, and Dee's face was swollen and mis-shapen with crying. The horrid little chant began again: 'Queen of the garden — '

'Dee,' I said softly, 'Dee, wake up. Dee, it's Miss Jan and Twice.'

Twice switched on the lamp by the bedside, and, as if drugged, she rolled over heavily on to her back while I kept repeating Twice's name and my own. Her eyes opened, flickered over us and: 'What'swrong?' she asked, sitting up. 'Is someone ill?'

The eyes were hard and distant, the voice cool and self-possessed; eyes and voice consorting oddly with the swollen plain little face and the tousled short hair.

'No,' said Twice, and, sitting down firmly on the edge of the bed, he pulled his pipe out of his overcoat pocket. 'Janet and I were bored and we came in for a little chat. After all, you were talking in your sleep and sounded pretty bored with yourself too.'

'Surely this is an odd time of night to be funny?' she enquired.

'No, I am frightfully funny all the time. By the way' — he nodded at the letter and ring on the table — 'I notice that you've thrown Mr. Stewart over?'

She stared at him. 'You — you have been reading that letter?'

'I learned to read when I was three-and-a-half. Why?'

'What do you mean, why?'

'Why have you thrown Mr. Stewart over?'

She stared at Twice, her eyes hard, her mouth compressed and showing the little vertical wrinkles at each side as it used to do when she was a child.

'That is none of your business,' she said.

'Oh yes it is! I am not going to have people jilting my wife's ex-fiancés without knowing why. Bless my soul, Alan Stewart is a relation of mine by non-marriage and I owe him a deep debt of gratitude!'

'What a fool you are, Twice,' she said and suddenly began to cry.

Twice looked up at me, rose from the side of the bed and said: 'I'm going down to the kitchen to make a pot of tea.'

'Y-you don't know where anything is,' Dee sobbed.

'I soon will,' he told her and went out and shut the door.

I took his place on the side of the bed, and while Dee lay back on her wet pillow, sobbing and with the tears pouring over her temples, I said: 'Dee, I am sorry. This is all wrong and silly. Alan's thing with me was nothing — he has probably forgotten all about it long ago and I didn't see the point of telling you either. But I am sorry. Still, you shouldn't be like this about it.'

'I am not like this about Alan or you or anything,' Dee sobbed. 'It's not about Alan — '

'Then what, darling? You were talking in your sleep and crying. That's why Twice and I came in. If it isn't Alan, what is it?'

'It's Rose — it's *Rose*! Oh, I dont know *what* it is!' She struggled up to a sitting position. 'Miss Jan, could you get me another handkerchief, please? In my case, in the left-hand side pocket. Thank you. I'm sorry.' She mopped her face in a blundering clumsy way that was pathetically unlike her. 'This is frightful. It's all so — so exposing. I'm sorry.'

'Never mind that,' I told her. 'What's this about Rose?'

'What *will* Twice think of me?'

'Dammit!' I said. 'He's making *tea* for you! Twice has never made tea for any woman except me!'

'Ow!' she said in a near-howl. 'You *are* nice to me!' and then she had another fit of crying.

I let her go on for a bit, and when the storm had subsided a little, I said again: 'What is this about Rose, Dee?'

She sat up again, mopped her face, folded her hands neatly in her lap, with the wet handkerchief between them. She stared blankly at the wall ahead of her and in a colourless voice she began to speak.

'Rose was quite right. I am an ugly brat. Alan is the only man who ever took the least interest in me, and he only did it to get a partnership in the firm. She is quite right. I have known it all the time, but I wouldn't face it. But I really knew it all the time. But you see, her *saying* it like that made it different. You can't cheat yourself when you are not cheating other people

. . . It's not that I *wanted* to cheat myself, Miss Jan—'

'Of course not!' I said.

'I've always tried not to cheat myself. I didn't do it over lending Rose this house. I told Lorna straight out that I was doing it to spite Father, and that was true or partly true. I lent it partly to help Lorna, because I like her. She was kind to me when I was small. I didn't do it for Rose, but I did it for Lorna. I like her.'

'I know you do.'

'But, Miss Jan, this is a dreadful thing. I don't *like* Alan Stewart. I have never liked him, not really *liked* him, but I cheated myself about him. You see, it's so easy to cheat yourself when everybody helps you to do it by being pleased about things. I mean, *he* was pleased, and Father and Aunt Angela and everybody, and I like people to be pleased. But I never really liked Alan Stewart.'

'Nether did I,' I said.

'Nor me neither forbye and besides,' said Twice, coming in with his tea-tray.

I looked at him. 'Honestly, Twice Alexander — ' I began.

'You know, Miss Jan,' Dee said with a slight hiccuping sob, 'Twice is not nearly such a fool as he tries to make out he is.'

'I'm not a fool at all,' Twice said equably. 'At least, I don't think so. But then, one never does, does one? Sugar, Dee?'

'Is anything the matter?' Lorna enquired, appearing in the doorway in a very ugly camel-hair dressing-gown and with her hair all rolled up in curlers which, I think because she was wearing her glasses, looked extrordinarily funny. 'What are you all doing sitting up making tea?'

'We are jilting Alan Stewart for the second time,' Twice said. 'I brought a cup for you because I knew that pop that gas stove made would wake you up. Sugar? You ought to have that stove looked at. It doesn't *have* to blow the roof off every time you turn it out.'

'I wish I knew what you are all talking about,' Lorna said, taking a cup and sitting on a spindly bedroom chair that creaked horribly.

'It's quite simple,' Twice said. 'We're talking about pops and poops.'

Dee hastily deposited her cup of tea on the bedside table and began to laugh as if she would never stop. At first I thought it was another attack of hysteria, and Lorna, blinking behind her glasses, looked very worried, but after a few seconds I realised that Dee's laughter was utterly carefree and as innocently natural as the fall of the water over the weir beyond the window.

Very soon she laughed herself to silence, mopped her face again and said: 'Gosh, I am sorry you are going away, Twice.' She swallowed some tea. 'I wish I could come with you!'

'Why don't you?' said Twice.

She stared at him. He stared at her. I stared at Twice. Lorna stared at all of us in turn. The river outside seemed to have been arrested in its flow over the weir, so complete was the silence.

'Put a P.S. on that letter' — Twice nodded at the sheet of paper on the table — 'saying "Gone west". That's all you have to do.'

'Twice!' I said.

'What?' said Lorna.

'Miss Jan?' said Dee.

Twice turned to me. 'Flash, don't you think it's a good idea?'

I smiled at him and then at Dee. 'Yes, Twice,' I said. 'I think it's a splendid idea. Dee, would you like to come for a holiday at Paradise? Actually, it's in St. Jago, but the place is called Paradise.'

'It isn't!' said Lorna.

'Yes, it is,' I assured her. 'It isn't of course, Paradise, I mean. But it would — would take Dee out of things.'

'I'd like to be out of things,' Dee said wistfully.

'Yes,' Lorna said to me. 'Dee has had a lot of — things.'

Twice put his cup on the tray and rose to his feet. 'I am going to bed. Good night' — he bent over the bed and kissed Dee — 'you — and' — he kissed Lorna on the nose — 'you.' He turned to me. 'Don't be too long, you,' and, picking up his tea-tray, he went away, shutting the door behind him.

'Lorna,' Dee said after a moment, 'have you ever seen a person like Twice before?'

'No, dear, I must say I haven't quite.' She stood up. 'I am for bed,' she said and went at once.

'Twice quite put me off Alan, you know, Miss Jan,' Dee said when we were alone. 'Even before Rose said that thing she said, I had started thinking and comparing. And I had sort of decided that Alan wouldn't do.'

'I am glad,' I told her. 'You see, he wouldn't do for me, either, and one always wants better than for oneself for the people that one really likes, if that makes sense.'

'I know what you mean. I really ought to let you get off to bed, Miss Jan, but would you mind staying a little longer?'

'Not me,' I said. 'It's nearly morning, anyway, but do you mind if I put my feet under your eiderdown?'

I got into the bed at the bottom, my back against the end, and lit a cigarette.

'This is like Tom and George at Reachfar holding a Parlyment in Tom's bed on a wet Sunday afternoon!' Dee said. 'Miss Jan, why do you suppose I get into so many muddles?'

'Everybody gets into muddles — it isn't just you.'

'Did you have muddles?'

'I had a frightful one over Alan Stewart, and the funny thing is that it was Rose who cleared me up too, with one of her acid remarks. That seems to be Rose's function, clearing up other people's muddles although she could never do anything about her own.'

'Miss Jan, *shall* I come to St. Jago with you?'

'Do you want to? If you want to, Twice and I will be delighted. But you don't have to make up your mind right now.'

'I *have* made it up, rather. I would like to come. I think it would be a good thing for everybody if I got right away from the family for a bit. I just don't know about families. I think somebody like you is luckier than somebody like me. I was just working out that when you came to Daneford you must have been just about the age I am now. If you had had a muddle at that time, at least you would have got peace to think it out for yourself. Father wouldn't be there nag-nagging at you or Aunt

Angela or anybody . . . Miss Jan, is it terribly important that one should get married?'

'I don't think so,' I said. 'I think people like your Aunt Angela are a little old-fashioned in that way. Mind you, being married is very nice if you get the right person, but you have to be terribly sure he is right.'

'But how do you know?'

'It just sort of comes over you.'

I was learning that in so far as relationships were concerned she was no more experienced than she had been at eight years old. She put her head on one side and looked at me studiously. 'I shouldn't say you were terribly pretty or good-looking or anything. I mean, you're not sticking out a mile for men to compete to dance with you at parties, like the Goldiloxes. Going to a party with *them*, you just knew you would be trampled underfoot in the stampede to get at them. It was sort of disgusting. But they liked it and wanted it that way. And honestly, Miss Jan, this isn't sour grapes or anything. I didn't *want* to be like that. I don't want to have compliments paid me and things. I know I'm not pretty, but I know I've got brains, too. It is very annoying when people keep on looking for the things you haven't got and taking no notice of the things you have, like Alan calling me "pretty little woman". I'm not pretty and I'm not really a little woman either!' she ended fiercely.

'No. You are an awkward brat and always were,' I told her. 'Look here, I am going to bed.'

'All right.' She gave a large yawn. 'I am sorry I caused all this uproar tonight. I know I talk in my sleep — I used to do it at school. What was I saying, by the way?'

'I don't know. It was just an uncanny, eerie noise, and then when we came in you stopped.'

'It was probably a lot of rubbish. At school I used to recite theorems from Euclid mostly. Thank you for everything. Good night, Miss Jan.'

When I went back to our room, Twice laid aside the detective story he had been reading and said: 'Well?'

'You've been and gone and done it,' I said, taking off my coat and getting into bed. 'We've got a passenger for the West Indies.'

'Flash, I'm sorry! But I was so darned sorry for that poor muddled little devil.'

'Lord, I don't mind. But it seems to me that in our home there is always what Martha would call a slew o'comp'ny . . . Golly, Rose is the end, isn't she?'

'Absolutely. I have never seen anything so vicious as that performance tonight. Was she always like that?'

'The motivation, if that is what one calls it, was the same. I think she always liked to hurt people, but she used to try to raise a laugh out of it as well, to get the applause of her claque, you know. The odd thing is that in my case and Dee's her cruelty has actually been helpful. It makes you think about the devious ways in which people make their contribution, doesn't it?'

'I suppose it does, but I prefer not to think about Rose.'

I did not expect that we should sleep any more that night, but sleep we did, and by the time we awoke, dressed and had breakfast, it was nearly eleven o'clock.

'You ought to stay for lunch,' Lorna said.

'No, Lorna,' Dee said firmly. 'I want to get back to Town. I intend to get a passage for myself and the car on this ship called the *Pandora*.'

'Don't you go setting yourself up a disappointment,' Twice told her. 'The *Pandora* only takes twelve passengers and if she is full there are other boats.'

'Not for me. And I ain't a shippin' woman for nothing,' said Dee firmly. 'I intend to sail in the *Pandora* with you and Miss Jan, if you don't mind.'

'Well, here you all are!' said Rose, appearing utterly unexpectedly in the doorway in tight black velvet trousers, a tighter pink sweater and pink satin mules. She was all hung about with heavy, clinking brass costume jewellery, including two enormous curtain rings that hung from her ears. 'My God, are you still stuffing your faces with toast and marmalade? Lorna, it's no bloody wonder your figure is a mess . . . It's cocktail time. Get the drinks, for heaven's sake!'

She put her hand on Twice's arm and led him to the sofa by the fire.

'Rose,' said Dee, 'we're just off back to Town.'

'All right,' said Rose, sitting down and inviting Twice with a coquettish smile to join her. 'Be on your way. You too, Janet. Don't hang about like a tart at a street corner.'

Helplessly, Twice and I stared at one another; and Dee, too, looked nonplussed.

'Twice,' said Lorna, 'please go and ask Perky for the drinks,' and she herself began to be very busy clearing the little table where we had had breakfast. 'It's time you went up and made the beds, you two,' she said to Dee and me, and we left the room, while Rose, on the sofa, adjusted one of her heavy bracelets.

The three of us piled into the car: I saw Perky go into the sitting-room with a glass on a salver and Lorna ran down the path to the gate.

'Off you go!' she said. 'And thank you for coming. Write to me, Janet!'

'Lorna!' came a raucous voice and Rose appeared in the hall. 'This drink is nothing but iced water! Do you think I am a bloody fool?'

'Goodbye, Lorna!' I called, and Lorna laughed as the car moved away before she went back into the house to my friend Rose.

THE END